NO REGRETS

NO REGRETS

JULIE MOFFETT

W✪RLDWIDE®

TORONTO • NEW YORK • LONDON
AMSTERDAM • PARIS • SYDNEY • HAMBURG
STOCKHOLM • ATHENS • TOKYO • MILAN
MADRID • WARSAW • BUDAPEST • AUCKLAND

Recycling programs
for this product may
not exist in your area.

No Regrets

A Worldwide Mystery/April 2019

First published by Carina Press

ISBN-13: 978-1-335-45538-3

Printed in U.S.A.

To Brad Moffett, muse extraordinaire, fixer of all things broken and the best big brother a girl could have. You're the greatest. oxox

ONE

THE EVENING BEFORE the wedding, I noticed something odd.

It's not that I go around *looking* for things out of the ordinary, but I have a photographic memory, and I'm also good with math and computers, so it's in my nature to look for meaningful patterns. When something seems off, I notice, perhaps more than most people.

My name is Lexi Carmichael, and first things first: the wedding I'm talking about is *not* mine. That honor goes to my best friend, Basia Kowalski. Tomorrow she's getting married to another of my best friends, Xavier Zimmerman, one of the most accomplished computer geniuses in the US. I have the honor of serving as Basia's maid of honor, a duty which has been stressing me out daily for the past few months.

People, parties, dancing and the beach are *not* my things. In fact, before Basia became my roommate at Georgetown University, I'd avoided all of them by never leaving my room. I lived online. Hacking, gaming and chat rooms. Virtual kingdoms and personal domains. Then Basia swept into our Georgetown dorm room and drowned the place in pink. She smiled at me every time I tried to ignore her, and offered to let me lecture her about password security if I'd just go to the cafeteria with her for an hour. She'd drag me to parties, and help me with my French homework. I still remember the day she introduced me to someone as her best friend. I'd been surprised and yet deeply touched, not sure how and when it had evolved to that. I owe a lot to her, more than I can ever repay. If she hadn't continually badgered me to "log off," I might still be stuck in a virtual existence. The transition hasn't been easy for me, but it's been worth it. Walking down the aisle as the maid of honor at her wedding is a small price to pay for a friendship I value highly.

Thankfully, the wedding rehearsal and subsequent dinner had gone off without a hitch. I hadn't messed it up, destroyed anything, or been shot at, kidnapped or tortured in the process. That sounds like a joke, but I'm not kidding. My life has been a statistically improbable whirlwind of all the above for the past year. My friends say I have a little black cloud of trouble that follows me around. Since I'm a computer geek and a math nerd, I started a spreadsheet noting specific events, actions and my involvement in them, so I could keep track. I called it my "Little Black Cloud" spreadsheet. I'd racked up a considerable number of entries in a less-than-one-year period. So much so, I'd mathematically proved beyond any question of a doubt that I'm a trouble magnet. My friends were right.

It concerned me more than I let on.

The fact the evening had gone as well as it had was a near miracle. Now I had only to survive the next twenty-four hours. Then my best friends would be happily married and the pressure for me to perform would be off.

Then, *bam*! My spidey senses went off when I saw them.

The *them* I'm referring to is three guys I passed in the lobby on my way to the hotel bar that faced the ocean. I was on my way to meet my boyfriend, Slash, who'd texted me he was waiting there. My boyfriend is Italian by birth, but American by heart. He's deep into computers and hacking like I am and was just promoted to one of the most sensitive spots in the NSA. He's so valuable to the agency, he's followed around the clock by his own Secret Service detail. It's been weird having my first real relationship in the prism of a fishbowl, but it is what it is.

I'd been in the bridal suite, because I was sharing a room with Basia on the night before her big day. I'd exchanged my dress and heels for jeans and a T-shirt because I couldn't handle the discomfort for one more minute. Then, walking through the hotel lobby on my way to meet Slash, I saw them.

They weren't doing anything illegal or overtly suspicious. They weren't even standing together. Instead, the three of them were spread out in the lobby crowded with people. But all were sweating like crazy, even though the hotel was well air-conditioned. They glanced around furtively, as if they were scoping the place or looking for someone. They never indicated they were together, but the regular eye contact with each other confirmed they were definitely operating as a team.

A team of what?

I supposed it could have been as harmless as three guys spreading out to look for a friend or a girlfriend, but that wasn't the vibe I got.

While processing all of this inside the span of about five seconds, my inner alarm went off and I froze in mid-step. The guy the farthest from me noticed first. His eyes met mine for a fraction of a second before he and his friends abruptly melted into the crowd.

I did a three-sixty in the middle of the lobby, but all were gone.

What the heck?

Frowning, I went into the bar. It wasn't hard to spot my boyfriend, especially when most everyone else in the bar was looking at him, too. Although he perched quietly on a barstool, he commanded attention. Maybe it was the way he sat, his back straight, his dark eyes constantly assessing the room. Although people didn't mind looking at his jet black hair, square jaw and well-toned physique, they seemed hesitant to meet his gaze. I suspected it was because he gave off a slightly dangerous vibe. Tonight, dressed in a white shirt and dress slacks, holding a drink in his hand, he could have easily been posing for a *Vogue Italia* magazine photo shoot instead of waiting at the bar for his geeky, jean-clad girlfriend.

His gaze landed instantly on me when I walked in. My heart skipped a beat when he rose to greet me.

When I reached him, he pulled me in for a kiss, running a hand down the back of my ponytail. He smelled good, like a mixture of citrus, soap and cologne. I leaned into him and pressed my lips against his, feeling the scratch of his five-o'clock shadow against my chin. It didn't matter that we'd been dating for months, every time he kissed me, I melted.

Still, he knew me well enough to immediately sense something was wrong.

"Cara," he murmured against my mouth. "What's up?"

It boggled my mind that he could tell that from one brief look. Either I was going to have to work on a better poker face or resign myself to the fact he'd always know what I was feeling.

I put a hand on his chest and lowered my voice.

"There were these guys in the lobby. They weren't doing anything…but I got a feeling."

He nodded. He trusted my instincts as much as I trusted his. "Descriptions?"

"Male, all aged between twenty to twenty-seven years, maybe. Two Caucasian, one Hispanic, all average height, no overt tattoos or markings. One of the Caucasian males had a navy blue knit hat on, a dark T-shirt and blue jean shorts. He had some facial hair, a partial beard, I think. The others both had dark hair, white T-shirts—sorry I couldn't see the front of them to see if there were any markings—and shorts. All of them were wearing sandals." My descriptions could have fit half the population of a hotel at the beach. "They're long gone now, Slash. They noticed me looking and disappeared."

"Wait here." Slash walked over to speak with two guys sitting at a small round table. His Secret Service tail. The agent on the right stood and went with Slash toward the lobby. The other stayed in his seat, his eyes on me. No question what his job was.

Sighing, I ordered a cranberry juice and spritzer water and stirred in a lime when the bartender set it in front of me. I read the latest tech news on my phone until fifteen minutes later when Slash returned and sat on the barstool next to me.

"No sign of anyone fitting that description," he said. "But I told hotel security. They'll be reviewing the security feed to check it out."

I set my phone on the bar. "Hopefully it's nothing."

"These days it's better to be sure than hopeful."

"I agree." I noticed he'd angled his stool to have a better view of all the entrances to the bar. Since one side of the bar was open to the beach and ocean, it was a lot of ground to cover. Still, Slash didn't seem outwardly concerned. He took my hand and squeezed it lightly.

"You did a good job at the rehearsal tonight, *cara*."

"I didn't trip over my feet or lose the ring, so I count it as a win." The rings had gone back to the safe in the bridal suite I was sharing with Basia for the night.

"Definitely a win."

"I don't know how you can be so calm," I said. "Doesn't it bother you to be on display in front of everyone?"

Slash had graciously agreed to fill in as a groomsman after Xavier's coworker, Manny, had caught the chicken pox three days ago. It meant a lot to me that Slash was going to be a part of the ceremony. When he was there to be my buffer, social interactions were much easier. I knew it meant a lot to Slash, too, because it signaled Xavier had started to see him as a friend, and not just my boyfriend.

Progress on all fronts.

"I don't let things like that bother me." Slash picked up his drink and took a sip. From the smell, I guessed it was scotch, two fingers, neat. "Not when I have more important things to worry about…like your parents coming to the wedding."

"Right." I sighed and stirred the lime around in my drink, thankful I wasn't the only one worried about it. "I'm going to tell them we're living together at the reception."

Slash raised an eyebrow. "How is it that I didn't know you haven't told them yet?"

My cheeks heated. "Well, I kept meaning to, but it was never the right time. There was the trip to Egypt, the last-minute wedding preparations with Basia…and here we are."

He gave me a look that even I could read. He wasn't impressed with my lame excuses. Easy for him to think that, because he'd already told *his* parents. But his mom and stepdad live in England, so he had distance as a cushion, if he needed it. Lucky him. Distance, a lot of it, always made conversations easier for me. Unfortunately, my parents live twenty minutes from our new place in Silver Spring, Maryland—not that they even *knew* I had a new place yet. If I tried to chicken out and tell them over the phone, they'd be at our house before I had unpacked the glassware and could offer them something to drink. I'd made my decision and intended to stick with it no matter what they might say, but even I knew telling them in person was the adult thing to do. It didn't make it any easier, though.

Technically, Slash and I had only been living together for about forty-eight hours. It was a big step for a geek girl who hates change, and a loner like Slash, but so far, it was working out better than expected. Difficult to derive any significant data from a forty-eight-hour stretch, though.

I'd prepared as much as possible for the talk with my parents because I always try to be ready with things to say for important conversations. According to the book I'd now read twice, titled *The Cohabitation Talk*, telling your parents you were moving in with your boyfriend was best done in person and with confidence in your decision. Despite the clawing anxiety now living in the pit of my stomach, I'd figure out how to do it right.

I worried the most about my dad's reaction. He'd met Slash several times, chatted with him (while secretly employing ill-disguised, lawyerly interrogating methods) and watched him interact with me. *Maybe* he liked Slash a little…even if he wouldn't admit it. Unfortunately, my dad is far too overprotective of his only daughter, even if said daughter can take care of herself just fine.

Luckily convincing my mother this was a good development wasn't going to be a problem. She'd be thrilled to hear Slash and I had moved in together. She adored him and had been mentally fitting him for a tuxedo for months while planning our two-thousand-guest wedding—which neither Slash nor I would ever attend, *if* we ever decided to get married.

I tried to push aside the anxiety. It wouldn't help to freak out when everything was going well. I took a sip of my drink just as Basia and Xavier walked into the bar holding hands. Basia was dressed in a bright yellow sundress with matching shoes and purse. She was glowing—literally—with happiness and the bit of extra sun she'd gotten this afternoon while tanning on the beach. She carried a package in one hand and beamed as Xavier spotted us and raised a hand in greeting.

She walked over and gave me a hug. "Lexi. There you are. You slipped out after dinner so quickly I didn't have a chance to speak to you."

"You were busy," I said. "I just got out of your way."

She noticed the jeans. "You changed already?"

"I hope that's okay. I figured I was off duty."

"It's fine." Slash slid off his stool and insisted Basia sit next to me. As there was no place left for the men to sit, they stood behind us. Basia perched on the stool and smiled. "Guys, I'm so happy. Everything was wonderful tonight. The rehearsal was perfect, and the dinner was spectacular. It all went exactly as planned."

"That's the part I liked best," I admitted. "The going-exactly-as-planned part."

The bartender came over and took Basia's and Xavier's drink requests—a glass of chardonnay for Basia and a beer for Xavier.

I tapped the package she'd laid on the counter. "Another wedding present?"

"Yes. The front desk handed it off to me."

For some reason, Basia wanted the packages to be on display for the reception and Xavier didn't care, so those of us who chose to get them something from the registry had our packages mailed to the hotel. Didn't seem logical to me, but I wasn't the bride, so I kept my mouth shut.

Since Basia and Xavier had apparently received an avalanche of gifts, the hotel ran out of room in their safe and storage area. So, upon our arrival at the hotel, Basia and I had taken several of the larger packages and stored them in our room. It was clear, however, if they got any more presents before tomorrow, we'd have to rent a room just for them.

Basia waved at Finn Shaughnessy, our boss at X-Corp as he strode into the bar, loosening his tie and carrying his suit jacket over his arm. He saw us and came over, joining our little party. After giving the guys high fives and the girls a kiss on the cheek, he realized someone was missing.

"Where's the best man?" he asked looking around.

"Elvis is in our room," Xavier explained. "He needed a little downtime."

I totally got that. Elvis was as much of an introvert as I was.

The conversation immediately turned to the rehearsal, how well the cute flower girl and ring bearer had carried out their duties, and how everything had gone swimmingly.

Eventually I figured I needed to participate a little, so I turned to Basia. "Tonight is your last time sleeping as a single woman. Remind me again, why you're spending it with me?"

Finn cleared his throat and Slash looked at me in amusement.

Okay, maybe that hadn't come out like I planned.

Basia swept her hand out in front of her, the diamonds in her engagement ring sparkling in the light. "Because you are my best friend and because the groom absolutely, positively cannot see the bride on her wedding day until the moment she walks down the aisle."

"That tradition is supported exactly how?"

"I'll answer that." Finn leaned against the bar with one hand, his Irish accent thickening, which it always did when he drank. "Traditionally, it was done in medieval times to ensure arranged marriages were completed. The bride didn't even meet the groom until the ceremony and wore a veil until after the vows were repeated and the deal was sealed, so to say. This prevented the groom from backing out until it was too late."

"Whoa. That's so sexist," Basia protested.

"Don't kill the messenger, lass," Finn said grinning and lifting his hands. "I'm telling it like it was."

"You wouldn't need a veil," Xavier told Basia. "You're stunning. There would be a rush of men to have you. But you're mine. Plus, you know I love you for your mind." Xavier bent down and kissed her. She laughed and slid her arms around him, kissing him back.

Jeez. Get a room already.

I glanced over their heads at Slash and Finn in exasperation. They look amused. It was totally unfair.

"Come on, guys, are you sure you don't want to spend tonight together? I'm more than happy to abdicate." I didn't want to admit it publically, but the truth was, these days I slept better when Slash was around. Seeing as how tomorrow was going to be an extremely nerve-racking time for me, I needed all the rest I could get.

Basia unwound her arms from around Xavier's neck and pressed her cheek against his. "Nope. We're sticking with my plan, mostly because I want to surprise Xavier with my dress."

"I'm going to be so floored, babe," Xavier said. "No doubt about it."

"That makes no sense," I said. "You can wait to get dressed until he leaves. He'll never see the dress."

"No," Basia said firmly. "My last night as a single woman will be spent with my best friend, without whom I never would have met my future husband. I'll never forget that moment when that huge wave crashed you into Elvis and you, ahem, pulled down his swim trunks."

Everyone laughed, including Slash.

My face heated. "You were the one who made me go swimming in the first place." I pointed a finger accusingly at Basia.

She just grinned. "I was. And look where it got us. You crashing into Elvis led to me meeting Xavier. Now I'm getting married to the most incredible man in the world, and I have my best friend to thank for it."

"That kind of reasoning, while understandably sentimental given the circumstances, still doesn't explain why you're spending tonight with me," I pointed out.

"It *totally* does," Basia said. "Trust me on this."

Since she was the bride, I knew I was on the end of a losing battle, so I refrained from arguing, no matter how illogical her position was.

Slash reached around me and retrieved his scotch, taking a drink. "Are you two ready for the honeymoon?"

Basia and Xavier had been planning their honeymoon since the day they'd announced their engagement. They'd be winging their way to a super-secret location for ten days of "just us" time. None of us knew where they were going—not even Elvis. Of course, we had their phone numbers in case of emergency, but they warned us they would only check their phones occasionally. I guess they wanted to unplug as much as possible. I got that, too, although I'm not sure it would ever be that easy for Slash and me.

"I'm *so* ready," Basia said with a sigh. "We need a break and time to be alone, no offense, guys. Weddings are so stressful."

That was the understatement of the century.

"The rehearsal was flawless," I reminded her. "That should relieve some of the stress. We just have to go through the motions tomorrow."

Xavier put his hand on Basia's shoulder. "Yeah, and Andy did a great job. That was one of the few unknowns."

Andy was Andrew Garrington, the Chief Operating Officer, or COO, of ComQuest in Baltimore and Xavier and Elvis's boss. He'd been tapped to officiate the wedding because he was a former district judge and had a special fondness for the genius twins who'd brought his company considerable profit. But more than that, he'd become a close mentor and friend to the twins. It was both fitting and bittersweet that he'd be the one asked to officiate, especially given the absence of the twins' father, from whom they were estranged.

"He's perfect for the officiant," Basia sighed. "It's all going to be amazing tomorrow. I just know it. The wedding of my dreams to the man of my dreams is finally happening."

To my alarm, she started to tear up. Xavier threw me a worried glance. Like, somehow, I'd be better at handling this. Which I wasn't. But since I'd been riding the wedding rollercoaster for the past several months, it didn't scare me as much as it used to.

"Maybe we should call it a night," I suggested. "Getting a good night's sleep is important so we're all good to go tomorrow."

Basia sniffled. "You're right, Lexi. It is getting late."

We finished our drinks and walked to the elevators together. Tonight, Basia and I were in the bridal suite. Tomorrow I'd move into Slash's room and Xavier would move into the suite in my place. It seemed like a lot of musical rooms to accommodate an outdated tradition, but it wasn't my wedding, so I played along.

Xavier, Finn and Slash got off on the eighth floor and Basia and I rode up to the bridal suite on the twelfth. I had the key card ready, so I swiped it and opened the door. I heard a slight rustle and a footstep just as I flipped on the light.

The three guys from the lobby were there waiting for us.

TWO

We were so surprised we barely had time to yelp, let alone scream, before the guys grabbed us, pushing us against the wall and covering our mouths with their hands.

"Make a sound and we'll hurt you," the guy holding me warned. It was the one with the navy blue knit hat. I didn't see any weapons, but that didn't make me feel a whole lot better. "Understood?"

I nodded and he slowly lifted his hand from my mouth. I glanced to the side and saw the guy holding Basia had released her as well. She was trembling, but in true Basia form raised her chin and glared at the guys.

"What do you want?" she said. "I'm getting married in the morning and you are *so* not ruining it."

Like that would convince them to apologize and leave. But still, I had to give her credit for trying.

"That's up to you," Knit Hat Guy said. "I need something from you."

That's when I noticed all the wedding presents had been opened. The boxes, wrapping paper and bows strewn across the suite common area, over the couch, chairs and coffee table.

"You're stealing wedding presents?" I said. "That's low even for petty thieves."

"We are *not* petty thieves and we're *not* stealing wedding presents. We're looking for a box that belongs to us."

"What box?" Basia asked.

"Let's say a client mailed us a box, but it didn't arrive. Instead, the shipping company screwed up by putting the label with *your* name and the address of this hotel on *our* package. All we got was a stupid can opener. We traced the box here to the hotel and now we want what's ours."

"Hey, the can opener was one of my most desired gifts on the bridal registry," Basia protested.

I shot Basia an exasperated look. "Just take your stupid box and get out of here. We aren't going to stop you."

"That's the problem. Our box isn't here, lady. Where do you have the rest of the presents?"

Basia glanced at me with worry in her eyes. "I think there might be some boxes still in the hotel safe in the reception area. They ran out of space, so that's why we've been storing the rest of them up here. How big a box is it?"

He made a size with his hands that indicated it was about the size of a breadbox. I thought the hotel had given us all the large boxes, but I couldn't be positive. For all I knew, Xavier had taken some to his room.

"Look, dude," I said. "We don't know where your box is. Maybe it hasn't even arrived. Or maybe it's in the hotel safe. All I know is that we don't have it here."

"That's why she and I are going to go down to the lobby and ask real nicely for them to give us all of the boxes in the safe." He loomed over Basia. I estimated his height to be about six foot four. He shook a finger at her. "If you scream or try anything funny, my friend will slice your friend's throat here."

The Hispanic guy advanced on me, pulling out a large serrated knife. I shrank back against the wall.

"So, little bride, are we clear on what we're doing?" Knit Hat Guy asked Basia.

She swallowed hard and nodded. "Perfectly."

Basia met my gaze across the room. "Just do what he says, Basia. I'll be alright." I nodded encouragingly even though my heart was doing the tango in my chest.

Nodding, she straightened her shoulders and headed to the door with Knit Hat Guy following close behind her. I tried not to act petrified, but being alone with two big guys who might hurt me in ways I didn't care to imagine wasn't helping much.

The guy with the knife motioned for me to sit in a chair. I slid into it and poked a gigantic white vase with pink roses that was lying sideways on the coffee table. A wedding present, I presumed. The guys must have yanked it out of the box, probably looking for whatever it was they'd lost.

"That's a big vase," I commented.

"It's butt ugly," the other guy said from his perch on the corner of Basia's bed.

He was right, but it didn't feel right agreeing with thugs, so I kept my mouth shut. Knife Guy paced back and forth in front of the door and I thought he might wear a hole in the carpet. I feared he might be juiced, and not with just alcohol. The other guy noticed it, too.

"Chill, *hombre*. We're going to get the package."

Knife Guy whirled around. I wished he would put that stupid knife away. If he were strung out on something, it might fly out of his hand and hit something. Me, for example.

"And if we don't get the package?"

"We will."

Knife Guy kicked at some discarded wrapping paper

that was on the floor. "If we don't find it, we're all going to be dead, man."

"No one's going to be dead. We know it's here somewhere. My bet is the broad's going to bring it back with her."

"Bride, not broad," I said helpfully. "Just trying to point out a more politically correct manner of referring to her."

Both guys glared at me.

I shut up after that and started chewing on my fingernails, which I always do when I'm nervous. Since I'd been nervous ever since Basia said she was getting married and had asked me to serve as her maid of honor, there wasn't much left to chew. Another fifteen minutes passed before there was a soft knock at the door.

"About damn time," Knife Guy said, jumping to the door and yanking it open. He took a step back, startled.

Slash stood there.

THREE

I'M NOT SURE who was more surprised.

Knife Guy, Slash, me or the other dude, who'd leapt to his feet with a shout. It all went down fast. Suddenly, explosively, Slash surged forward, his fist connecting with Knife Guy's elbow with a sickening crunch. Knife Guy dropped his blade with a screech of pain and reeled backward as his buddy ran past me, throwing himself at Slash. Without even forming a plan, I hoisted the heavy vase and swung it at the back of his head. It connected with his skull and shattered into pieces.

"Who's butt ugly now?" I shouted.

The guy staggered a couple of steps before Slash kicked out with his leg, striking him so hard in the stomach with his foot, he fell backward over the coffee table, hit his head and lay motionless. Knife Guy tried to swing at Slash with his one good arm, but Slash easily blocked it and gave him a right hook under his chin. Knife Guy crashed into the wall and slid down, his eyes rolling back in his head.

It was over in a few terrifying seconds.

Slash yanked me to him in a one-armed hug. "*Cara*, what's going on? Are you okay?"

"I'm fine. But just so we're clear, this is not my fault." I squeezed against him in the hug, taking a second to close my eyes and relish his warmth and strength. Then, not wanting to distract him too much from the situation at hand, I straightened and stepped back.

"Are they dead?"

Slash's hand lingered on mine for a moment more before he knelt next to Knife Guy. "He's unconscious."

He patted down the guy all the way to his feet, presumably looking for more weapons. He was clean, but Slash took the guy's wallet and knife. He did the same to the other guy, who, according to Slash, was still breathing.

"Where's Basia?" he asked, straightening.

"The third guy took her to the lobby to get the rest of the wedding packages."

"Third guy?" Slash's eyes quickly swept over the carnage of opened presents and wrapping paper. "Packages?"

"These guys are looking for a package—their package. They said the address label got mixed up and adhered to a package that was mailed to Basia and Xavier at the hotel by accident. They think maybe it's still in the lobby safe and took Basia with them to retrieve it."

Slash pulled out his phone and called someone, barking out a couple of commands. He slid the phone back in his pocket.

"Who were you talking to?"

"My Secret Service detail. They'd already retired to their rooms for the night. They'll contact hotel security and check the lobby for Basia. We'll wait here in case they return."

The adrenaline began to disappear and my legs got shaky, so I sat on the couch while Slash ripped up a couple of pillowcases and tied both the guys' arms behind their backs. I wondered how much would be added to the bill for shredded pillowcases. I bet the bridal suite wasn't used to seeing *this* kind of action.

"Why did you come up?" I asked him.

He finished testing the last knot with a hard jerk, then rose. He reached into his pocket and held out my phone. "You left it in the bar."

I slapped my forehead. "Oh, wow. I totally did. How did you remember?"

"I didn't. The bartender took it to the receptionist. I'd picked up the tab, so he had my name and room number. The receptionist called me, so I went down to get it and bring it up to you."

There was a knock at the door, so Slash held a finger against his lips and headed to the door. He looked out the peephole and then opened the door. Three guys dressed in hotel security uniforms, Slash's Secret Service detail, Knit Hat Guy in handcuffs and Basia entered the suite. Everyone was talking at once.

Basia ran to me and for a moment, we simply hugged without speaking. A huge lump had formed in my throat. She was okay, thank God. She was alive and unharmed.

Basia pulled back and looked at me. "Oh, Lexi, I was so worried about you." Her eyes swam with tears of relief and concern.

"I'm fine," I lied. My legs still felt weak. The truth was I'd been far more terrified something would happen to her than me on the eve of her wedding. "You're okay and that's what's important. I'm sorry, but one of your wedding presents—a vase—is a lost cause."

"Forget the vase. I'm just relieved no one got hurt." She looked at the guys tied up on the floor and then at Slash. "How did you get away from them?"

I dipped my head toward Slash. "I forgot my phone in the bar and he came to return it to me. You can imagine the rest."

"Oh, Slash." She walked into his arms. "You're our hero."

He held her tight, resting his chin on her head. Our gazes met over her head and he smiled at me. I smiled back in both relief and love. In this crazy mixed-up world, I knew I'd always be able to count on him to have my back.

"All's well that ends well," he said.

For the next hour, Basia, Slash and I spoke at great length with hotel security, the hotel manager, the Secret Service, and the state police who showed up about fifteen minutes later. A few minutes after that, the bellhop arrived with all Basia's and Xavier's wedding packages on a rolling cart, and we all watched as the police started unwrapping the rest of the boxes, hands clad in plastic gloves. Less than ten minutes in, the police opened the box in question. Neatly wrapped plastic bundles were stacked in two piles.

It *definitely* did not look like a wedding present.

Another policeman took several photos before the guy who had initially discovered it unwrapped the top bundle. He looked at the tablets, smelled it and looked at one of his colleagues. "Mandrax, I think."

"What's Mandrax?" Basia asked.

"A popular synthetic drug originally prescribed back in the 1960s and '70s as a sleeping pill," a policeman explained. "It was also used as an antidepressant and a treatment for high blood pressure. It causes a severe psychological and physical dependency. It's been banned in most of the world, which, naturally, makes it a favorite among crime syndicates."

"Ewwww…" Basia said.

Yep. It was certainly not an appropriate wedding gift unless you were off your freaking rocker.

The police took the Mandrax and left. The Secret Service and hotel security departed shortly after that, and Basia was finally permitted to call Xavier. He and Elvis arrived at the suite minutes later to join the party and make sure we were okay.

After hearing everything that had gone down, Xavier didn't want to leave. But Basia insisted on keeping with the plan.

"I'm fine. I've got Lexi, and I'm not letting a bunch of losers change one single thing about my perfect wedding. Are we all clear on that?" She stood with her hands on her hips, her eyes flashing fire. No one, not even Slash, was going to argue with that, so we did what she wanted. By the time we got everyone out of our room, it was nearly two o'clock in the morning. The place looked like a tornado hit it, but we were too exhausted to do anything about it.

"Shall we call it a night?" I yawned and stretched my arms over my head.

"Definitely." She plastered a tired smile on her face and kicked off her shoes. "One for the books, right?"

"Yep. You do realize that all of this means tomorrow is going to be smooth sailing, right? The crazies are gone for good. Finished, done, bye-bye. All out of our system."

She slipped out of her dress and hung it up in the closet before reaching for her pajamas. "I hope you're right."

"I *am* right. The statistical improbability that anything else could go drastically wrong is now quite small…even with me involved. Simple math."

"And *that's* why we're best friends."

I laughed and we took turns in the bathroom, showering and changing into our pj's. When we were both safely tucked in bed with the covers up to our chin, Basia rolled to her side, propping her head on her hand, and looking at me.

"It was fun being your roommate at Georgetown. It was like a slumber party every night."

I lay on my back, staring at the dark ceiling. "I agree, although before I met you, I'd never even been to a slumber party before. Being your roommate was fun and a learning experience. Despite my initial reservations, we turned out to be a good match as roommates. Except for the snoring part."

She gasped and sat up straight in the bed. "*What?* I do not snore."

"You do." I chuckled. "But it's a cute little snore. Surely Xavier has said something."

"He certainly has not."

I smiled. "Wow. Xavier is even smarter than I thought."

A pillow hit me in the face. I laughed and held my hands in front of my face to fend off further attack. "Fine, fine. I won't tell Xavier."

"I do *not* snore. Admit it."

Still chuckling, I rolled over onto my stomach and punched my pillow a couple of times to fluff it up. "Maybe you've grown out of it."

"Or maybe I never had it."

"Either way, my lips are sealed."

We were silent for a moment before Basia spoke. "Lexi, thanks for spending tonight with me. It means a lot to me."

"You're welcome. I'm lucky you chose me to be your best friend. You are one of the nicest things that's ever happened to me. I hope we continue to be friends for the rest of our lives."

"We will." Basia spoke with such confidence, I believed her.

A smile crossed my face as I closed my eyes. "Good. Now let's get some sleep and make sure we do this wedding thing right tomorrow."

Basia yawned loudly. "I'm totally down for that."

FOUR

I WAS IN the middle of a weird dream where I was being chased around the ocean by a bunch of sharks with gnashing teeth and knit hats when I abruptly sat up in bed. The room was too bright, the bed felt different and the windows were all wrong. Then I remembered I was in the bridal suite in Ocean City, Maryland, on the morning of Basia and Xavier's wedding.

I pushed the hair off my shoulders and tried to calm my galloping heart. I glanced at the clock and saw it was just after six. Only four hours of sleep, but I was surprised I'd slept at all. Basia's wedding dress hung in a clear bag on the back of the door. Despite the drama that had surrounded obtaining the perfect dress, she'd ended up with a beautiful gown, fitted at the waist with pearls and crystals sewn into it, and a plunging V down the back. I wasn't into dresses or clothes and even I thought it was pretty.

Moving quietly so I didn't wake her, I slipped out of bed, grabbed my laptop and slid open the balcony door. The sound of the ocean crashing on the beach greeted me, the warm breeze carrying a hint of salt. The sun, a gorgeous orange, rose over the horizon as I sunk into one of the plastic chairs and opened my computer.

While it booted, I rolled my neck to ease the tension stored there. Despite my aversion to sand, sun and water, I had to admit the bridal suite had a pretty sweet view from the hotel. Basia and I had met Elvis and Xavier at this very beach. It seemed like a lifetime ago. But now Basia and Xavier were getting married. I hadn't seen that coming—not that I ever saw *anything* coming—but it was a good thing. A very good thing.

In the distance, I could make out the silhouette of a man running along on the beach, his arms and legs pumping. It was a beautiful morning for a run. A quick check on my laptop confirmed the weather forecast for today was perfect—sunny, clear skies and only a two percent chance of rain.

So far so good.

I'd just pulled up my spreadsheet and was putting in the data from last night's events when I heard a noise at the balcony door.

"Lexi?"

Basia stepped out. I shifted in the chair, putting the laptop on the small white plastic table. "I'm sorry. Did I wake you?"

"No." She ran her hand through her tousled dark bob and smiled sleepily. She'd grabbed a silky blue robe and belted it around her waist. "It's hard to sleep when I'm so excited about today."

"You're not nervous at all?"

She sat in the chair next to me, drawing her knees to her chest and wrapping her arms around them. "No, strangely, I'm not. I'm at peace." She looked at the ocean and sighed. "I'm marrying the man of my dreams today. All the details are decided and arranged. Now all I have to do is show up."

I sincerely hoped she meant that. Still, I was afraid she might freak out at the last moment. I wanted to be prepared for that mentally, but I was so anxious about my other responsibilities, I wasn't sure I could manage that kind of emotional flexibility.

She looked over at me. "How did you sleep?"

"Me?" I tried to open my eyes wide and look perky and awake, but probably ended up looking more like a cross-eyed owl. "Ah, great."

"You are such a bad liar." She laughed. "I'm sorry, Lexi. I know this is stressful for you. It's just I couldn't imagine having anyone else by my side today."

"Well, there's no reason everything shouldn't go perfectly today," I said.

"I know." She sighed in contentment. "I'm not even going to think about what happened last night. The venue is lovely, the weather is perfect, the flowers are going to be gorgeous, and all the people I love are going to be here."

"Undoubtedly, it will be the best wedding ever."

She grinned. "So, are you ready to get this day underway?"

It would be a cold day in hell before I was ever ready, but I sucked it up and summoned a smile. "Sure, let's get this thing done."

WE WERE SCHEDULED for a manicure and pedicure at eight o'clock in the morning at the hotel salon. It was a bit early in my opinion, but it was the only time I could get us a double appointment. I'd initially wanted to watch Basia get her nails done, but she insisted we had to do it together. I'd never had my nails, fingers or toes, done before because I don't like to put myself in situations where strangers touch me. But this was a special occasion and I didn't want to ruin it for her.

After we'd both showered and changed, we headed

down to the salon. I was hungry. Unfortunately, brunch was scheduled for *after* the salon visit. While I'd managed a cup of coffee from the room coffeemaker, my stomach rumbled as we walked through the lobby to the salon.

A trio of lovely dark-haired women greeted us when we entered. "Hello, ladies. Welcome to Starfish Nail and Salon. We're glad to have you. Which one of you is Basia?" She pronounced the name Ba-see-a instead of Ba-sha, but Basia was used to that and stepped forward. As if on cue, two of the ladies whipped out white party horns and blew them. The one on the right pulled out a tiara and placed it on Basia's head. Another one pulled out a bottle of champagne and two flutes.

"Congratulations. Today is your wedding day, yes?"

Basia nodded and the one with the champagne took her by the arm, steering her to some large chairs. "We're going to make your nails look good. Your groom is going to love it."

The woman who greeted us looked at me. "You're Lexi Carmichael?"

I pulled my credit card out from my back pocket. "Yes. I'm paying."

She took the card. "We'll give her deluxe bridal treatment. It's very special. You'll get it, too, right?"

"No, I don't need a bridal treatment. I'll just take the minimal service. In fact, I would be happy to just sit next to her and smile. No one has to touch me."

She narrowed her eyes. "Let me see your hands."

I almost sat on them, but instead, reluctantly handed them over.

She examined my nails. "No good. Go sit in the

chair, right now. You need the deluxe treatment more than her. I'll bring you your receipt."

I stood by the door, trying to decide if I still had time to make a run for it, when Basia waved me over. She had already stuck her feet in the bubbling water and was sipping a glass of champagne. Her chair was vibrating.

"Come on, Lexi. It feels great."

I didn't have the heart to bolt or tell her I'd never had a pedicure or manicure before or I'd rather have a root canal twelve times over than let people I didn't know touch my hands and feet.

I walked over and climbed into the chair next to Basia. Other than another woman sitting at a table and getting her nails done, we were the only three customers in the salon. The lady who took my credit card handed me my card and the receipt. I signed it and returned my card to my pocket.

"I got us the deluxe," I told Basia. "Whatever that means."

"It means it's going to be good." She smiled. She looked pretty with the tiara sparkling in her hair. "Oh, thank you, Lexi. This is going to be so much fun. You're the best wing woman ever."

The lady, sitting at my feet on a little stool with wheels, pointed to the bubbling water. "Roll up your jeans and put your toes in. The water feels good."

I gingerly lowered my toes in. The water did feel good. Maybe this wouldn't be so bad after all. The chair massaged my back and I sipped champagne. My feet warmed in the bubbly water.

Not bad at all.

Another woman appeared out of nowhere and started examining my hand. "Hey, hey! What's going on?" I said, trying to snatch my hand away without success. She held on and flipped my hand over to look at my palm. "We'll do a manicure and pedicure at the same time." She frowned. "Your nails are too short. You chew them."

It wasn't a question, so I flushed guiltily. "Well, sometimes I do when I'm nervous. And I've got a lot on my plate right now."

"You have a boyfriend?"

"What does that have to do with my nails?"

"Men like long nails."

My knee-jerk reaction was to dispute that statement, but the truth was I had no idea if it were true. The thought had never crossed my mind even *once* in twenty-five years. I would have googled it right then to see what, if any research had been done on that topic, but she wouldn't let go of my hand.

"I work with computers," I explained. "I don't care if men like them long or not. I can't have long nails." Not that I *wanted* them, but I felt it important she understood the logic behind my reasoning.

"What's more important?" she asked. "Computers or a boyfriend?"

"Ah…"

"It's simple. If you have boyfriend, you need long nails because he likes that. If you *don't* have a boyfriend, you need long nails."

Now my head hurt. "What? That's not simple. That's ridiculous. I don't need long nails, and I'm pretty sure my man doesn't care." I flushed because technically, I had no idea if Slash got turned on by claws or not. It wasn't like long, short or fingernails in general had ever come up in a conversation between us.

"Ah, ha! So, you *do* have a man. What's his name?"

I sighed. *This* is why conversations were so hard for me. "Slash."

She frowned. "What kind of name is Slash?"

"Well, it's not his real name. It's hacker lingo for *backslash*. Look, Slash is just what everyone calls him."

"Doesn't he have a real name?"

"Of course, he has a real name. But not many people know it. It's complicated."

"So, you have boyfriend with no real name. You definitely need long nails. I'll give you an extra good price."

"No! Long nails are *not* happening. Seriously. Okay?"

"Okay." She sighed. "Just a regular manicure, then. How about adding a waxing to that? Bikini, eyebrows, toes. I'll give you good price on all three."

"Whoa." My heart skipped a beat in terror. I'd been there, done that with the bikini wax, and would *never* do that again. Yet something she'd said stuck in my head. "Wait. Did you say toes? Why would I need wax on my toes?"

"Men don't like hair on toes."

"I don't have hair on my toes…do I?" I tried to look at them. The lady doing my feet hissed something in a language I didn't understand and gripped my feet tighter.

Panic started to grip me. "Okay. Here is the deal. No waxing on toes or any other part of my body. No long nails, no extra anything. Just paint the nails with as clear a polish as possible and pour me more champagne, please." I chugged the rest of my glass. I was going to need a lot more alcohol to get through this.

The woman must have sensed I was one step from

going nuclear because she patted my hand and smiled. "Relax. We'll help make your boyfriend happy." Thankfully, she poured more alcohol into my glass before she and the other technician disappeared, undoubtedly to discuss their strategy with me. A minute later one of the technicians returned, sitting on the small stool. She watched my face as she carefully took one of my feet from the water, dried it off and began clipping my toenails. I grit my teeth and tried not to watch her.

Basia was happily chatting with the woman doing her toes, drinking champagne with one hand and soaking the nails of her other hand in a small bowl. She looked relaxed, while I was cranky as an ogre and fighting the overwhelming urge to tell the woman to stop touching my feet before I ran out of the place screaming.

Basia saw me looking and lifted her champagne glass. "Cheers, Lexi. Thanks for always being there for me."

"May you have great nails and a long, happy marriage." I lifted my glass and clinked it against hers.

She laughed. "Is that practice for your toast tonight?"

"I only wish it were that short."

I took another drink. The champagne had started to go to my head especially because I had no food to cushion it. I felt a little light-headed, which wasn't necessarily a bad thing, because it made the feet touching at least a little more tolerable. That's when the woman doing my feet held up something that looked like a handheld cheese grater.

"I'm going to buff your heels, okay?"

"What does 'buff my heels' mean?" I asked.

She mimicked rubbing the grater back and forth on

my heel. "It won't hurt. Tickle a little, maybe." Before I could respond, she rubbed it for real against my heel.

Just like the last time I was at the doctor's and he hit me with a rubber mallet in the kneecap, my foot jerked upward, catching the nail technician right below the chest. The force of my kick propelled her, and her little stool with wheels, spinning backward with alarming force. She hit the pedicure chair behind her, slid off the stool and landed butt-first into the bubbling spa water.

"Ahhhhh!" she screamed, along with some other phrases in a foreign language that made me glad I couldn't understand what she was saying. Her butt was wedged into the basin as water splashed all over the floor.

I leapt from my chair to help her. Unfortunately, my feet were wet, the floor was slippery, and I was a bit woozy from the champagne. I took two steps, skidded, and promptly slipped, sliding across the floor on my back and butt. My left hip hit the stool on wheels and sent it careening wildly toward two technicians who rushed to our aid. Amazingly, the two jumped over the stool like a pair of freaking track stars while I, unfortunately, finished my slide by crashing, butt-first, into a manicure table. Nail polish, clippers, acrylic nails and cotton balls rained down on me as I covered my head with my hands.

For a brief moment, the salon was deadly silent. Then I heard Basia yell my name and the salon was filled with anxious shouting. By the time I'd been helped to my feet, and the technician who'd been working on my toes un-wedged from the foot basin, we were all wet, panting and thoroughly traumatized.

On the upside, it appeared no one had broken any

bones, nor had the salon suffered irreparable material damage. I counted only two bottles of nail polish, a container of polish remover and an undetermined number of cotton balls as complete losses. On the downside, I was a bit worse for the wear. A quick glance in the mirror indicated my hair was damp and stuck to my head on my left side, there was a splash of purple nail polish on my right earlobe and jaw, I smelled like nail polish remover. My dignity had suffered a significant hit. The technicians, with great efficiency, picked up everything, making it look perfect again in just minutes. The woman who'd been working on my feet and ended up with her rear soaking in the foot basin, however, had disappeared... to change her underwear, I presumed.

When I finally managed to get a good look at Basia, she sat in her pedicure chair staring at us with her hand clapped over her mouth. Not exactly a leisurely, relaxed and pampered salon start to the day of her wedding.

I should have known better.

FIVE

I APOLOGIZED PROFUSELY, to Basia, the technician I kicked and everyone else in the salon. No one protested when I said I didn't want to finish the pedicure and manicure. After being permitted to wash up the best I could in the bathroom, I'd sat in a corner chair near the entrance. I drank the rest of my champagne in peace, my cheek and ear pink from where I'd scrubbed the nail polish off. The technicians finished painting and buffing Basia's toes and nails so she looked perfect.

Since I didn't ask for a refund *and* I gave the injured technician a big tip for her trouble, everyone seemed happy. Especially when we left.

Thankfully, Basia didn't seem at all disappointed that I didn't have sparkly toes or fingers. She was, however, concerned I seemed a little tipsy.

"It's a good thing we're going straight to brunch." She held my elbow as we steered our way to the dining room. "You drank too much champagne and you still smell like nail polish remover."

"Basia, I'm sorry about the nails. I should have just watched you get it done."

"That's on me. I wanted us to do it together. I shouldn't have made you go out of your comfort zone, for the manicure or for any of this wedding stuff, but I appreciate that you have. That's what friendship is all about. Thank you."

When we arrived at the restaurant, the hostess led us to a table after wrinkling her nose at my smell. "It's just the two of us?" I asked.

"Yes, the rest of the girls are meeting us in the bridal suite at one thirty for hair and makeup. To be perfectly honest, I'd rather just spend the morning with my best friend, no matter what it brings."

I lifted my water glass and clinked it to hers. "Well, I'm good with that."

"I figured you would be."

We ordered our food and after the waiter left, I reached into my pocket and pulled out a dark blue velvet pouch. I set it on the table in front of her.

"I know you already have the jewelry picked out. But I wanted you to have something special from me that you could wear at the wedding or during the honeymoon, if you wanted."

She picked up the pouch and shook the contents into her hands. Two small diamond and pearl studs fell into her palm. I'd figured since she had multiple holes in her ears, she might want to add these to her display.

Her breath caught in her throat. "They're beautiful! I love them, Lexi." She reached up and put them on. "They'll go perfectly with my dress."

"Now it's your turn." Basia dug into her purse and pulled out a little box, laying it on the table. "This is for you."

I looked at the box, stunned. "Me? But I'm not getting married."

"You're the maid of honor. I wanted to thank you for everything I've put you through. Open it, please."

I carefully opened the box. Inside was a tiny platinum feather with sparkling crystals hanging on a thin silver chain.

To my astonishment and slight horror, I felt tears spring up behind my eyes. "It's beautiful." I took it out of the box and put it around my neck. Basia got out of her chair and came around to help me fasten it.

"The feather because you helped me spread my wings," she said, returning to her seat. "I can't tell you how much your friendship has meant to me. We've been through it all, from surviving college to nearly dying together in a jungle. I'd never have made it without you. You've changed my life. You know that, right?"

I touched the necklace with reverent fingers. "Likewise. I'd still be online, playing 'Hidden Kingdoms' or something. I would have missed out on all of this."

"Don't look so wistful about that." She laughed. "I'm proud of you, Lexi. I mean it."

"Look at us. You're getting married and I'm living with my boyfriend. I mean, it's huge."

"It is. It really is. By the way, how is the living together thing going?"

"Well, it's only been a couple of days, but so far so good."

Then I remembered I still hadn't told my parents we were living together, not to mention my secret fear I'd do something to screw it up. But even beyond that, there was still another concern worrying me that I'd never told anyone...not even Basia. But on the morning of Basia's wedding wasn't the time to discuss it.

Unfortunately, Basia knew me too well. She leaned forward. "But..."

"But what?"

"Don't play dumb. You're terrible at doing that.

There's something on your mind. Best friend, remember? Spit it out."

Apparently, everyone could expertly read my inner-
most thoughts by simply looking at me. I needed to
work on a poker face if I wanted to have any chance at
privacy. "We can discuss this another time."

Her eyes flashed that fire I knew all too well. "We'll
discuss it now."

There was never any arguing with Basia when her
mind was made up. I sighed. "Well, you know the NSA
had to clear Slash to go to Egypt with Elvis and me,
right?"

"I figured as much."

"I didn't think about it much at the time because
there was so much going on, but when I look back now,
how did he make that happen? I mean Slash works in
a top secret job, is watched 24/7 by the Secret Service
and, boom, he gets approval to go to a dangerous place
like Egypt just like that? How is that possible?"

She shrugged. "He's Slash. He makes things happen."

"I know. But I think it's more than that."

She stared at me for a long moment. "What are you
getting at, Lexi?"

"I think the NSA cleared Slash to go to Egypt because they approved his trip as a mission. His superiors
weighed the danger and decided it was worth the risk. I'll
be honest, Slash was acting a bit strangely the whole time
we were there. I thought maybe his feelings for me had
changed, but I realized later he was acting that way because it wasn't about me at all. It was about the mission."

"And that surprises you?" Basia leaned forward on
the table, staring at me intently. "That's the nature of

Slash's job. He couldn't tell you one way or the other, even if it were true."

"I'm aware of that. But how do I know when he and I are living *our* life and when we're living the mission?" I folded my napkin into a small square.

Basia thought for a moment and then sighed. "The mission—yours or his—is always going to be a part of your relationship. You and Slash have become too valuable, too integral to the safety of this country for it to be any other way. Whether you can live with this as a couple, I don't know. It's a lot of pressure and secrecy to manage. Trust is going to have to be paramount. It's going to be hard on this relationship or any relationship you may have. You'll have to decide if it's worth it. One thing I'm sure of—Slash loves you. I had my doubts at first, but not any longer. Whether that's enough is up to you."

"Thanks, Basia. I guess I still do need your advice."

"You've got it whenever you need it. Remember, I'm getting married, not dying."

"I know. But I'll have to survive without you for two weeks while you're on your honeymoon."

She laughed. "Just don't get into any trouble while I'm gone, okay?"

"Believe me, I'll try."

SIX

AFTER LUNCH, BASIA and I returned to the bridal suite so I could shower (again), pack up, then move into Slash's room. Xavier's suitcase, minus his tuxedo, was already parked in one corner. I left my red bridesmaid dress and shoes hanging in the closet as I would be joining Basia, the bridesmaids and the stylists here for hair and makeup at one thirty. Ugh. For now, however, I needed a break. As much as I loved Basia, I was on social overload.

I rolled my suitcase to Slash's room and used the key he'd given me to get in. He wasn't there, so I unpacked and took my laptop to the balcony to work on the spreadsheet. I needed to unwind and get to my happy place—the one that involved numbers, order and data. I was still on the balcony when Slash arrived. He was dressed in running shorts and a black muscle shirt. He had a white towel around his neck.

He kissed the top of my head. "Finished with all the girl stuff?"

"For the moment, thank God."

He noticed my necklace. "That's pretty."

"Basia gave it to me at brunch. I don't know why I'm getting presents when I'm not the bride. She said she wanted to thank me for being the maid of honor."

He slid a finger under the chain, examined it. "A feather?"

"It signifies flight. She said I gave her wings and changed her life, although I don't really know exactly how I did that."

He smiled. "You do that a lot."

"I hope that's a good thing."

"It is."

I shifted the laptop so it rested more on my knees. "So, what are you up to?"

"I just had a run on the beach. I'll take a shower and join you out here in a few minutes."

"I'd like that."

While he was in the shower, I continued working on the spreadsheet. After a short while, he returned to the balcony dressed in jeans, a white T-shirt and bare feet. His dark hair was damp and curling slightly around his ears. He carried two bottles of water. He placed one beside me on the small side table before taking a seat in the plastic chair next to me. Sighing, he stretched out his long legs in front of him and balanced the water bottle on his thigh. He motioned with his head to the laptop. "What are you working on?"

I angled the laptop toward him. "The spreadsheet."

"What spreadsheet?"

"It's a spreadsheet that compiles the data on all my troubles over the past year. I call it my 'Little Black Cloud' spreadsheet. Before you say anything, I know the word *trouble* can be subjective, so I've limited it to verifiable events such as getting kidnapped, shot at, knifed and tortured. I've added in plane, car and motorcycle crashes as well. That's not all-inclusive, but you get the idea. I've also added peripheral dangerous events involving people I love such as my parents, brothers, close friends and you, of course. That all counts as trouble in my book."

He lifted an eyebrow, but said nothing.

"I understand that look, you know. You're wondering the purpose of such a spreadsheet. Well, the answer is I wanted to see for myself what the data showed. Because data doesn't lie. Data never lies. It is what it is."

He took a swig of water and smiled.

"What?" I shifted in my chair. "Why are you smiling?"

"No reason other than I adore you."

"While that comment is appreciated, I fail to see how they connect. How do you extrapolate adoration from hearing about my spreadsheet?"

"Because only you would rely on data to prove to yourself that a little black cloud follows you around."

"It does."

"I'm not disagreeing with that. Just admiring that logical mind of yours." He ran his finger up and down the neck of the water bottle, wiping off the condensation. Watching him reminded me what nice hands he had—elegant hacker hands—and *that* made me think of the manicure this morning.

"Um, Slash, can I ask you a question?"

"Of course."

"Do you like long fingernails on a woman?"

That apparently caught him off guard. I could almost see him trying to figure out how and why I'd asked that question.

I decided to help him out. "My nails are short." I held up a hand. "Sometimes I chew on them when I'm nervous."

He was still looking at me, kind of freaked out now. "Okay, and that's important why?"

"I'm not sure. It was a question posed to me today and I didn't know the answer. I guess I just wanted to know."

He considered for a lot longer than I thought necessary. It wasn't rocket science, after all. "Long nails have never been criteria for me." He spoke carefully, as if walking a minefield.

"That's what I thought."

He leaned over and took my hand. "Who asked you this question?"

"It came up in conversation during Basia's and my nail salon experience today."

"Really?"

"Really. The nail technician insisted men like long nails. But I'm glad they're not important to you, because I'm not sure I could ever get a manicure or pedicure again. I'm perfectly capable of trimming my own fingernails and toenails."

"Of course, you are. What exactly happened at the salon?"

"Well, there was this one small accident involving a nail technician and something that looked like a cheese grater, but no one got hurt…badly. It's all sorted out now."

He opened his mouth to speak and then closed it without saying anything. Instead, he stood, closed my laptop and tucked it under his arm, and used his other hand to pull me out of the chair.

"You didn't get much sleep last night," he said.

"No, I didn't. Not without you. And I may have drunk a little too much champagne this morning. I think you should know I think I'm pathologically unsuited to nail salons. That won't be a problem with our relationship, will it?"

A smile touched his lips. "No, it won't. Come now, you need a nap. You have time, so come to bed, *cara*. Rest and conserve your energy. You'll need it for later. I'll stay with you and wake you when it's time to go get dressed."

The idea sounded heavenly, even if I rarely took naps in the middle of the day.

We left the balcony door open. The crash and ebb of the ocean was soothing, despite the normal noises from hotel and beach below. Slash sat on the bed, resting against the headboard. I sat between his legs, my back against his chest. He massaged my shoulders and neck lightly until I began to feel the knots unwind.

"That feels so good. I don't know why I don't mind when you touch me, but when anyone else does, it freaks me out."

"Good. I don't want anyone else touching you anyway."

"That wasn't exactly what I meant."

"I know what you meant. Close your eyes, and I'll wake you when it's time to get dressed."

I rested my head back against his shoulder and closed my eyes. "I'm glad you love me, Slash. You know that, right?"

"I know," he said, rubbing my shoulders as I fell asleep. "And I thank God for it every day."

THE BRIDAL SUITE was in complete chaos when I walked in. Basia's mother was helping her fasten her specially-made bra. One of Basia's cousins, Victoria, was having her bridesmaid dress zipped up by a woman I didn't recognize. Victoria hollered at her two young children to stop jumping on the couch while her younger sister and Basia's other bridesmaid, Jolka, tried to chase them down and get them dressed. A woman I assumed was the makeup artist was arranging cosmetics on a table. A female photographer was everywhere snapping candid photos. She aimed the camera toward me, but backed off when she saw my expression.

Mrs. Kowalski waved at me from across the room and I smiled and waved back.

Curling irons, clothes, bras and shoes were scattered everywhere. Open suitcases were spilled in a half-dozen spots. An unopened bottle of champagne sat on one of the tables. Just looking at it made me feel queasy.

The mystery woman who'd zipped Victoria in her dress marched up to me.

"Are you Lexi, the maid of honor?"

I almost said no because of the intense way she was looking at my hair, but I sucked it up and nodded. "That would be me."

"I'm Monique. You're just in time. Let me look at your hair."

She released it from my ponytail and spread it around my shoulders. "It's long, thick and healthy. That's good. You should get highlights."

"Not today," I answered. "If I'm honest, probably never."

"Well, you should consider it, since some strategic highlights would be pretty. But you're right. We don't have time today." She pointed to a chair in front of four plugged in devices. "Sit. That's your spot right now. You're mine for the next half hour."

I gulped. "Wait. You're not using all of those contraptions on me, are you?"

"Not all at the same time. Park it."

"Yes, ma'am."

She worked on my hair with a special curling iron that supposedly gave me beach curls, whatever the hell that meant. I just closed my eyes and didn't look. Finally, she was done with me. When I dared a look in the mirror, my hair was curly, but in a soft way and it swished every time I moved my head. It wasn't as bad as I'd expected. I waited patiently until the bathroom was empty and snuck in there with my dress. There was no way I was dressing out there in the chaos with people running around, including someone with a camera.

When I came out, Mrs. Kowalski was waiting for me.

"Lexi, I know it's traditionally the maid of honor that helps the bride with the final touches of hair and makeup, but would you mind if I joined you girls?" Her voice held a trace of wistfulness. "I haven't had much of a chance to help out Basia today."

I suddenly realized that in the scramble to get Basia ready, she'd kind of been pushed aside. "Of course not, Mrs. Kowalski. I don't mind at all. In fact, if you want it to be just the two of you, I'm totally on board for that."

She blinked. "Really?"

"Really. As long as Basia doesn't mind. But it's her show, so let me talk to her first."

I couldn't even see Basia since she was surrounded by a sea of people fussing with her hair, undergarments and makeup. I had to push my way through the crowd to get to her. She was leaning back in a chair, eyes closed, while someone I'd never seen before put foundation on her chin and throat.

"Um…excuse me, Basia."

She opened her eyes and smiled. "Lexi. You're dressed and your hair looks gorgeous, but you don't have makeup on."

"No, not yet. Look, I have a question for you. Would you mind if I passed on the last-minute hair, dress and makeup duty?"

She looked puzzled, so I continued. "I know it's just supposed to be the two of us until your dad comes to get you, but I think there's another person far more suited for the role." I tipped my head toward her mom and lowered my voice. "I think she's feeling a bit left out. It would mean a lot to her and I'm happy to back out so she can have you to herself. I know you'll be in good hands."

Basia's eyes softened. "It sounds great. Thank you."

"Hey, what are best friends for?"

I endured another twenty minutes with Renee, the makeup artist, before I was finally done. The noise, perfume, hairspray and craziness were driving me nuts. I slid toward the door, hoping to step out for a bit of fresh air and quiet. It wasn't like anyone would miss me. Mrs. Kowalski now seemed to have things well in hand with Basia, and the other bridesmaids were taking their turns with Renee and Monique.

I just wanted the heck out.

I had my hand on the doorknob, when Victoria rushed over. "Oh, Lexi, are you finished getting ready? Would you mind taking the kids down to the venue and letting them run around to blow off a bit of steam? My husband should be ready shortly. I'll text him you're waiting down there."

I looked at the two little hellions. Sophia was dressed

in a fluffy white dress with a red bow. Her blond hair was a mass of curls. She looked like a perfect angel. Teddy was dressed in a mini tuxedo with a red bow tie. They were beyond cute, but they were kids and I had exactly zero experience with pint-sized humans.

"Ah… Um…" I stammered.

"Oh, thank you so much." Victoria mistook my hesitation for acceptance. She turned to the kids. "Sophia and Teddy, come here this instant. You're going to go out with your Auntie Lexi for a bit. You listen to her and do what she says until Daddy gets there, okay?"

"Yes, Mama," Teddy said. Sophia giggled and planted a kiss on her mom's cheek.

Before I could say another word, Teddy opened the door and Sophia shot out at full speed with Teddy close behind her.

"Hey, come back," I yelled and darted after them.

Just like that, I was stuck with two munchkins.

SEVEN

"WAIT! SLOW DOWN," I bolted after them.

Thank God, they had to wait for the elevator or I would have lost them. Who knew two tykes could run so fast? Sophia was standing in front of the elevator, pressing the button as fast as her little finger would go.

"Pressing it once is sufficient," I said, but she didn't pause for a second. I sighed as her brother shoved her out of the way and started pushing it on his own.

"Hey, once is enough," I repeated. Sophia hit her brother and tried to move him out of the way.

"Whoa! Time-out. Stop fighting over a button. It's already pressed. See the little light? That means the elevator is coming. All of your pushing isn't making it come any faster."

I might as well have been talking to a brick wall. They ignored me and kept pushing the button and each other.

Thankfully, the elevator opened and the two of them jostled each other getting on. Luckily the elevator was empty. Before I could open my mouth, Sophia and Teddy had pushed every button between them on the elevator keypad.

"Why did you do that?" I asked, exasperated.

They grinned and stood in the elevator looking supremely proud of themselves. Other people got on and

I smiled brightly as we stopped at every freaking floor before making it to the lobby.

When we got off the elevator, I knelt next to the little girl. "How old are you, Sophia?"

She held up three fingers.

Teddy shook his head. "No. She's not three until November first."

"I'm a big girl," she insisted.

"Yeah you're getting there. How old are you?" I asked Teddy.

"I'm four."

"Wow. Practically in kindergarten. Look, I'm counting on you to help me out with your sister, okay?"

"I don't like her."

"That's not very nice."

"She eats her boogers."

I shrugged. "Eating boogers is pretty subjective criteria. Come on, let's go see how things are looking for the wedding."

We headed to the spot where we'd rehearsed the ceremony last night. To get to the main area, we had to walk through a waiting area. Last night it had been empty, but today there were long tables with white tablecloths on each side of the room. The waiters were bringing glasses of water, orange juice, iced tea and lemonade and setting them on two long tables that were pushed back against the wall. Off that room was the main area which was a wide-open space with doors to a huge wooden terrace over a private beach. A white awning stretched across several rows of white plastic chairs. There were a lot of people running around, putting last-minute touches on the venue.

"Look what I found." Sophia held a basket with red rose petals. "The flowers."

"Right." I ran my finger across the velvety petals. "You're going to scatter those right before Basia walks in. Just like you practiced last night, except today you get to use the real thing."

"Here's my pillow with the rings," Teddy said proudly.

"Exactly." Except those were not the wedding rings. Basia and Xavier were too smart to give wedding rings to a four-year-old. Instead they'd entrusted them to me and Elvis. I glanced down at my right hand, where I wore Xavier's wedding ring on my third finger. The platinum band shone brightly.

"So, Teddy, you and Sophia walk out together. Remember? Be sure to hold the pillow like this."

I demonstrated with a walk up and down the aisle before Sophia tugged on my hand.

"Auntie Lexi. I have to go potty."

"Right now?" I looked around. "I'm not sure where the bathroom is."

"I have to go right *now*."

"Okay. Just hold it. You don't want to have an accident in your nice dress. Let's go ask someone where it is."

"Hurry."

I flagged down a harried hotel worker who told us a bathroom was around the corner. When I turned around to tell Teddy, he was gone.

What the heck? It had been exactly 0.12 seconds. How could a four-year-old vanish in that amount of time?

"Teddy?" It was physically impossible for him to

have disappeared so quickly. Except I didn't see him anywhere. "Where are you?"

"Potty. Now!" Sophia screamed in my ear with the decibel level of DEFCON 2. "Hurry, hurry, hurry."

I couldn't go without Teddy. But I couldn't let her pee on her flower girl dress.

Where the heck was Teddy?

Panic gripped my throat. Pee or not, we couldn't go anywhere without Teddy.

"Teddy?" I shouted, running back the way we came, pulling Sophia with me. "Where are you?"

I ran through the waiting area and out onto the terrace where the wedding would take place. "Teddy? Teddy?" I shouted like a lunatic.

"I have to pee," Sophia wailed at the top of her lungs. "Now, now, NOW!"

Teddy suddenly crawled out from under one of the tables. "Surprise." He threw his arms up in a grandiose gesture.

My heart resumed its normal beat. "That wasn't funny, kid. Come on, your sister has to go to the bathroom."

I grabbed them both by the hand until we got to the bathroom. When we got there, Teddy refused to go in.

"I'm not going in the girl's bathroom. I'm a boy." He crossed his arms over his chest.

I narrowed my eyes. "You're four. I'm bigger and stronger than you. Get in the bathroom or I'll carry you in."

He must have sensed I meant business because he stomped in.

"Now, wait here and don't move." I pointed at a spot

by the sink, then pulled Sophia into a stall and stood there. "Ah, you know what to do, right?"

"I have to go now," she wailed in the loudest, most dramatic voice ever. "I can't hold it."

Holy emergency.

"Can't you get your underwear down by yourself?"

"No." Tears welled in her eyes as she shook her blond curls.

"Okay, okay. Don't cry. Jeez." I bent down on one knee, which wasn't easy in my bridesmaid dress, and reached under the dress to get her underwear down. I lifted her onto the toilet and held her because I was afraid she'd fall in.

She sat there, but I didn't hear anything happening. After a few seconds, I asked, "What's wrong? Why aren't you going?"

"Mommy always sings the song to *Frozen* when I pee."

"What?"

"You have to sing or I can't go." Tears spilled from her big blue eyes and her lower lip trembled.

Oh, dear God, no. This can't be happening to me.

I tried to reason. "Look, Mommy's not here and I don't know the song, so you're going to have to pee without it. You're a big girl. You can do this."

"Noooooooo." Tears kept sliding down her cheeks. "I can't."

One thing was certain. This kid had a lock on the drama thing when she grew up. Unfortunately, there was no logic in this discussion. There had to be a way to make sense of this.

"Look, how is that possible that you can't pee? You just said you couldn't hold it."

"I don't know." She started crying harder.

It was becoming abundantly clear reasoning was not going to work on a toddler. "Fine. Okay, don't cry. How does this *Frozen* song go?"

She sniffed. "Like this." She started singing. I did my best to sing along, relieved beyond measure when I finally heard her tinkle. Eventually I got her off the toilet and she hiked her underwear up. We were washing hands when I realized Teddy was gone.

Again.

EIGHT

"ARE YOU KIDDING ME?" I whirled around. Was this a never-ending nightmare? How hard could it be to keep track of two kids who weren't even in kindergarten yet?

"Teddy?"

Silence.

I looked under a stall. An elderly lady threw her handbag at me. "Pervert," she shouted.

"Sorry," I said, rubbing my forehead. "I'm looking for a missing child."

A quick look confirmed there was no one else in the bathroom. I dragged Sophia out of the bathroom in search of her brother.

"Teddy?" I shouted. We rushed back into the venue, but didn't see him. I ran past the dais and out onto the beach. There were a lot of people, but I didn't see a little boy in a tuxedo.

OMG.

What if he'd been kidnapped? What if he'd drowned in the ocean? What if he got lost?

It would all be my fault.

I asked every waiter, every person I saw, but no luck. In a panic, I ran back into the reception area and found Teddy standing next to the table with the liquid refreshments.

For a moment, I stared at him like he was a mirage. "Teddy?"

"I was playing Hide and Seek," he said proudly. "I hide. You seek. Except you aren't very good."

"We're *not* playing a game," I shouted and then felt bad for doing so. I had the strangest urge to sit down in the middle of the room and cry. What the heck was wrong with me? These kids were making me crazy. "You're supposed to stay where I can see you."

He pouted. "I got thirsty."

"I don't care how thirsty you are. Don't *ever* run away from me again. You took ten years off my life, bud, and the way my life has been going lately, I don't have a lot of years to play around with."

"Down," Sophia insisted as she wiggled in my arms. I was holding her rather tight. "I want down."

"No freaking way." I held on tighter even though my arms were aching. Who knew a two-and-a-half-year-old girl could weigh so much? "I'm not letting either one of you out of my sight again until your dad gets here. I don't care if you have to pee on the floor."

Speaking of their dad, where the heck was he?

"I don't feel so good." Teddy rubbed his stomach. "I dranked the orange juice. It tasted funny."

"Which orange juice?"

He pointed to a table where a bunch of glasses with orange juice sat. Right next to the sign that said Adults Only.

"Oh, no." I picked up one of the orange juices and took a sip.

Holy mimosa!

"Teddy, how much of the orange juice did you drink?"

He lifted his shoulders. "I don't know."

"Which glass is yours?"

He pointed to a glass on one end of the table. I picked it up. Thankfully, it looked mostly full. I calculated his body weight, the amount he drank, the average alcohol content of the champagne and how much was likely to be mixed in with the orange juice and concluded he'd be okay.

Just then a waitress walked in and arranged some glasses of lemonade on the table. She patted Teddy on the head.

"Aren't you so adorable in your tuxedo, little man?"

He threw up on her shoe.

She gasped, staggered backward, and knocked several glasses of lemonade off the table. I gagged, not only because I was grossed out by the sight and smell, but because I am also a sympathetic vomiter.

"Teddy throwed up," Sophia observed, holding her nose. "It smells bad."

I gagged again because she was right. It reminded me of the time Devlin Mackleberry threw up after ingesting six pieces of sausage and ground beef pizza and three Red Bulls during a marathon gaming session of 'Swords and Scythes.' Four of us had hurled right along with him. I pressed my lips together hard, praying I wouldn't add to the mess in my bridesmaid dress.

I grabbed Teddy by the back collar of his tuxedo, pulling him away. By some miracle, none of the vomit had gotten on his tuxedo. Still holding Sophia, I grabbed some napkins from a nearby table, shoving them at the waitress, all the while dry heaving.

"Why are you making that funny noise, Auntie Lexi?" Sophia asked.

I gagged. "I can't stand the smell." I glanced at the waitress. "I'm sorry. Are you okay?"

"I'm fine." She was acting a lot calmer than I would have if some kid had thrown up on my shoe.

The waitress slipped out of her shoe and left it there before tossing some of the napkins on the floor to cover the mess. She wobbled away on one shoe, wagging a finger at me. "Keep the kids out of the mess."

Seriously? Like that would be a problem? Then again, maybe it would. How the heck could I predict what these two adorable hellions would do next?

I moved us down to the other end of the room where the lemonade, non-spiked, was located. I leaned back against the wall, panting. I was going to have a nervous breakdown if their dad didn't get here soon. Epic babysitter fail.

"Lexi?"

I looked to see who was calling my name, hoping I was finally relieved from duty. Unfortunately, it wasn't the kids' father.

"Elvis?" I said, then frowned. "No, Xavier." For the first time in pretty much forever, I couldn't tell.

"You were right the first time. It's me, Elvis." He looked nice in a black tuxedo with a red bow tie and matching red rose pinned to his left breast pocket.

"Wow, Elvis. I'm so stressed out right now I probably wouldn't recognize my own mother."

"You look different. Pretty. What did you do to your hair?"

"I didn't do anything. But I couldn't stop the army of stylists from swarming me. They're beach curls, whatever the hell that means."

"No idea." He looked at Sophia, who had suddenly taken an interest in my hair and was winding it around her finger. "What's that smell and why do you have two kids?"

"It's barf and they're Victoria's. How do people manage kids without completely losing it?"

"I suspect parental duties are kept largely secret by those who have children because otherwise the human population would never increase."

"That's no kidding." Teddy was pulling on my hand, wanting a closer look at his stomach contents, but I wasn't budging. "What are you doing here, Elvis? Why aren't you getting ready with Xavier?"

"Probably for the same reason you aren't with Basia."

"Good point."

"I need a drink." He walked down the table, careful to avoid the napkin-covered part of the floor. He picked up one of the mimosas and downed half of it before carrying the other half back to me. I was beginning to see how stress could turn people into drinkers.

"Whoa. Go easy, Elvis. You drink even less than I do."

"I'm nervous, okay?" He ran his fingers through his hair. His skin did look a little gray.

"I get that. What's going on in Xavier's room?"

"He's still in the suite. Finn and Slash are talking him down from the ledge."

"Xavier has cold feet?"

"Not really." Elvis finished off the glass and picked up another one. "He's just terrified in general. It's a big thing pledging your undying love to someone until the end of time. He'll be fine. He loves Basia."

Before I could comment, Teddy shouted, "Daddy!" and yanked out of my grip, running to a man in a blue pinstripe suit and tie. The man scooped him up with a kiss on the cheek. "Now, don't you look handsome."

"Daddy." Sophia kicked her legs and squealed, so I released her.

"Oh, I see a princess, too," he said, smiling.

The man strode toward me holding Teddy and leading Sophia by the hand. He made it look easy. "Hi, I'm Tadeusz Nowak. Are you Lexi?" He stuck out a hand, so I shook it.

"Yes, I am. Listen, I'm sorry, but Teddy drank a little of the orange juice before I could stop him. It was spiked—a mimosa. He didn't drink much, but he said his stomach hurt right before he threw up."

"Threw up? Is he okay?"

"He seems fine now that he got it out of his system. I'm sorry. I was helping Sophia in the bathroom. Well, we were all in the bathroom at one point, but he ran out while I was in the stall helping Sophia."

"I was a bad boy," Teddy said proudly.

Tadeusz frowned at his son. "We're going to have to talk about that."

"Daddy, let's go see the beach," Sophia shouted and ran past the dais. Her dad followed, hot on her heels, still holding Teddy.

Better him than me.

I sunk into one of the chairs that was pushed against the wall. A clean-up crew of two guys with a special trash can, rug cleaner, air spray, broom and brush arrived to deal with the barf fest, thank goodness. They looked at me suspiciously. I waved, but they didn't seem cheerful about having to be there.

"Okay, babysitting has now officially passed hand-to-hand combat with a terrorist in terms of difficulty." I pushed the hair off my shoulders. I was sweating from a combination of heat, nerves and stress. "Toddlers are the most irrational creatures in the universe."

"Their brains aren't fully functional yet." Elvis

grabbed another mimosa and started to chug. I decided I needed to either distract or join him. Since my stomach was still queasy due to the barf and too much champagne from this morning, I decided to abstain.

Distract it was.

"So, how's it going with you and Xavier?" They'd had a recent falling out over their long-estranged father, who had showed up requesting their help. Elvis had assisted his father, but Xavier had refused any contact with him. The issue had driven a wedge between the twins, which was painful for me to watch since they'd always been so close.

Elvis sat in a chair next to me, leaning forward and holding the orange juice between his legs. "I don't know. We're pretending it's okay. I don't know how to fix it or if I can. He probably feels the same way."

I didn't know either, but I wanted to be supportive. "Just give him time. He's got a lot going on right now. Weddings are not good times to try and talk reasonably about things. You're brothers, you'll figure it out. So, take the nervousness down a notch."

"If that was it, life would be a lot better. That's not the only thing I'm nervous about."

"What else? The ceremony? You'll do fine. You aced it last night. Just remember, it's not about you. It's about them. Smile and be supportive, which isn't as easy as it sounds, but you can manage."

"No, it's not just that either, although I'll be honest, I'm anxiety-ridden about those things, too."

"Then what's wrong?"

"Bonnie thinks she's my date tonight."

"Okay. How's that a problem?"

"Gwen thinks she's my date, too."

I paused a beat, making sure I'd processed that right. "How did that happen?"

He shoved his fingers through his hair. "Well, earlier this week Bonnie came down with the flu. She told me she wouldn't be able to make the wedding. Since Xavier and Basia couldn't get their money back, I figured I might as well invite Gwen to come in her place. Problem-solving, right? I asked Xavier if he minded, and he didn't, since he sort of knows Gwen from work. What he doesn't know, however, is that Gwen accompanied me to Egypt and met Father. He's not clued into our connection at that level. Yet. But before you say anything, it's not like I purposely avoided telling him about Gwen going with me, it's just we haven't had the opportunity to talk about anything except the wedding these past few days. Unfortunately, last night after the rehearsal, Bonnie called and told me she was feeling better and would be able to come to the wedding after all."

"Oh, crap, Elvis. That's why you were hiding in your room."

"Yeah, I was thinking what the hell I should do."

"So, what *are* you going to do?"

"I have absolutely no idea. Continue hiding?"

"You're the best man. Not a good plan."

"I know. That was a failed attempt to inject a small measure of levity into this discussion." He threw back the rest of his drink.

I studied him for a moment. "Elvis, does Gwen even know about Bonnie? Are you and Bonnie dating exclusively? Did you invite Gwen as a friend or is there something more there? Not that I'm prying—okay, maybe I am—but the answers might factor into the solution, if there is one, so it's legit for me to ask if you want my advice." I shifted in my seat. I wanted to help him, but this was way out of my range of expertise.

He pressed his hand to his forehead. "To answer your questions, Lexi, no, Gwen doesn't know I'm dating Bonnie. No, Bonnie and I are not dating exclusively. I told her I wasn't ready for that. But I honestly didn't think I would date someone else because…who the hell can deal with the stress and management of that kind of thing? Look at me. I'm Exhibit A for why no one should *ever* do this. I just wanted to take things slow with Bonnie…and now look what happened."

"What about Gwen? Is there something between the two of you? More than friendship, I mean."

"Yeah, there is." His cheeks flushed slightly. "I… slept with her. It wasn't planned. It just happened. I really like Gwen, Lexi. She's amazing. But I like Bonnie, too. So, what do I do?"

I truly had no idea what to say. I should have seen it coming after our Egypt trip, but I'd been too preoccupied with my own issues that I hadn't thought ahead.

I blew out a breath. "I'm not sure *what* to say. Let's try to dissect this logically. I guess technically, you didn't cheat on Bonnie if the two of you weren't in a mutually exclusive relationship and you were both up front and honest about that. Just the same, I'm sure Bonnie will be devastated to find out about Gwen. And when Gwen finds out about Bonnie, she'll be upset you never told her about that relationship, not to mention, you remain undecided between her and Bonnie."

"What should I do?"

"I don't know. I feel…awful for everyone involved, but I don't see how you can get out of this without hurting them both."

"They're going to think I'm a first-class jerk."

"I don't envy you their reactions." I couldn't think of anything to say to make him feel better. He'd made choices that had led to this moment, but his choices were adversely affecting two people I liked. It was a no-win situation.

"You can't be the first man this has ever happened to, Elvis. Did you google what to do in such a situation?"

"Of course, I googled. Apparently, I'm an MDMW."

"A what?"

"A Man Dating Multiple Women. MDMW." He tugged on the collar of his tuxedo, as if he were being strangled. "And, in one stroke—yeah, inappropriate pun intended—I violated the number one rule of MDMW."

"Which is?"

"Never let your circle of women intersect."

I might have laughed, but he looked genuinely miserable. "Oh, Elvis. I don't see an easy way out of this. You're going to have to come clean with both and then sort it out."

"Unfortunately, that was my conclusion as well."

"Why don't you talk to Slash? If nothing else, he's a trained operative. That might have some value here if you need to make a lifesaving exit."

He smiled wearily, then stood and patted me on the shoulder. "Good idea. Thanks for listening. I've got to get back to the room." He set his empty glass on the table. "Wish me luck."

He looked so forlorn, I pulled him into a hug. "I wish you luck, bud. I really do. If nothing else, I'll always have your back."

He hugged me tight. "True. Thank God for that."

NINE

THE BRIDAL PARTY, minus Elvis, Xavier, Basia and officiant Andrew Garrington, stood in the waiting area of the venue in exactly the spot I'd found Teddy hiding under the tablecloth. Right now, Teddy was chasing his sister around the room. She was squealing loudly and slapping at his hands as he tried to tag her. Since Victoria was there, I let her handle them. My nerves were stretched thin as it were.

I'd already caved and gulped down one of the pre-prepared mimosas, despite my queasy stomach, and was thinking about having a second, but I refrained. I had to keep my faculties about me to stay sharp. I didn't want to trip over my dress, set anything on fire or knock anyone out…even by accident. I just wanted this wedding to be as perfect as possible for my best friend.

I stood at the doorway and peeked into the venue. The large raised dais at the center of the terrace had been undecorated last night for the rehearsal. But today it held a gorgeous white and arched trellis intertwined with red and white roses. A tall crystal vase on a stand was filled with a lovely white and red rose display and positioned to one side of the dais. The sparkling blue of the ocean and the golden sand provided a spectacular background. I had to give it to Basia—it was a sweet setup.

The first two rows had been cordoned off with a red

ribbon for family members. A woman I didn't recognize in a black skirt and sleeveless blouse was setting up small place cards on those seats. At least I didn't have to worry about where I'd be sitting since I'd be one of the bridesmaids standing on the dais. Although I'd rather just be one of the crowd.

A hand landed on my shoulder. When I turned around, Slash stood there. Without a word, he lifted my hair off my shoulder and pressed a kiss on my neck.

"Belle donne," he murmured, wrapping a finger around a strand of my hair. "You are beautiful."

I smiled. "You don't look so bad yourself."

Understatement of the day, of course. Every female in the room, including the two-almost-three-year-old flower girl, was looking at him. I didn't blame them. His tuxedo fit perfectly, his expensive cufflinks gleaming silver against his white shirt. His black hair had been slicked back behind his ears and his brown eyes, while regarding the venue, always returned and lingered on me. Although he'd shaved, he still had a bit of dark scruff on his chin that made him even sexier. When he looked at me like he might devour me, my stomach fluttered in a way only he seemed able to make happen.

He took my hands in his, lifting them up, examining my right hand where I wore Xavier's wedding ring on the third finger. He lifted an eyebrow.

"I figured it was the safest place to keep it," I explained.

"Ah, smart move." He lifted my hand to his lips. Instead of kissing the top of my hand, he turned it over and kissed where my wrist and hand joined. It was an especially sensitive spot for me. My breath caught in my throat from the promise behind that kiss.

He leaned over, putting his mouth against my ear.

"Later," he murmured, then gave my hand a final squeeze and walked over to join Finn in greeting the wedding guests as they arrived.

I touched my wrist. Now I'd be thinking of little else until the wedding was over. Maybe that was his plan all along, to take my mind off the pressure and to make me think of something else more pleasurable than the next few hours. Pretty face aside, he was a smart guy, that boyfriend of mine.

I glanced outside. The weather was certainly cooperating. The sky was a brilliant blue and the sun shone brightly. It was hot, but not as humid as it might have been. Although, after having been in Egypt recently, I wasn't sure I'd ever consider humidity in the same way.

I could smell the salt in the breeze. Soft, soothing music was playing on the speakers. Slash, Finn and Elvis began their usher duty, offering drinks and seating guests as they arrived. I said hello to a few. There were a few people I recognized from Xavier's and Elvis's work with ComQuest. My parents arrived with my brother Rock and his new girlfriend, Lacey. My other brother, Beau, is a policeman and was on duty. He was going to try and make the reception later.

I spoke with my parents briefly, promising to chat with them more at the reception. A couple of minutes later, I waved at Gwen when she arrived, dressed in a sky-blue gown that fell to her ankles and complimented her long red hair and blue eyes. She came over to say hi.

"Lexi, you look incredible."

"Well, it's easy when you have a team of professionals fixing and hiding every flaw. You, on the other hand, are glowing naturally. What's up with that?"

She smiled. "I'm super happy these days."

I bet she was, and I hated to think it wouldn't last. But it wasn't my place to interfere, not that I wanted to.

"Well, you should hang on to that feeling of happiness, Gwen, no matter what happens, because you deserve it. The happiness, I mean. So, see you at the reception?"

She gave me a strange look. "Sure, Lexi."

Slash strolled over and kissed her on the cheek. "Hello, Gwen. You look lovely."

She blushed. "Hi, Slash. Thanks. Are you my escort?"

"I am." He held out an arm. "Shall we?"

Gwen threw me a smile over her shoulder. "See you later."

Not one minute had passed before a tap on the shoulder made me jump. Bonnie was dressed in a red cocktail dress with matching red shoes and a clutch purse, her blond hair swept to one side.

"Hey, Lexi," she said. "How's it going?"

"Fine. It's all going fine. No worries about anything." I put a hand on my hip and tried to look casual, neutral and like I knew nothing about a potential love triangle involving her boyfriend. "It's great to see you here. Glad you're feeling better. Hope you'll continue to feel better because…everyone deserves to feel better. Especially at a wedding."

Gah! I was a guilty, blubbering idiot who needed to shut her mouth.

Bonnie gave me a puzzled smile. "Thanks, Lexi. Good luck today." She looked around the room. "Where's Elvis?"

"Ah, he went to get his mom. He should be down shortly."

"Okay. See you later."

She took Finn's arm and he walked her to her seat.

After she left, I blew out a breath. Holy girlfriends. I didn't envy Elvis his situation and had no idea how he'd figure things out.

I spoke to a few more guests until Elvis arrived, escorting his mother on his arm. Ottilie Zimmerman recognized me at once. She was lovely and her eyes, as piercing blue as both of her sons', lit up when they saw me. Though she was nearly seventy years old, her long brown hair held only a few strands of gray. Her skin was as pale as porcelain with just a few wrinkles around her eyes. Today she was dressed in a brilliant royal blue dress that fell to her ankles and a matching blue pendant around her neck. A pretty corsage of red roses was on her wrist. A touch of color had been added to her cheeks and lips.

Ottilie suffered from a rare form of dementia and lived in a care facility not too far from the twins' house. The reasons for the onset of the illness weren't a happy story and my heart hurt just thinking about it. But for now, I plastered a smile on my face and put those thoughts away.

"Lexi," Ottilie said, touching my cheek. "Your hair is different. I'm glad you came today."

I gave her a hug. "Of course, I came to the wedding. Xavier and Basia are two of my very best friends."

"Yes, indeed, they are. Do you have any books for me?"

"Not today. But I'm going to bring some to you soon. Okay? I promise."

"I will look forward to that."

Ottilie looked at Elvis, momentarily confused. "Why are we here again?"

"Xavier is getting married today, Mom." He gently patted her hand. "Come on. Let's get you seated." He started to lead her down the aisle.

A gray-haired woman followed them, lifting a hand in greeting when she passed me. "Hi, Lexi. Nice to see you again. Almost didn't recognize you in a dress and your hair out of a ponytail. You clean up nicely."

"Thanks, Marilyn." Marilyn Para was the Day Administrator at Garden Springs Resort where Ottilie lived. She took good care of Ottilie, so I always made a point of stopping by to say hi when I visited. "Thanks for coming and helping out with Ottilie."

"It's my pleasure. I love those boys as much as I love their mama. Good luck today."

"Thanks."

After a minute, Elvis returned alone and gave me a thumbs-up. Mrs. Kowalski, Basia's mom, entered the room, looking pretty in a silver floor-length gown and a wrist corsage.

"Is Basia ready?" I asked.

Mrs. Kowalski smiled. "She's ready. Thanks for letting me do it, Lexi. That meant a lot to me."

"No problem. I got the better end of the deal," I said.

She laughed, patted my cheek and took Slash's offered arm as he held it out to her. They strolled down the aisle to her seat in the front.

Behind me, Victoria was busy corralling both the excited flower girl and ring bearer, making sure they were standing in their places and holding the flower basket and ring pillow, respectively. Jolka was checking her reflection for the thousandth time in a glass window. I just closed my eyes and leaned back against the wall. I wanted to get this thing underway. I needed to wash my face, get out of the dress and shoes and return to my regularly scheduled life as soon as possible. Performance stress was difficult for me to handle.

The room suddenly quieted. I opened my eyes and saw Basia standing there, arm-in-arm with her father. She looked like a vision—sparkling in her pearl-and-crystal-encrusted dress. The dress, tight at the waist with a scoop neck and plunging V in the back, highlighted all her attributes and looked as if it were made just for her. Her dark bob had been smoothed and styled so it fell just above her shoulders. Her makeup was subtle and fresh, and she was wearing the pearl earrings I'd given her. They matched the dress perfectly. She looked stunning. There was something about her, a contentment that took my breath away. I could only stare at my best friend, completely tongue-tied.

The expression on my face must have surprised her, because she approached me, her eyes brimming with tears.

"So, Lexi, what do you think?" she whispered.

To my surprise, I felt tears prick my eyes as well. I didn't normally get emotional over things like weddings. "I think you're the most beautiful bride I've ever seen," I whispered.

She hugged me and I hugged her back. For a moment, we stood there, friend-to-friend, heart-to-heart. Finally, she stepped back, dabbing the corner of her eyes with a perfectly painted fingertip.

"It's time," she said.

"It's time," I agreed, as nostalgia swept over me. "It's the *right* time."

TEN

Mr. Kowalski stepped forward and took Basia's arm, tucking it into his. His voice caught slightly. "It's really happening. How has this day arrived so quickly? My little girl is flying away."

"I'm not going anywhere, Papa." Basia patted his arm, but she started to get teary again. "And I'm not a little girl anymore."

"I know, Poppie. It was just a way of saying you are all grown up now." He dipped his head at me. "Hello, Lexi. You look lovely."

I liked the sound of his clipped British accent. Although his first language was Polish, he'd learned English in Great Britain and had adopted the accent.

"Thanks, Mr. Kowalski. I appreciate your contribution to the effort."

"What do you mean?"

"I assume you paid for all of those makeup artists and stylists that did this to me. If so, you deserve the kudos."

He chuckled. "Ah, how kind of you to point that out."

"Anytime."

Elvis, who had been standing at the doorway, suddenly turned around, his face paling. "Take your places everyone. Xavier and Andy just went out. We're a go."

Inhaling a deep breath, I took my place. I glanced at Slash's back. He stood in front of me and next to Jolka. Somehow, he must have known I was looking at him, because he turned around and smiled. I knew that was his way of letting me know I could do this. I appreciated the vote of confidence.

Slash held out an arm and Jolka took it. They walked down the aisle together, followed shortly thereafter by Victoria and Finn. They made it look so easy.

Elvis stepped forward and held out his arm. "It's our turn."

"I know. Don't let me trip." I took his arm and held on tightly.

"Don't let me throw up."

"Deal."

I plastered a fake smile on my face as we walked down the aisle. After a few steps. I relaxed. I noticed no one was looking at me. Sophia and Teddy had started their walk, and since they were a thousand times cuter, no one paid us any attention. Except for Slash. I looked up at the dais where he already stood and saw he was, indeed, watching me. He always had eyes for me.

As planned, Elvis and I split at the bottom of the dais and stopped at the bottom of the stairs on opposing sides. A quick glance at the water and beach confirmed everything remained perfect in terms of setting and the weather. There was even a light breeze to give us some relief.

I was waiting at my spot at the bottom of the stairs when the guests all rose. Basia and her father began to walk down the aisle. Xavier gasped when he saw her. At that moment, I kind of understood the motive behind Basia's obsession regarding finding the perfect wedding dress.

They also split at the bottom of the dais and headed toward opposing stairs. As Basia reached the stairs, she smiled at me and handed over her bouquet. I picked up the back of her gown with one hand as she went up the stairs. She crossed the dais and stood next to her father, who stood between her and Xavier. I took my place between Basia and Victoria. I slid a glance at the couple. The expression on Xavier's face was a mixture of disbelief, extreme happiness and nervousness. His face was so pale, I thought he might faint. In stark contrast, I'd never seen Basia so serene.

As soon as everyone was in place, Andy stepped forward. "I'd like to welcome you today to this beautiful outdoor wedding to celebrate the joining of Xavier Zimmerman and Basia Kowalski in matrimony. Today, on this beautiful afternoon, we will have the privilege of seeing this special couple joined in marriage. As their family and friends, we intend to support and love them as they start their journey together. So, let us begin the celebration of one of life's most significant moments, the union of two souls through the most sacred of vows—marriage."

Andy addressed Mr. Kowalski. "Since I've never met a man willing to give away his daughter, I'll ask you this instead. Piotr Kowalski, do I have your blessing for this union?"

Mr. Kowalski's voice caught as he said, "You do."

He stepped back from between Xavier and Basia and left the dais, returning to his seat next to his wife.

"Basia and Xavier, do you freely enter into this union of your own will and desire?" Andy asked.

"We do," Basia and Xavier answered together.

Andy took one of Basia's hands and one of Xavier's hands and joined them. Xavier's hand was shaking badly. "Xavier, from this day forward, do you choose Basia to be your lawful wife, your best friend and your one and only true love? To support her, in sickness and health, to dream in her arms and always look for the best in her? If so, say, 'I do.'"

Xavier swallowed hard and nodded. "I do. I *really* do."

"Basia, from this day forward, do you choose Xavier to be your lawful husband, your best friend and your only true love? To support him, in sickness and health, to dream in his arms and always look for the best in him? If so, say 'I do.'"

Basia smiled encouragingly at Xavier and said, "I do."

"Then it is time to say the vows."

Basia turned to Xavier and took both of his hands in hers. She took a deep breath. "Xavier, you are the sweetest, smartest man I've ever known. Here are my vows to you. I vow to never stop growing in love with you, because growth and change are inevitable. I won't be afraid of changes if we face them together. On a more practical note, I promise to be patient and understanding about the thermostat setting, which is freezing, by the way. I'll also try not to be jealous of the time you spend on your computers and I'll even learn to play an online game or two, if you'll teach me. I'll listen to your advice and occasionally take it. Xavier, you know me better than anyone ever has, and you still love me. How lucky am I? In your eyes I found my home, and in your heart, I found the love I was always looking for. Wherever this journey takes us, so long as we're together, it's going to be a wonderful life."

Xavier blinked hard. His legs were trembling. Whether

it was from nerves or emotion, I just hoped he held it together for the rest of the ceremony.

He removed a hand temporarily to push his glasses
up on his nose and then took her hands again. "Basia,
you are the logic to my processor. The battery to my
circuit. My love for you is like dividing zero—it can't
be defined. I loved you from the moment I saw you.
You were the most beautiful girl I'd ever seen, and I
couldn't believe you spoke to me—you *saw* me. You
will always be so incredibly beautiful to me—inside and
out." His voice was shaky and filled with emotion, but
he pressed on. "Now, we're together. If I'm dreaming,
I hope you never wake me up, because I'm the lucki-
est guy on the planet. So, keeping that in mind, here
are my vows to you. I promise to love you with all my
heart. To live in truth and respect with you. To do my
best to communicate with you, even when I don't know
what I'm doing, which will likely be most of the time.
I believe in you. I believe in us. I vow to love you and
stand by you. Always."

Basia's eyes shimmered with tears. I had to swallow
the lump in my throat. They grasped hands and took a
step with Andy toward a unity candle which they would
light.

I glanced over at Elvis to see how he was doing and
was surprised he wasn't looking at the happy couple.
Instead, he was focused on something above his head.
I followed his gaze. A big brown pelican had perched
atop of the flowered arch, directly over the spot where
Xavier and Basia were now standing. The guests noticed
it, too, as murmurs and whispers were getting louder.

Elvis caught my eye and dipped his head toward the

pelican, as if asking me how to get rid of it. I shrugged. This was *not* my area of expertise.

"Get rid of it," I mouthed.

Elvis made some flapping motions with his arms to try and get the pelican to fly away.

It didn't.

People were murmuring louder now. Another glance over my shoulder indicated the guests had become way more interested in the pelican than the ceremony. Some had even started snapping photos of it with their phones. I suddenly had an awful thought. What if the pelican pooped? It would land directly on either Xavier or Basia. I glanced at Elvis in alarm, wondering if he'd considered that. Elvis was still looking at the pelican, but this time Slash made eye contact with me. He shook his head slightly.

I wasn't sure if he were shaking his head to signal that waving arms wouldn't be enough to get the pelican to fly away or whether he was telling me to leave well enough alone. It wasn't like I could ask him for clarification. I just kept having this horrible vision of the pelican taking a crap right on top of Basia's pretty veil and dress. After all she'd, no *we'd*, been through to get the dress, there was no way I was letting a stupid pelican ruin everything. But the longer the bird sat there, right over her freaking head, the greater the chance he might take a crap on her.

Elvis must have been thinking along the same line as me because his hand movements became more animated as he tried to get rid of the pelican. Still no luck. The pelican wasn't going anywhere.

Basia and Xavier turned around from lighting the unity candle and faced us. Elvis quickly dropped his hands to his side and smiled. The bride and groom had no idea of the danger directly above them. By now the whispering and the murmuring from the guests had reached a crescendo. Basia looked around, wondering what was going on. My blood began to boil. The pelican was stealing the show from my best friend.

But what to do?

Andy took both of their hands, just as we had practiced it last night, in preparation for the exchange of rings. As Basia's hand rested lightly on top of Xavier's, the pelican let out a loud, rude screech. Basia, Xavier and Andy looked up in surprise.

Furious at the interruption, Elvis waved his arms. "Shoo. Get out of here, you, stupid bird."

The pelican didn't move.

More whispers from the crowd and some nervous laughter came from the audience. The pelican seemed to be enjoying the attention, stretching his wings and cocking his head.

Realizing there was nothing we could do about it, Andy continued the ring exchange. The show had to go on, unwanted guest or not. "Bless the giving of these wedding rings so those who wear them may live in peace and harmony."

That was my cue. I turned to my left to pass Basia's bouquet, as well as mine, to Victoria, so I could get Elvis's ring off my finger. That's when I got an idea on how to get rid of the bird.

Before I gave the bouquets to Victoria, I plucked the head off one of the roses. She looked at me as if I'd lost my mind, but I shoved the bouquets at her and closed my hand over the blossom. I stepped to the center of the dais next to Elvis so the four of us stood together.

Xavier held out a hand to his brother waiting for the ring. Elvis fumbled in his tuxedo pocket, finding, then passing, the ring. Xavier took the ring and held it like a bomb between two trembling fingers. I just hoped he didn't drop it, although the way he was shaking, I was afraid he might drop first.

Andy turned to Xavier. "Xavier, as you place this ring on Basia's finger, I ask you to speak the words on your heart."

While this was happening, I gently bumped Elvis with my shoulder. He glanced down and I opened my hand so he could see the rose head. I cocked my head toward the pelican to indicate my thinking. After a moment, he smiled and nodded. The nice thing about Elvis is that we're often on the same wavelength. I was sure he understood immediately what I had in mind. I would have done it myself, but a second later he slipped the rose head from my hand.

In the meantime, Xavier was trying hard to remain calm, but he was awfully unsteady on his feet. "B-Basia Johanna Kowalski, you are the love of my life and…"

The pelican squawked several times and Xavier lost his concentration. We all glared at the bird's rude interruption. "And…um… I…" His sentence trailed off and he swayed a bit before catching himself.

Mrs. Zimmerman abruptly stood and shouted with her fist raised at the pelican, "How dare you interrupt my son's wedding. Be gone, you foul bird."

Pun intended, I guess.

There were more muted laughter and whispers. Marilyn whispered something and tugged on Ottilie's arm before she sat back down.

Xavier glanced nervously at the pelican, but cleared

his throat and continued. "Um, well, what was I saying? Oh, right. Basia, you're my very b-best friend. I give you this ring to—"

The pelican stretched his wings and let out a sound between a croak and a fart. Xavier's confidence was clearly flagging, as was his ability to stay calm. The pelican moved along the arch, but refused to fly away. The distraction was taking a toll on all of us.

Elvis took one look at me and nodded with determination. He was going to do it. Before I could react, he threw the rose head in the air just in front of the pelican.

Bingo.

For a geek, it was a damn near perfect throw, and it had exactly the desired effect. The pelican, thinking the rose was food, flew off the arch and caught the rose in its gullet before flying away.

The guests cheered. The bridal party cheered. Andy shook a fist in the air. Xavier sighed in relief. Mrs. Zimmerman leapt to her feet, waving her hands with joy.

Disaster averted. Elvis was a hero.

Except…suddenly we had a new problem. When the pelican pushed off, he'd loosened the arch.

It now swayed precariously above us.

ELEVEN

EVERYTHING HAPPENED IN slow motion after that. The arch started to come down, not toward the beach, but toward us and the guests. Elvis gasped in surprise and jumped sideways, knocking into his brother. Xavier, who was already unsteady on his feet, fell backwards, flinging the ring into the air. Andy tried to catch him as he fell, but Xavier's elbow smashed into Andy's nose and blood spurted everywhere. Finn slipped and went down, taking Elvis with him. The bridesmaids screamed and scattered, but had nowhere to go on the small dais. For one brief, suspended moment amid the chaos, I met Slash's gaze. In that nanosecond, I knew exactly what he was going to do. He jumped, stomach first and arm outstretched, to try to catch Basia's wedding ring before it fell between the wooden slats on the dais and disappeared to the beach below.

That left me with saving everyone else.

Despite my high heels, I moved with the agility of a wide receiver and pushed Victoria and Jolka aside, barely catching the edge of the arch before it landed onto the dais and subsequently into the crowd. Surprisingly, it wasn't as heavy as I expected.

Thank God for small miracles.

For a moment, I thought all was well until the guests gave a collective gasp. Jolka had staggered too close to the edge of the dais. She teetered for a moment on her high heels and then fell off the dais with a shriek, landing directly onto Mr. Kowalski's lap. The chair he was sitting on collapsed under the weight of them both. Wedding guests screamed and scattered.

Mrs. Zimmerman, however, leapt to her feet and started clapping wildly. "Bravo! Bravo! Encore!"

I lowered the arch to the dais as Slash's Secret Service detail stormed the dais.

After an initial moment of chaos, Slash waved them off, assuring them he was fine. He got to his feet, brushing his tuxedo pants. "You okay, *cara*?"

"I'm fine." I examined my gown. It had some dirt, sand and errant flower petals on it, but nothing torn or stained, much, thank goodness. "What about you?"

He lifted an eyebrow and held up the wedding ring.

I breathed a sigh of relief. "Wow. You're good. You might want to consider a side career in football or baseball, if the NSA gig doesn't work out."

"Thanks, but I've got other plans." He glanced down at the arch. "Not a bad catch yourself."

"It's plastic, but you knew that, right?"

"I had a strong suspicion, which is why I went for the ring instead."

"Good thing, because I don't think I've ever caught a baseball in my life despite the six dozen which have been thrown at me."

We took a moment to look around. Everyone had stopped shrieking and running around. The Secret Service was corralling people, calming them down. Damage control from the hotel was in full swing with staff checking on the guests and examining the dais and the arch. Basia, holding up the sides of her dress, climbed down the dais stairs and rushed to her father where a Secret Service agent was helping him to his feet. Xavier followed close behind her.

"Papa. Jolka, are you okay?" she asked.

"We're fine, lamb," Mr. Kowalski said in his clipped British accent. He patted his daughter's arm. "Don't you worry."

Jolka stood nearby smoothing down her dress, looking none the worse for wear. "I'm okay, Basia. Your father broke my fall. A true gentleman."

Mr. Kowalski pulled down the sleeves of his suit and straightened his tie as his wife brushed down the back of his jacket. "Frankly, it's a bloody good thing my arse has a lot of padding."

For a moment, there was dead silence. Then Basia started to laugh. She laughed so hard, her eyes started to stream with tears. After a moment of indecision, we all took our cue and joined in. I just hoped like hell it was a good thing she was laughing hysterically and not because she was becoming unhinged.

Hotel staff swarmed the dais, checking the structure and the arch and making sure everything was still structurally sound. The Secret Service agents were trying to be inconspicuous, but they were giving everyone the eye. When Slash stepped across the dais to give Andy a handkerchief to stem the blood from his nose, Elvis walked up next to me, crossing his arms against his chest.

"Well…we sure showed that pelican, didn't we?"

"We sure did." I sighed. "At least the intent was good and no one got hurt…much."

"True. Andy insists he's fine, although I'm not sure what it means that Xavier gave our boss a bloody nose. I hope neither one of them disowns me." Elvis watched as his twin procured a fresh chair for his *almost* father-in-law and set it up.

"You were just trying to help. Blame it on me. It was my idea."

"Yeah, but the execution was mine."

"Which was perfect, I might add. Who knew the arch was so flimsy and made of plastic? If I'd known that, I might have calculated things differently."

"Yeah, well, you know what they say about hindsight."

After a few more minutes, the staff hoisted the arch back into place, minus several flowers, and we all took our places again on the dais.

Before the ceremony restarted, Xavier turned to his brother and clapped a hand on his shoulder. No words were exchanged, but the simple gesture seemed to signal no hard feelings. I breathed a sigh of relief. That relationship was hanging by a thread as it was, so the fact that Xavier had made an open sign of forgiveness meant a lot.

Carefully holding Slash's handkerchief to his nose, Andy reminded Xavier and Basia they had been ready to exchange rings before they had been interrupted. While that was happening, Slash reached around Finn and discreetly handed Elvis the ring.

"Thanks, man," Elvis said to him in a low voice. "You saved me."

Slash dipped his head.

Andy made sure we were all correctly repositioned and then he turned to Elvis. "Tell me that after all that, you have the ring."

"I have the ring," Elvis replied. He handed it to

Xavier. This time Xavier took it with a steadier hand and gave his twin a grateful look.

"Just so we're clear, this time, short of a nuclear explosion, nothing is going to stop me from making you my wife," Xavier said. "Basia Johanna Kowalski, you are the love of my life and my very best friend. This ring is a symbol of my abiding love and a reminder of our unity. With this ring, thee I wed."

He slipped the band on her finger and I could see Basia was fighting back tears. She glanced over at me and held out her hand. I quickly slid Xavier's ring off my finger and gave it to her.

Basia closed her eyes as if to calm herself and then said, "Xavier Barnabas Zimmerman, you are the love of my life and my very best friend. This ring is a symbol of my abiding love and a reminder of our unity. With this ring, thee I wed."

She slid the ring on his finger and smiled shyly at him.

Andy spread his hands. "I now pronounce you husband and wife. Thank God. Mr. Zimmerman, you may, at last, kiss your bride."

Xavier gave a small whoop and pulled her into his arms. Basia kissed him back with equal enthusiasm.

There was some good-natured catcalling from the guests until they broke apart, grinning.

Andy maneuvered them front and center on the dais, a hand on each of their shoulders. "Ladies and gentlemen, I present to you, Mr. and Mrs. Zimmerman."

Everyone cheered, including me.

It hadn't been easy, but my two best friends were finally married.

TWELVE

AFTER WHAT SEEMED like an eternity of taking pictures, we finally headed into the reception. My cheeks hurt from fake smiling, my feet ached from the high heels, and I wanted people to quit telling me how I should cock my head, drop my shoulders and quit snarling. We'd taken pictures in front of the hotel, on the dais and on the beach. We had to pose as a bridal party—both serious and fun poses—as a large group, just the bridesmaids, and a few of just Basia and me. The entire time we were in the sun. By the time it was over, I was hot, cranky and thirsty.

I never wanted my picture taken again. Ever.

I just wanted to relax, but all I could think about was how in just a short time I was going to have to stand up in front of all the people at the wedding and give a lame toast. The pressure was crushing me.

Slash disappeared to make a call, so I headed for a small room off the main reception to have a few minutes of peace and quiet to collect myself. As I entered, I saw the back of someone sitting on a circular couch alone.

"Elvis?"

"Really, Lexi?" He turned around.

"Oh, sorry, Xavier. I couldn't tell it was you from the back."

"Basia can tell the difference between us from the back."

"Well, yeah. She's probably spent a lot more time canoodling and examining your neck than I have. Not that I've *ever* canoodled or examined your neck, but you know what I mean."

Xavier chuckled. "I know, but the image you've now planted in my head is priceless."

"I'm glad you're amused. What are you doing in here anyway? Aren't you the star of this party?"

"I guess, but I figure I'm here for the same reason you're here. I just need a breather. It's been the best day of my life, but it's a lot to take in. Need a little processing time."

"Yeah…about that. I'm sorry about the crazy pelican thing."

"Not your fault." He shrugged. "Wildlife is one of the perils of an outdoor wedding. We knew that going in. No worries."

"Thanks. I appreciate you being good to Elvis about it, too. Just so you know, it was my idea to toss the rose head at the pelican. Elvis just ran with it."

"A rose head? Is that what it was?" He smiled. "Smart thinking. I figured you had a hand in it. But, seriously, it was all good. Brilliant, actually. It was a wonderful day surrounded by the people I love…including you and my brother."

I let out a breath. "Thanks, Xavier. Back at you. I just hope you and Elvis get everything sorted out soon. It's been hard on him, you know."

"It's been hard on me, too. We'll figure it out."

"I never doubted that." I sat down beside him, glancing at the shiny platinum band on his finger. I bumped shoulders with him. "So, it's now official. You're a married man. It's been a wild ride with all the twists and turns, right?"

He laughed a little. "Yeah. Crazy is an understatement." His face got momentarily serious. "You know, Lexi, sometimes I worry I'll wake up and this will all have been a dream. How can a girl like Basia fall for a guy like me?"

I leaned back on the couch. "You really have to ask me that? Didn't you hear her when she said her vows? Basia loves you. You're a great guy, and you're perfect for her. Trust me, she knows she's getting a good deal."

Before I could say anything else, Elvis rushed in looking panicked. "Oh, my God. They're both following me. I need to do something."

"Who's they?" Xavier said, confused.

"The girls. Lexi, can you do me one and talk to whichever one comes in here first. Just keep her busy for five minutes. That's all I need. I need to come clean, but I'd prefer to do it one at a time." He dashed out of the other exit before I could say a word.

Xavier looked completely confused. "Come clean with what? What's he talking about?"

Before I could answer, Gwen walked in. She was swaying a bit, which led me to believe she'd had a drink or two. It probably didn't take much; she was such a tiny thing.

"Hey, Lexi. Heck of an exciting wedding ceremony. Beautiful, exciting and fun. I loved every minute of it." She looked at Xavier. "But *you* have been avoiding me."

"I have?" A puzzled look crossed his face. "I'm sorry. I've been kind of busy."

"I know. I just missed you."

Before I could say a word, she plopped onto his lap and pressed her mouth against his.

Xavier froze, eyes widening in shock.

"Gwen!" I yelled when I could find my voice. "What are you doing?"

She turned to face me, her arms still around Xavier's neck. "What does it look like? I'm kissing him."

"And why exactly…" Basia stood in the doorway, her eyes open in disbelief "…are you kissing my husband?"

Xavier moved faster than I'd ever seen him, jumping to his feet and dumping Gwen to the floor. His expression was so panicked, I thought he might stroke out. "Basia, babe, let me explain. This is *not* what it looks like."

"Xavier?" Gwen glanced up in horror, finally catching on. "You're Xavier?"

"That's Xavier," I confirmed.

Gwen's cheeks flushed scarlet, which was especially noticeable since she was a redhead. "I'm *so* sorry. I've had a little to drink, obviously, and I… I thought you were Elvis."

Slash walked into the room from the other entrance and saw us all standing around staring at each other. He spread his hands. "So…what's going on?"

"Well…" I started.

"Excuse me, Lexi?" Bonnie stood in the doorway peering over Basia's shoulder and waving a hand at me. "I'm sorry to interrupt. Is that you, Elvis?"

"I'm Xavier," he shouted.

Bonnie blinked, clearly taken aback at the vehemence of his tone. "Oh. Well, of course you are. Identical twins, dressed identically, and it's hard to tell from a bit of a distance in the dim lighting. I apologize. Congratulations on your wedding. It's just I can't seem to find your brother. Do you know where he is? I think he might be avoiding me. It's odd, seeing as how he's my date and all."

Gwen stood up, brushing down her dress. "*You're* Elvis's date?"

Bonnie frowned and crossed her arms. "Yes. Who are you?"

"Gwen. *I'm* Elvis's date."

The room fell abruptly silent and the temperature may have dropped a frosty twenty degrees. Every eye in the room turned to me as if I had the answers. I stood there wishing I were anywhere else. I lifted my hands. "Ah…nope. I've got nothing. At this exact moment, I can't think of a single thing to say."

"You don't have to."

To my enormous relief, Elvis stepped past Slash and into the room. "If the rest of you ladies and gentlemen will allow me time alone with Gwen and Bonnie, I'm sure we'll get it all straightened out."

I looked at Elvis with sympathy, but I'd never been happier to leave a room. Slash took my hand as we followed Xavier and Basia out. Xavier was trying to explain his version of the mix-up to Basia. He spoke so quickly he was tripping over all his words. Thankfully, Basia laughed and shut him up with a kiss. After, they started whispering. Since neither of them knew about Gwen and Elvis, I'm sure they were confused.

Slash quickly steered me toward the drinks and then leaned me against the wall, resting a hand to the left of my shoulder. "I leave you alone for five minutes and look what happens."

"Not my fault," I said in a low voice. "I'm worried about Elvis."

"He's a big boy. He'll handle it."

"How?"

"That I don't know. But I have faith in him."

"I'm glad you're so confident. Did he ask you for advice?"

"He did. I told him to tell the truth. I just didn't think he'd do it with both women at the same time." He paused. "Perhaps I should have made that part clearer."

"It's too late now."

Slash tugged at his bow tie, loosening it. "I'm afraid so."

I sighed. "No matter how many scenarios of this I play in my head right now, I can't imagine how it could go well for Elvis."

"Unfortunately, I'm in full agreement with you."

"I just hope he holds it together for the toast."

"He will." Slash patted my arm. "Elvis is a lot stronger than he looks. He'll deal. As his friends, we'll support him."

"Yes, we will." I took his hand, linking my fingers with his before leaning into him and kissing him lightly on the mouth. I never, in a million years, imagined myself showing PDA with a boyfriend, but I was feeling more and more comfortable in my role as his girlfriend. I liked the physical connection we shared. Our little stolen moments of affection were becoming surprisingly natural and easy for me. I could tell Slash liked it, too, because he pulled me closer, pressing his mouth to my forehead. For a moment, we just stood there, face-to-face, a small fortified island of introverts in the whirling midst of a sea of partygoers.

Just then, my mom swept over to us dressed in a floor-length, shimmering gold gown, my father in tow. I stepped back from Slash quickly, my cheeks heating, wondering if they'd seen our little public display of affection. Wasn't sure how they could have missed it.

"Lexi, Slash. It's so good to see you both." My mom air-kissed my cheek. "You look lovely, darling. You should wear red more often. It's a bold color on you. Are you both okay after that crazy problem with the arch?"

"We're fine. Thank you."

"Well, I'm glad everyone is okay and no one was harmed." She turned to Slash and beamed. "Slash, I must say you are a statement of European sophistication."

I rolled my eyes, but Slash smiled and lifted her hand to his lips for a kiss. *"Grazie, bella signora."* He shook hands with my father. "Sir."

"Good to see you this evening, Slash." My dad, dressed in a steel gray suit with a blue tie, regarded us. He had a certain way of looking at you that made you want to confess all your secrets, which was a good trait for a trial lawyer to possess, but not so beneficial if you were his daughter and hiding something, like moving in with your boyfriend.

"Mom, Dad, you guys look great." I spoke with way too much enthusiasm. "Did you enjoy the ceremony?"

My dad shifted on his feet. "Heck of a ceremony with that bird and all. Nice catch on the ring, young man."

Slash dipped his head. "Thank you."

"I'd never recommend an outdoor wedding," my mom said, lowering her voice. "Too many things could go wrong. I think a wedding should take place in a controlled environment."

"Well, I think it turned out great," I said. "Pelican and all."

Silence. There seemed to be some weird tension in

the air. I couldn't figure it out, not that I could *ever* figure things like that out. But even my mom wasn't talking and my dad kept giving me the eye. Alarm bells were ringing in my head.

"So, how are things with the two of you?" my dad finally asked.

"They're great." I watched his expression cautiously. "Actually, I'm hoping to have a chance to speak with you and mom…alone…after the toasts."

"I see," my dad replied pleasantly. "Is that when you were planning on telling us you'd moved in together?"

THIRTEEN

MY MOUTH DROPPED OPEN. This was not the way it was supposed to go down. According to *The Cohabitation Talk*, it was better for me to speak to my parents alone, which had been the plan. But it was supposed to be *after* the toasts because I wasn't sure I could handle that kind of stress at the same time.

Obviously, it was too late for that now.

"You…know?" I slid a panicked glance at Slash. He stood perfectly relaxed, his eyes on my father, his expression not changing one iota. How could he be so freaking calm?

"We know," my dad confirmed.

I swallowed hard, tried to keep things light. "Well, it's funny you bring it up, Dad, because that's what I was going to talk to you guys about tonight. See, there's been a lot going on these last few days, so I hadn't had a chance to tell you because the book suggested I do it in person." I paused and realized I sounded nervous and guilty. "Wait. How did you know?"

My dad still hadn't taken his eyes off Slash even though I was the one talking. "Basia might have mentioned it to her mother who mentioned it to *your* mother. Imagine our surprise."

My mom kissed my cheek. "Oh, never mind your father. I'm so happy for you, darling. I suppose this means the engagement is not far behind."

"Whoa." I held up a hand, my face heating. "No. No, no. Do *not* start hiring caterers or ordering dresses or flowers. We're just living together, okay. Checking things out, so to say."

"Checking *what* things out?" my father asked, still looking at Slash.

Wow. Was it getting hot in here or was it just me? I lifted my hair off my neck, shook it a little. "Just regular stuff, Dad. You know, are we compatible, does he leave wet towels on the floor, does he put his underwear in the hamper..." I let my sentence trail off.

Okay, bringing up underwear probably hadn't been a good idea. But my perfectly prepared conversation was *not* going as planned.

"I presume, young man, this means you're serious about my daughter." I opened my mouth to answer even though the question hadn't been addressed to me.

Slash put a hand on my arm, indicating he wanted to answer. He met my father's gaze evenly. "I've never been more serious about anything in my life, sir."

For a long moment, we stood in awkward silence until I decided it was time to put an end to the testosterone staring match.

I put a hand on Slash's arm. "Um, Slash, would you mind if I spoke with my parents alone for a few minutes?"

"Of course." He tore his gaze away from my dad's and pressed a kiss on my hand. Dipping his head politely at my parents, he stepped away.

When he was out of earshot, I turned to my dad in exasperation. "Dad, what are you doing? I was planning on telling you guys tonight. I swear. What's with the third degree?"

"I'm your father. I have a right to know his intentions."

"Then ask me. I'd tell you *our*, not just his, intentions are that we're taking our relationship to the next level. That's it."

"How many levels until he's going to make it official?"

"I don't know. I've never done this before. We'll figure it out when we get there, okay?"

His face softened. "I don't want to see you get hurt, pumpkin."

"I don't want to see me get hurt either. You know I'm a careful person. I'm also twenty-five, gainfully employed, and fully in charge of my own life. I've calculated the risks—you know me and my spreadsheets—and I decided Slash is worth it."

My dad studied me. "Do you love him?"

"I do. But I won't lie to you. Our relationship is complicated. I guess most relationships are. Ours might be more complex due to the nature of our jobs, but we're going to give it a go. It's a big step for him and a big step for me. But we feel safe doing it together."

My mom took my hand. "Oh, he's such a catch, Lexi."

"No one caught anyone, Mom. Moving in together was a mutually agreed upon decision. No one ran, therefore, no one was caught."

She sighed. "You make it sound so…logical."

"That works for us."

"Well, at least you found someone. A handsome someone, to be exact." She patted my shoulder. "I suppose this means Slash must really love you. Why else would he put up with us?"

Now *that* made me smile. "Come on, Dad. Take a cue from Mom. Can't you ease up a bit?"

My dad crossed his arms against his chest. "Your heart is on the line, so he's going to have to prove himself to me."

"What else does he have to do, Dad? He saved our lives the first time you met him."

"Yes, I'll admit he's courageous and adept with a gun. That doesn't change my concern about his intentions toward you. I'm sorry, Lexi, but I still consider it suspect that he wants to move in with you without a formal commitment of any kind."

"Dad, this is not the 1950s." I narrowed my eyes. "And the commitment being expressed is that we want to live together. That's a huge commitment in my book."

"To you, yes. But to me, no. I won't deny that Slash strikes me as a capable young man who is quite fond of you. How fond is yet to be determined, however."

I hated that this conversation had started to sound like one of his trials, but I knew I wasn't going to change his mind at this point, so I let it go. For now.

"Lexi!"

I glanced over my dad's shoulder. Basia waved frantically at me to come into the room where they'd started serving dinner.

Holy cow. Showtime.

I swallowed the panic that rose in my throat. We were being seated for dinner. People would eat and drink and then I'd have to stand up in front of everyone and give a toast. A toast that took several minutes, where no one else in the room was speaking but me. What if I forgot what to say? What if the words came out garbled? What if everyone started laughing so hard they couldn't hear me?

What if I couldn't visualize a single person naked, including Slash?

I should have never agreed to this. It was so far out of my comfort zone, it might as well have been in the outer stratosphere. My breathing started coming faster.

I excused myself from my parents and headed into the dining area. There was a main table, which faced out to all the guests, who sat at long tables on either side of the dance floor. I hated being on display and my stomach started to churn. At least Slash was seated next to me, which was a huge relief. He didn't ask how the rest of the conversation with my parents had gone and I didn't offer to tell him. We both knew that would be better discussed in a private venue without my parents looking on.

While the servers brought our salad, Slash got up to talk to Mr. Kowalski. Elvis stopped by and slipped into his empty chair. He was holding a drink. Whiskey, by the smell of it.

"Are you ready for the toast?" he asked.

"I'll never be ready for the toast. I wish I could just get it over with. Why can't we toast first and then eat? Who made this stupid rule that the toast must come *after* the meal, but *before* the dancing. Where's the logic in that?" I pressed my hand to my forehead. "Why does a new couple need a toast anyway?"

"All excellent questions."

I blew out a breath. "You're drinking whiskey. You never drink whiskey. I take it the conversation with Bonnie and Gwen was difficult." I looked around the room, but didn't see either of them. "What happened?"

He sipped his drink, shrugged. "I apologized for being an idiot, then told them the truth."

"Which is?"

"I like them both, but I need time to get it all straight in my head."

"And?"

"They left. Both. Neither spoke a single word, to me or each other. I may not have a decision to make. After this, I'll be lucky if either of them will ever talk to me again."

I sighed. "I'm sorry, Elvis. At least you were honest."

"I'm sorry I put you and Xavier in the middle of my mess. On his wedding day, nonetheless."

"It was inadvertent, and he'll forgive you."

"Maybe. It will probably require an excess of groveling and favors."

"You'll do it."

"Yeah, I will."

Finn walked over from the other side of the table where he was seated next to Jolka. He'd removed his bow tie and opened his shirt to his throat. "How's it going?" he asked, leaning over Elvis and me.

"Ask us after the toast," I replied.

"Ah, lass, you'll do fine. You will, too, Elvis. I wish you both *ádh mór*. That's Gaelic for good luck." He grinned, his Irish accent deepening. "Or as they say in Texas—or maybe it's Montana, because how the hell would an Irishman know—knock 'em dead." He paused, as if in reflection of his words. "Ah, Lexi, you do know that's just a saying, right?"

"Not helpful, Finn."

He laughed, patted the top of my hand. "I'm sure you'll stun us with your wit."

I rolled my eyes as he and Elvis returned to their seats. Just as Slash was heading back to his, Andy stopped by to talk to me. It was like Grand-Freaking-Central Station at the head table.

"You did a good job catching that arch today, Lexi." Andy lifted his drink to me. "Quick reflexes. Can't say I've ever officiated a wedding with a pelican crashing the ceremony."

"I bet. How's your nose?"

"A little tender, but I'll live. All in a day's work."

"If you say so."

He clinked his glass to my water glass. "By the way, good luck with the toast. I'm looking forward to it."

"I wish you wouldn't," I said, but he was already walking away.

Slash took my hand under the table and squeezed it. "Focus and breathe," he murmured. "Just like you practiced."

After everyone had eaten, and I'd successfully pushed all the food around on my plate, Basia's mom handed me a microphone and told me to get ready for the toast.

Showtime.

FOURTEEN

"CALM, COOL AND COLLECTED," Slash said, patting my leg under the table. "You've got this."

I really didn't, but seeing how I didn't have a choice, I took a deep breath and stood. I clinked my fork against the glass until the room quieted. I was acutely aware every eye was on me. I froze in panic and then looked over at Basia and Xavier. They were both smiling at me, relaxed and in love.

I could do this. For them.

I didn't need a piece of paper for the speech. My photographic memory would remember it for me, not to mention I'd gone over this speech more than a hundred times already. All I had to do was hold the microphone and speak.

Still, my hands shook badly as I set the water goblet and fork down and picked up the mic. I took a few breaths to steady myself before I started. "Hi, everyone. I'm Lexi Carmichael, Basia's maid of honor. First, a disclaimer. I've never given a toast before, and certainly never a wedding toast, so I hope you'll bear with me. I reviewed more than three hundred toasts in preparation for this evening. During that research, I discovered I'm supposed to deliver an original and carefully tailored speech briefly mentioning the bride's and groom's past, but focusing on their future. Some sources recommended using humor, but since that isn't my forte, I'm not going down that road. The best toasts are said to be between five to seven minutes, which, I'll be honest, seems like an eternity to stand up here talking. So, with all that in mind, Xavier and Basia, I hope I do this right for you."

Basia's eyes filled with tears, which scared me even more. What if I failed her? What if my toast was the most epic fail in bridesmaid history? It wasn't a stretch to imagine that could happen, especially since I was involved. My hands were so sweaty I was afraid I would drop the microphone. It felt like a giant fist was squeezing my abdomen. Every eye in the room was on me, but I glanced at Slash. He nodded slightly, encouraging me. As practiced, I took a deep breath and imagined him naked. I don't know how or why this worked, but it gave me the courage to continue.

"Although approximately six thousand, two hundred and twenty-two other couples are getting married today in the United States, you two are truly unique. I calculated the odds of another five foot three inch brunette who speaks a dozen languages and owns over one hundred pairs of shoes, getting married to a five foot eleven inch, twenty-seven-year-old identical twin with an IQ over 180, as being approximately 12.357 trillion to one. Therefore, I can say with great certainty, you two, as a couple, are one of a kind. In fact, I can't think of a single other person either of you should marry—that's how perfect you are for each other."

Xavier laughed and gave me a thumbs-up, while Basia blew me a kiss, her tears kept at bay, at least for the time being. Their happiness loosened the tightness in my chest.

"Luckily for you two, the odds for a long marriage

are better than average. While 44.2 percent of all first-time marriages in the US currently end in divorce, because of your age, backgrounds and dating experience, I am thrilled to report you have a greater than seventy percent chance of celebrating your thirty-fifth wedding anniversary. Therefore, by my calculations, your long, married life should allow you many years to rejoice in your 3.12 children. Please note there's an error factor of 0.2 based on the 500 simulations I ran, so it could conceivably be either two or three kids."

There was laughter from the entire room. I looked up in alarm, but Xavier now had his arm around Basia and they were beaming and blushing like two people in love...which they were. Their smiles seemed to indicate they were enjoying my toast, but in case they were just being polite, I forged ahead determined to get this over as quickly as I could.

"Anyway, Basia and Xavier, today is the first day of your happily ever after. It doesn't seem that long ago when Basia and I first met as college roommates. Not long after that, Basia, you met Xavier on this very beach, on a sunny summer day, with me and Elvis nearby. None of us realized at that moment how the encounter would change our lives so dramatically, and so much for the better. Therefore, guys, I wish for you, on your wedding day, that your love be lasting and your friendship never ending. And on that final note—thank God—I raise my glass and ask everyone to join me in honoring this very lucky and special couple."

Basia stood and hugged me tightly. The waterworks had commenced. "Oh, that was beautiful, Lexi. Thank you." She sobbed, wiping beneath her eyes with her fingertips. I felt like crying, too, but mostly with happiness the toast was over. Before I could sit down, Xavier stood and hugged me, too. The three of us remained locked in an awkward group hug for several seconds before I was finally released.

As I walked back to my seat, I handed Elvis the microphone, which he reluctantly took. He looked as if he might throw up any minute. I totally felt his pain.

He stood and waited until the talking died down. The expression on his face remained one of panic, but he held it together.

"Okay, so I admit I'm pretty nervous right now." Elvis loosened his tie. "Like Lexi, talking in front of people isn't my thing either. I can honestly say, it's been an incredibly emotional day. Even the cake is in tiers." He paused a beat and finally the crowd laughed.

"But, I'm going to give it a go. Most of you know Xavier and I are identical twins. Apparently, some of you can't tell us apart when we dress alike. However, I'm happy to report that Xavier is the smarter one. Trust me—you always want him on your team for strategic and tactical decisions. He's fearless. He's faced down vicious mages, dragons and orcs from the worlds of Azeroth, Makanda and Darkscape. He can wield swords, axes and magic potions with amazing efficiency and accuracy. But when he's off duty, he's just a regular guy who likes computers and Mountain Dew, and was smart and courageous enough to score the girl of his dreams."

Laughter filled the room. Slash slid his hand into mine under the table and squeezed.

Elvis took a couple of breaths and then continued. "We've had our own ups and downs, like most families do, but I'm proud to call him my brother. He's going to make a great husband, a fantastic father—if you decide to go that route—and a good friend to you, Basia, for one simple reason. He's just that kind of person."

There was a slight pause while Elvis collected himself and Xavier blinked hard a couple of times. I felt my throat tighten. Regardless of their recent rift over their father's surprise reappearance in their lives, these two brothers were still two of the most closely connected people I'd ever known.

"Now, although I'm probably the least qualified adult in this room to offer marriage advice to them, I'm still going to do it," Elvis continued. "After considerable research of my own, I believe I've discovered the best words of wisdom to give my brother in terms of keeping his marriage a happy one. So, Xavier, listen carefully. Use these three words often to ensure continued wedded bliss, 'You're right, dear.'"

We all laughed, some people clapped, and Basia and Xavier kissed. When the room had settled down, Elvis continued.

"So, finally, I would like to say congratulations to this very special couple. May you continue to fall in love with each other for the rest of your lives." Elvis lifted his glass and we raised ours in a toast.

While Xavier and Basia stood and hugged Elvis, I polished off the rest of the champagne in my glass.

Thank God. My duties as maid of honor were officially over.

FIFTEEN

DANCING COMMENCED SHORTLY THEREAFTER. Thank God and all the stars above, Basia had decided *not* to throw the bouquet, because there would have been no way in hell I would have stood up for that. Instead, she presented it to the couple at the wedding who had been married the longest, which happened to be her adorable grandparents. I thought that a fitting and touching salute to their lasting wedded bliss. Since I had a few moments alone with Slash, I filled him in on what Elvis had told me about the girls while Basia and Xavier whirled around the floor for the first dance of the evening.

Just after I'd finished filling Slash in, Elvis walked over to us. "You slayed it with that toast, Lexi." He gave me a high five. "Perfectly written and executed."

"You were better," I insisted. "You employed humor to great effect, even though your speech only ran four minutes and forty-seven seconds, including pauses."

"Good work all around." Slash slapped hands in a cross between a handshake and a high five with Elvis. "Heartfelt and perfect—the both of you. I'm impressed."

"I'm just glad it's done," I said. "I survived. Barely."

"Right there with you," Elvis said. "I'll be honest. I was on the verge of a nervous breakdown. I'm just glad I won't have to do that again."

"I'm so with you on that."

I heard someone calling my name. When I looked

up, Xavier and Basia were waving me toward the dance floor.

"Oh, heck, no," I said, trying to hide behind my water goblet. "I'm done with maid of honor duties, right?"

Elvis sighed. "Guess not. Come on. We've got to be supportive."

"No!" I wanted to shout it, but didn't see how I could do that without making a scene. "How can this be fair? I've performed my duties admirably. I rode the wedding roller coaster, shopped for a wedding dress, caught the wedding arch in my bare hands, gave an appropriate toast, and babysat the ring bearer and flower girl. Now I have to dance?"

"Yep." Elvis shrugged and then headed for Mrs. Kowalski. He gave a slight bow and gallantly asked her to dance. I was impressed by his chivalry, in spite of myself.

Slash stood and took my hand. "He's right. Let's dance, *cara*."

"Seriously? Is my work here never done? Do I really have to?"

"You really have to. I promise to make it as painless as possible for you."

Since there was no escape, I reluctantly stood. "Sorry to be so cranky. I appreciate your support."

He only smiled as he removed his jacket and placed it on the back of the chair. Holding my hand, he led me to the dance floor. It was already crowded, and a lot of people looked downright happy to be shaking their body all over the place. Personally, I didn't get how people enjoyed doing this.

Thankfully, the music had slowed a little. Slash slid his hand down my arm, letting his hand rest on my hip.

He placed my hand on his left shoulder and my right hand on his waist. His right leg slid between mine as he pulled me close.

At five foot eleven, I often tower over other women and even some men, too. But with Slash standing about six foot two, we fit together nicely, as if we'd been made for each other. His arms were a comfortable and safe place for me. I let myself relax into his warmth. He pressed his cheek against mine.

"This is nice," I murmured, closing my eyes.

"It is." His hand rubbed small circles on my back. "It's been a stressful day for you. A lot of pressure, under which you performed admirably. It's mostly over now."

"*Mostly* being the key word here. I really appreciate you helping me through it, though." I considered for a moment. "So, why do you do it?"

He lifted his cheek to look at me, his eyes questioning. "Why do I do what?"

"Stick with me. Put up with all my crap and neuroses. This relationship stuff…it isn't easy for me."

He laughed softly. "You think it's easy for me?"

"It does seem to come more naturally to you." We continued to dance, our hips swaying from side to side, our feet moving in the rhythm that Slash set.

"It doesn't." He shook his head. "But it's worth every minute of it. *You're* worth it. In fact, your toast tonight made me contemplative. What makes a strong couple— a couple that will last all the trials and tribulations of normal, or in our case, not-so-normal, life? Is it simply a luck-of-the-draw, statistics, a constant redefining…or is it something more? I don't have the answer. But I do know before I met you, I might have accepted another kind of woman. Now I know, without a shred of doubt, I'd never have loved her like I love you." He trailed a finger down my cheekbone and across my jaw. "You're what makes me happy."

A warmth spread through me. Happiness, but also a kind of contentment. His words resonated with me. "You make me happy, too, Slash. But I'll be honest. I'm still struggling with the logic of it. A guy like you— mysterious, good-looking, secretive—with a geek girl like me who grapples with the simplest of social interactions. How do we make it work for the long haul?"

His brown eyes were thoughtful as they looked at me. "First, I'm as much a geek as you are, and the secretive part is job-related only. No one has ever known me as well as you. Second, why should you struggle with the logic? Biology and procreation aside, a search for a mate is an inner quest of the soul. I believe we're constantly looking for what is good, honest and pure within ourselves, so we search for someone who can reflect that back to us. Until I met you, I'd never known anyone who could do that. I trust you on all the levels that matter to me—physically, emotionally, mentally and spiritually. In my opinion, a union borne of such wholeness is likely to last and create an unusually strong, loving and intelligent family. That, *cara*, is what I see in your eyes when I look at you. I see my future."

I swallowed hard. His eloquent explanation had touched me deeply. I reached up and tucked a strand of hair behind his ear. "I'd never thought of it that way. I'm not sure what to say."

"You don't have to say anything. Just trust my feelings for you are genuine, as are my instincts about us. I am certain I've met my match."

I studied his face, his warm brown eyes, the soft touch of amusement in his expression. "So, *that's* why you put up with me?"

"*Si*, that's why." He smiled and pressed a kiss on my cheek. "Because you're the light, and I've been in the dark all my life."

WE LEFT THE hotel the next morning bright and early. After a quick breakfast in the hotel buffet, we headed home. It was Sunday and we had a lot to do before the work week started. Piles of laundry had to be attacked, not to mention the dozens of moving boxes that needed to be unpacked.

Unfortunately, it took us over three hours to get home due to heavy traffic on the Bay Bridge, so when we finally pulled into the driveway of our house, and I saw my red Miata sitting there, I gave a sigh of relief.

"We're finally home." As soon as I said the words, I paused. It seemed significant that this house already felt like home and I'd lived there all of two days.

It wasn't the house that made it a home, it was Slash.

He reached over and squeezed my hand. Somehow, he knew what I was thinking. "*Si*, we're home." For a moment, we sat there together, looking at the house together.

When the Secret Service pulled up behind us and parked at the curb, we finally unloaded the suitcases from the trunk and pulled them behind us to the front door.

"Do you think Xavier and Basia will miss us?" I asked as Slash punched in the key code on the alarm system.

"No." There was a beep and he unlocked the door.

He opened it and pulled his suitcase inside. "Not in the slightest."

"That's what I thought." I sighed and followed him in. It was strange, but I missed Basia already.

We emptied our suitcases and I put in a load of laundry to wash while Slash took our suitcases down to the basement storage. On the way back up, Slash took my hand.

"Let's forget about unpacking the moving boxes and do something else," he said. "I want to show you something. It requires workout clothes."

I didn't feel like working out, but nothing new there. I *never* felt like working out. Still, I felt like unpacking boxes even less, so I followed him to the bedroom and pulled on a pair of soft gray shorts and a blue T-shirt. I was reaching for a pair of socks when Slash shook his head.

"Stay barefoot, okay?"

He'd already changed into a pair of black shorts and white muscle shirt. He was barefoot, too. "Ready?"

"Almost." I went into the bathroom and pulled my hair back into a ponytail. When I came out, he was gone. I went down the hall to the second bedroom on the right, our exercise room.

He'd pushed aside some of the workout equipment so we had a large empty space on the mats facing the mirrors. I usually hated looking at myself while I worked out, but Slash told me it was important to see how I did things to make sure my form was proper. I think it was also because he didn't want me to hurt myself, but he was too polite to say so. It was weird seeing my awkwardness up close and personal, but I didn't have much choice, so I went with it.

Slash came up behind me and slid his hands onto my hips. "Given the way your life has been going lately, I want to start teaching you Krav Maga. It's a defensive art used by the Israeli military that focuses on real-life scenarios. It's an excellent, easy form of self-defense."

I'll be honest. Given his proximity to me, it was hard to focus on anything except the heat from his hands burning through my shorts. He probably didn't even realize that each flex of his fingers against my hip bone was driving me crazy. I tried to get my mind out of the gutter and back on the matter at hand, but he wasn't making it easy. "I'm not completely new to this kind of thing, Slash. I did take a couple of classes in tae kwon do."

"How could I forget?" He smiled at the memory and leaned over, whispering in my ear. "You challenged me once to a sparring match, remember?"

I'd just met him and he'd taken me down in less than two seconds. Ugh. "Oh, yeah. I forgot about that. So, is this Krav Maga something like tae kwon do?"

His hands dropped from my hips as he came around to face me. "Not exactly. It developed from a mixture of aikido, judo, jujitsu and boxing. It's like tae kwon do, but it trains you to injure rather than defeat. Forget the argument that you can't come out on top because your opponent is bigger, stronger, faster and/or male. You *can* be smarter, quicker and better prepared. Krav Maga is about self-empowerment regardless of gender or physical size."

"Okay." I tensed, lifting my fists. "Are you going to flip me on the mat now?"

He shook his head. "No, *cara*. I'm going to teach

you how to disable someone, man or woman, so you can get away safely if you're ever confronted…again."

I blew out a breath. "Okay. What's first?"

"Learning the body's most vulnerable spots." His breath was hot against my hair as he touched my ear. His fingers traced the lobe and then trailed across my cheek. "The ears and eyes are first, followed by the neck, throat and face, solar plexus, groin, knees, fingers and hands. There are more, but let's start with those."

He lingered on each spot, making sure I felt it. I swallowed hard. I wasn't sure if this was a seduction or a self-defense lesson. If he were trying to distract me, he was doing a bang-up job of it.

"How do I decide what to go for first?" I managed to say.

"Logic. Your first choice should always be conflict avoidance. If that's not an option, your first goal is to stay calm, shut down the panic and fear, and study your opponent. Think of it as a chess game on steroids. If you're able, let your opponent make the first move, so you can assess their skills, and predict what they might do. You also have to maintain situational awareness at all times to see if there is anyone else in play or how you'll escape once you hurt your opponent enough to get away." His voice was calm and confident, as if he wasn't concerned at all that I could pull this off. He took a step back and bent his knees slightly, rolling up onto the balls of his feet. His arms were close to his body, but hanging loose, so that he could move them in any direction quickly.

He saw me observing his stance and smiled. "Good. You're paying attention to my body language."

It was hard *not* to pay attention to his body, but I

didn't think that was what he meant. "That's a lot of things to remember when confronted with danger," I said.

"Exactly. So, you practice until it becomes natural."

We started with stances—passive and neutral—before moving into fighting stances. From there we worked on reactions to attacks involving no warning.

I'd barely prepared myself before Slash came at me hard from behind, pinning me with an iron grip. "So, what are you going to do now?"

I considered, mentally reviewing all the information he'd taught me so far. "You're bigger and stronger, so pure physics dictates I need to shift my center of gravity to get you off-balance, right?"

"*Si*. How are you going to do that?"

"Crouch down, I guess."

He nodded, but didn't loosen his grip. "*Si*, but not too much. Don't make it easy for me to get you to the ground. Shift your hips to the side. Your goal is to make space between us."

I did as he instructed and noticed I'd made a small space. "I did it. Now what?"

"What's the most vulnerable part of my body closest to your elbow?"

"Your groin?"

"Exactly. You'd put your elbow into my groin with all your might, as often as you can, until my arms release or loosen enough for you to do a full twist toward me. As you twist, smash your elbow up and into my neck, under my chin or in my face. When you are turned toward me completely, knee me again in the groin, as hard as you can. But you must act, *bam-bam-bam*, no hesitation, pause or doubt. By this point, you should be free to run. Trust me, I'll have a hard time keeping up if you've hit me there hard enough."

We practiced it several times, although I didn't really hit him. This kind of self-defense made sense to me. Krav Maga was logical and simple—self-defense using the science of anatomy, physiology and physics. I liked that.

We worked on escaping a wrist grab, a hair grab, how to break a fall if I were being brought down to the ground and a couple of other things.

I'm not sure how long we practiced, but, at some point, I realized my T-shirt was soaked and I'd finished off two bottles of water from the mini-fridge. I'd just wiped my face with a towel and tossed my bottle in the recycling bin when Slash yanked me toward him.

"Okay, what now?" I asked as he held me face-to-face, pinning my arms to my sides. "A front hold?"

His mouth curved into a smile. "A *kissing* front hold."

I barely had time to breathe as his mouth crashed down on mine, hot and demanding. After a minute, he released me and I almost fell.

"You didn't try hard to escape," he said with amusement.

I definitely hadn't. "*You* didn't play fair."

He grinned and grabbed a towel, tossing it to me. "You did well. You remembered what I said and acted without hesitation."

"The moves and theory are logical, which helps."

"I figured this style of self-defense would be a good fit for you. Shower?"

"Does this mean we're done?" Disappointment tinged my voice. I guess I was kind of hoping he'd throw me to the mat and have his way with me. Which probably meant I had this self-defense thing all backward.

He wiped his brow with the towel. "For now. It's just a start, *cara*. I'm not always going to be there to protect you. To be honest, you're smart and perfectly capable of protecting yourself."

That was my boyfriend for you. He got me a gun and GPS-locator earrings for Christmas, took me to a shooting range on the weekends, and taught me Krav Maga on our downtime. Somehow, despite my extreme klutziness, he still believed me capable of defending myself. After reviewing the statistics on my spreadsheet and seeing how often trouble followed me around, I appreciated his faith. As he stripped off his wet shirt, I also appreciated his *other* gleaming attributes.

Who knew self-defense lessons could be so sexy?

"We could still practice a hold or two in the shower, right?" I said slowly. "What if I'm attacked in the rain? I should practice that. The water in the shower will make me slippery and harder to hold, which means I should have a bit of an advantage."

He bent down to grab another bottle of water from the fridge and threw me a smile so hot, my heart skipped a beat. "Ah, *cara*, did you just challenge me?"

"Just switched up the environment. You up for it?"

He strode toward me, then slid his hands beneath my shirt, playing with the hooks at the back of my bra. "What do you think?"

"I think I'm going to be hard to hold." I stepped back and snapped my towel at him. "I only have to escape once to win. Loser does the dinner dishes tonight. Deal?"

His smile widened. "You're on."

SIXTEEN

I ENDED UP doing the dishes, but it hadn't been a complete loss. Trust me on that. Besides, Slash did the cooking, so it was a pretty sweet deal anyway. I could get used to this living together thing.

Monday came bright and early. The alarm blared and I turned it off, sitting up and yawning. Slash's side of the bed was empty. No surprise there. He often liked to do tai chi before breakfast. I grabbed my robe and went across the hall to the exercise room. Sure enough, he was standing in a perfectly balanced pose on the mat, his eyes completely closed. He cracked an eye open.

"Buon giorno."

"Good morning, Slash. I know I've said it before, but how can you be so coordinated before coffee? You're aware that's not natural, right?" I stretched my arms above my head. My arms and shoulders were sore from the workout yesterday.

He grinned. "Coffee's on. I'm almost done here. I'll be down in a bit."

I trudged downstairs. Sure enough, the coffee was on and it smelled good. I poured myself a half cup, added a half cup of skim milk and sat down at the kitchen counter, reading the newspaper on my phone.

Twenty-five minutes later, Slash came down. He'd showered and shaved and dressed in black slacks and a light blue shirt. His hair was still a bit damp and curled behind his ears. He walked toward me at the counter, then stopped in the middle of the room.

"Is that a box of Pop-Tarts?" He pointed at the box next to my left elbow.

"Double fudge." I set down my phone and lifted the box. "You want one?"

"You know I bought a cantaloupe, right? It's in the refrigerator."

"I know. I saw it in there. But I'll be honest with you, Slash—especially since honesty is the cornerstone of a solid relationship—Pop-Tarts taste better."

Slash sighed and walked over to the counter. He grabbed one from the box, took a bite. He winced.

"You didn't heat it up," I said. "It makes a big difference."

He must not have believed me, because he set it aside and poured himself some coffee. Black, strong Italian roast. "So, what's your workday look like?" He took the cantaloupe from the fridge and cut it into pieces, placing it into two bowls. He put one of them in front of me.

"I'm hoping it's a quiet day." I speared a piece of cantaloupe. "Paperwork, catching up from missing the past few days because of the wedding. You?"

"Same. But mostly meetings. A quick glance at my schedule indicated I have four. My least favorite thing."

"Ugh. I'm with you on that."

We ate our cantaloupe and drank our coffee, chatting about the new developments in quantum computing. He left first, pressing a lingering kiss on my lips. He smelled great and tasted like coffee and cantaloupe. I guess I tasted like chocolate fudge Pop-Tarts. Hope that wasn't too much of a turn-off.

I got dressed and left shortly thereafter, driving to

work with the top to my Miata down and enjoying the warm sun on my face and shoulders.

Once in the office, I poured myself a cup of coffee and read through my email. I then requested a debrief on the past week from my assistant, Kenji Kurisu, on the Hott-Beckett case we'd been working on when my phone rang.

I picked up the receiver. "Hello?"

"Good morning, Lexi," Finn said, his voice cheerful. "Will you meet me in Conference Room #1?"

"Sure." I perked up. A summons to the conference room usually meant we had a new client. The day might turn out to be more interesting than paperwork after all. "On my way."

I gave Ken some new instructions, unplugged my laptop and tucked it under my arm, I also grabbed my now-empty coffee mug, swinging by the kitchen to get myself a cup. Glinda, Finn's administrative assistant and family friend from Ireland, was the only person in the kitchen. She tossed her dark red hair over her shoulder, her eyes narrowing when she saw me. She loathed me, mostly because Finn and I had once been an item and she was hot for him. For some reason, she blamed me for Finn never showing an interest in her, even after we'd broken up.

I tried to be friendly. "Hey, Glinda."

Her bloodred fingernails tapped the handle of the carafe for a moment before she turned to face me, her eyes narrowing. "Lexi."

She carefully poured herself a cup of coffee, then holding the carafe, walked to the sink and poured the rest down the drain. Returning the empty carafe to the coffeemaker, she threw me a smile over her shoulder before stalking out. "Have a good Monday."

I sighed and left my coffee cup on the counter. No time to wait for a new pot to brew.

I headed to Conference Room #1, surprised to see Andrew Garrington sitting across the conference table from Finn. He stood as I entered and we shook hands.

"Hey, Andy." I set my laptop on the table next to Finn and leaned forward. "What are you doing here?"

He loosened the tie at his throat. "Business."

"It's not about the wedding, is it? I hope Basia and Xavier are still married and there are no problems or legal snafus because—I'll be honest—if there's a problem, there's no way I'm doing the wedding again."

He chuckled. "Everything is fine, Lexi. They remain legally wedded. I would also like to think they're happily enjoying their honeymoon."

I exhaled in relief. "Whew. Thank goodness. I'm always worried that something could go wrong, especially when I'm involved. How's your nose?"

"Sore, but not broken. No shiners. Thanks for asking."

"Glad to hear that. I know I told you this before, Andy, but you did a great job as an officiant. I never knew you were a judge before Xavier and Elvis told me. I bet that's quite different from being a COO of a large tech company."

He smiled. "They both present their sets of challenges, that's for sure."

Small talk exhausted, I sat down and opened my laptop. "So, what's up?"

Andy folded his hands and placed them on the table,

leaning forward. "I want to hire X-Corp, and specifically you, Lexi, to take care of something for me."

I glanced at Finn. He didn't know what Andy was talking about. "Computers?"

"No. This is regarding a prototype of a biomedical scanner, similar to the kind you might have seen in *Star Trek* and other science fiction movies. It's a device you can hover above a body and it detects problems and, in some cases, heals them."

My eyes widened. "Wow. That sounds totally cool, not to mention way out of my league."

"I don't need you to work on the project, Lexi. I need you to retrieve it for me."

"Why? Where is it?"

"It was supposed to be delivered to a client on Friday, but the shipping company mixed up the delivery, and my package went elsewhere."

"Another package screwup?"

He looked at me strangely. "Another? You're saying this isn't the only one?"

"I don't know if it's the same company, but there was a problem with an errant wedding gift at Basia and Xavier's wedding. Packages got mixed up. Police were involved." I gave them a brief rundown on what had happened on the eve of the wedding.

"Seriously?" Finn looked hurt. "No one told me?"

Oops. Crap, I had to remember to keep him updated on everything. "Sorry, Finn. There wasn't time," I explained. "It was all resolved sort of peacefully, so I put it out of my mind."

"That's interesting," Andy mused. He drummed his fingers on the tabletop. "Anyway, this is a *very* important package for ComQuest. I want this in my hands straightaway."

"Understood. So, what exactly do you need me to do?"

"I need you to pick up this package for me in person, open it up to make sure the device is in there, and bring it home."

"That's it?"

"That's it, along with keeping this request strictly confidential. It goes no further than the three of us."

"What about Elvis and Xavier?"

"Just the three of us," he said firmly.

I thought it over, wondering what would be so important he would conceal it from the twins. "No offense, Andy, but couldn't you get someone from your company to do this? I mean, it's essentially a messenger job. X-Corp charges a lot per hour, so you could save a bundle of money by going with one of your own employees or simply asking the shipping company to retrieve and re-route to you."

"This is a highly confidential matter. I cannot stress that enough. Money is of lesser importance than the assurance of complete privacy on this matter, as well as the integrity of the device. I trust you, Lexi. I've worked with you before. I need to feel comfortable with the person I choose to do this task for me. I am willing to pay for your time. It's more important for me to know I have someone I can trust implicitly."

It seemed weird that he felt he couldn't trust Elvis or someone else from his company for such a routine job, but I didn't see how I could bring that up and remain polite.

I exchanged a questioning glance with Finn. He knew what I was asking.

He rose from his chair. "Andy, will you excuse us for a moment?"

"Of course."

Finn took my elbow as we stepped out of the conference room. Finn shut the door behind us and studied my face. "So, what do you think?"

"I think it's a super odd request. Anyone could do this job. Why would he purposely go outside his own company for what's essentially a courier pickup?"

"Obviously, there's something else going on."

"Obviously. Regardless, I feel obligated to at least hear him out, seeing as how he's Xavier and Elvis's boss and an acquaintance. That kind of makes it personal, you know?"

"I know. But if you don't want to do this, I also understand. It's not your normal line of work."

I lifted an eyebrow. "No kidding."

"On the other hand, it seems to be a relatively straightforward assignment. For a change. I like that."

"I like that, too." After what I'd been through at the wedding, straightforward sounded attractive. "I guess I can do it, Finn, if you can spare me."

"Well, we don't have a lot going on. I was going to tell you this morning that Ben is going to take a two-month sabbatical starting next week. If I'm honest, I think we'll be lucky to keep him for another year before he retires. Again."

The Ben he referred to was Ben Steinhouser, a legendary computer guru at the NSA who had started X-Corp with Finn just a year ago. Ben's name had been critical in getting X-Corp the early credibility we'd needed as we got the company off the ground.

"He's earned his retirement," I said.

"He has, indeed. So, other than the McCafferty security breach and the security probe at Hott and Beckett I'm not sure what else we have on the docket. How's that case going, by the way?"

"It's on track. Ken's been doing a good job and can manage it for a couple more days. Plus, he's got some pretty smart interns to help him if he needs it."

Finn grinned, slapped me on the shoulder. "That he does, lass. Okay, it's settled, then."

He opened the door and we walked back into the conference room. I picked up my laptop since I wouldn't be using it.

"So, Andy, when and where am I going?"

SEVENTEEN

ANDY WAS DEAD serious about the confidential part. Before he would reveal any further information, Finn and I had to sign a strict confidentiality agreement he produced from his briefcase. Our signatures legally committed us to not sharing the information about this assignment with anyone outside the three of us. Finn, a lawyer himself, reviewed the entire document before signing. I did so on Finn's assurance, since the legalese could have been in Vietnamese for all I understood.

After that, there was one more matter to discuss.

"There should be a letter, an envelope, that's included with the package," Andy said. "That letter is to remain sealed. It's confidential. But you must make certain it is there and let me know if it's been opened."

"Okay." That sounded simple enough.

"If it's been opened, you are to let me know immediately. Anything contained within that envelope is not to be discussed."

"Understood."

After we signed the required documents, Andy asked if my passport was current.

"Yes. Why? Am I going abroad?" I hadn't expected that. I don't think it had occurred to Finn either.

"You are. The package was diverted to the Caribbean."

Oh, jeez. More sand, water and sunshine. I'd had

more than my fill of all three at Basia's wedding. I just hoped it wasn't hurricane season. I'd have to google that to make sure when I got back to my office.

"Where exactly in the Caribbean?" Finn asked.

"The British Virgin Islands."

I gulped. "I don't have to bring a bathing suit, do I?"

He looked at me strangely. "Not if you don't want to."

My cheeks heated. Maybe that hadn't been an appropriate comment. "Oh, good."

"Anyway, I'd like you to meet with me tomorrow at ComQuest to learn how to operate the device," he continued. "You'll leave for the British Virgin Islands on Wednesday. I want to ensure you'll get there in plenty of time to meet with my contact at the hotel where you'll be staying on Friday. I'll provide more on the particulars once you get there."

"You've already made arrangements?" Finn asked in surprise.

"Just the hotel. There's a business conference of some kind on the island this weekend. I was lucky to secure a room before they were all booked. Got the last room, in fact. I'll let you make travel arrangements, however. Just add it to my bill."

Finn jotted a note. "Will do."

We said our goodbyes and I headed back to my office to work. The rest of the day was spent clearing my desk and calendar, as well as working with Ken on current cases. It was nearly seven o'clock before I finally left the office. I almost headed to my old apartment in Jessup out of habit before I remembered to drive to the new place in Silver Spring.

Our new place.

Traffic wasn't bad at that hour and yet, I got home

before Slash. After changing my clothes, I surveyed the refrigerator and tried to decide what to make for dinner. It was kind of weird to realize I was no longer cooking for one. Or that I was cooking at all. After deliberating for a few minutes, I decided on macaroni and cheese. But not from a box. Homemade. One of the few recipes I could make well.

I rooted through a couple of the unpacked boxes in the kitchen until I found the pots and utensils I needed to cook. While the water was boiling, I connected my phone to some Bluetooth speakers and played music by Hai Tsang, a pianist whose music Slash had introduced to me. It had an immediate relaxing effect. I began to hum along while I started preparing the food.

Slash came home about fifteen minutes later and saw me in kitchen. He slid up behind me and kissed my neck. "You in the kitchen? Hai Tsang on your phone? Those are welcome surprises." He sniffed the air. "An additional surprise. Nothing is burning." He grinned and leaned back against the counter.

I scooped up a stray elbow noodle, turned around and chucked it at him. It landed in his hair. "The night is young," I said, narrowing my eyes. "Burning the food is still a possibility." I turned back to the stove.

He pulled the macaroni from his hair and tossed it in the sink. Laughing, he came up behind me, sliding his arms around my waist. "Whatever are you cooking, Madam Chef?"

"Mac and cheese. And before you ask, no, it's not from the box. It's my mom's special recipe and it's in the oven right now."

He lifted an eyebrow. "I'm looking forward to trying it. I'll make the salad."

"Thanks. I already washed the lettuce. It's sitting in your colander in the sink."

After he changed, he returned to the kitchen, dressed in shorts and a T-shirt. He found the wine glasses first and poured us both a glass of chardonnay. We sipped it while making the salad. He diced up the carrots and tomatoes while I split the lettuce, putting it into smaller bowls. It seemed so natural, cozy, to be cooking dinner in *our* house, humming to music we both liked using my silverware and his bowls. Something inside me shifted, a feeling I couldn't name yet. I filed it away for further examination.

We sat down to eat at the kitchen bar because we didn't have a dining room table yet. Slash got a fork-ful of the macaroni and chewed. He lifted an eyebrow. "Hmmm…it's good, *cara*. It's really good."

I fake-glared at him. "You don't have to sound so surprised."

He chuckled, set down his fork. "But it's a *good* surprise."

Just to make sure he wasn't being polite, I took a bite. Yum. "It's the first thing I ever learned to cook," I admitted. "It's my favorite comfort food…aside from anything Nonna cooks."

Nonna, Slash's grandmother who lives in Italy, is the best cook in the world, probably the universe. I'm not sure what she puts in her food, but whatever it is, I'm totally addicted.

"I'm in for cooking duty and sharing recipes," he said, tapping his wine glass to mine before taking a drink. "I'm sure cooking will be just another adventure for us."

"Just so we're clear, I'm up for any adventure as long as it doesn't involve kale or brussels sprouts."

He smiled again, but I noticed he didn't agree. The cad. Instead, he splashed a bit of balsamic on his salad before spearing a tomato. "How was work?"

"Great. I, um, caught a new case."

"Really? Will it be difficult?"

"No, surprisingly easy. But I'll have to travel. I'll be gone Wednesday through Friday. I'm sorry I'll be leaving you to do the unpacking by yourself for a few days. I should be back by Friday evening."

"No problem. I'll manage. Where are you going?"

I had been anticipating this question, but my stomach tightened anyway. "I...can't say. I signed a confidentiality agreement. Sorry."

"Ah, understood."

We fell silent. There it was again, that secrecy between us.

His job.

My job.

The mission.

It didn't matter. It would always exist between us. Basia said trust would be key. But how would we handle it? How did other couples with top secret jobs manage?

Looking down, I pushed the macaroni around on my plate. Slash reached across the table and took my hand. "Did you hear about the new preprocessor QT Tech released on Friday that reduces redundancy with variables and mix-ins by nearly one-third?"

My eyes widened. "One-third? Really?"

"Really, and you can reuse the code across multiple projects."

Just like that our awkwardness vanished as we excitedly explored the possibilities the new technology would bring to the computing world, as well as our own jobs.

After dinner, we started doing the dishes. Slash rinsed and I put them in the dishwasher. I'd just put the last plate in the bottom rack when he asked, "I've been meaning to ask, did you hide peanut M&M's in the slow cooker?"

I froze, guilt surely streaking across my face. "Me? You're asking me?"

"No, the other person who lives in this house. Of course, I'm asking you."

I put my hand on the counter and faced him. "Why were you looking in the slow cooker?"

"It's mine and I happen to cook with it on occasion." He washed a wine glass and set it in the drainer. "I was thinking ahead to dinner tomorrow night."

"Oh. Couples do that. Plan meals ahead of time, I mean."

"They do." He paused, studied me thoughtfully. "*Cara*, it takes time to figure out how to live together… to get into a rhythm. You don't have to be nervous."

"I'm not nervous…much."

His expression softened. "I remember how it felt when I moved from the hospital to my new mother and brother's flat. It took time for us to figure out how to live together, including taking turns cooking and cleaning."

I'd forgotten about that, and how hard it must have been for him to make that adjustment, especially as a child. I wanted to ask him more about that and how he'd handled all the secrecy and adjustments in his life after joining the NSA, but I couldn't bring myself to do it quite yet.

"Cooking duties are also number eleven on the Relationship Checklist," I said. "Too bad we can't have macaroni and cheese every night. I suppose offering you Cheerios for dinner more than twice a month wouldn't be appropriate. Right?"

I probably sounded too hopeful because Slash chuckled and laid the dishtowel over the corner of the sink. "Twice a month with Cheerios for dinner is two times too many. What's the Relationship Checklist?"

"It's a personal checklist of items that make a relationship successful. I compiled it mostly from psychology textbooks—and one popular online blog run by a PhD scientist about couples living together. Since relationships are complex and involve two people who may have differing and complicated needs, as well as expectations, I felt it was important to get a handle on what I need to do to make this relationship as successful as possible."

He studied me for a moment. "This checklist is separate from the 'Little Black Cloud' spreadsheet?"

"Completely. The LBC spreadsheet focuses on my mishaps. The Relationship checklist is all about healthy relationship behaviors that I can expect to encounter. I want to make sure I'm doing everything I can to bring out the best in you and advance your evolution as an individual while strengthening our bond as a couple and as friends."

He seemed as if he were trying not to smile. "That's admirable, *cara*. However, sometimes relationships develop organically and without a checklist."

"Of course, they do. But you should know me well

enough to realize I perform better when I'm prepared for as many contingencies as possible."

He tugged on my ponytail, pulling me in close. He wrapped his arms around me, resting his chin on the top of my head. I loved it when he did this, securing me in his circle of warmth and strength. The two of us against the world. "I do know you well enough to realize that." His tone held a mixture of amusement and affection. "But what does any of this have to do with the M&M's in the slow cooker?"

I leaned back in the embrace so I could look up at him. "Right. About that…" I paused, tried to come up with a plausible explanation and then realized I didn't have to. "I have no defense."

He lifted an eyebrow. "You don't have to hide food from me."

"I'm not hiding food from you. I'm hiding food from me. If I can't remember where I put them, I can't eat them."

"Nice try, but I'm not buying that. You have a photographic memory."

"Busted." I sighed. "Okay, the truth is I just pretend I don't know where they are. Don't judge me."

He laughed and lowered his head for a kiss. Just before pressing his lips to mine, he whispered, "Better find a new hiding place. I ate them last night."

EIGHTEEN

LATER THAT NIGHT when we were in bed, relaxing in each other's arms, I knew I had to say what was on my mind.

I hated to do it because at this moment, everything seemed just right. Slash lay on his back, his expression relaxed and contented. His arm was bent behind his head, cushioning it, while his hand made lazy circles on my back. I lay sideways in the embrace, my right hand on his bare chest. If we were going to make this relationship work, we had to talk openly about the things that bothered us, no matter how uncomfortable.

"Slash, may I ask you something?"

Maybe it was the tone of my voice or maybe he was just incredibly in sync with me, because he instantly looked down, his brown eyes alert. "What is it, *cara*?"

"Something has been bothering me about our time in Egypt."

There was a brief pause and a flash of concern in his eyes, before it disappeared. "Okay. What is it?"

"Well, when we were there, you sometimes acted in ways I didn't expect. It wasn't bad, it was just different. Sometimes you were remote and preoccupied, and you didn't treat me like your girlfriend, not exactly. You kept me at a distance, sometimes physically, more often emotionally. Before you express surprise that I even noticed, I'm getting better at reading your moods. At the time, I thought maybe you were losing interest in me, especially since there was a more beautiful and accomplished woman hanging around. But after I thought about it, I began to suspect why you acted that way. I think you were there to help Elvis because he's your friend, but I also think you were on a mission for the government to figure out what was going on with his father and assess the threat it posed to the US. It wasn't until we got back, and I had time to really think about it, that I came to this conclusion. I don't expect you to confirm it, because I know you can't, but it's important to me that you know I know." I tensed waiting for his response, but Slash remained silent. His hand on my back had stilled, too.

I swallowed hard and pushed ahead. "So, just days later, I'm taking an assignment that requires me to sign a confidentiality agreement. I can't tell you where I'm going or what I'll be doing. Suddenly, I'm doing to you what you did to me, except at least I can tell you I'm on a case. All of this should feel normal because it's just the nature of our work, right? We're not being secretive or exclusive on purpose. But I'll be honest with you, Slash. It doesn't feel normal or right. I'm worried it's going to put a strain on our relationship. How are we going to deal with this? More importantly, when we're together, how do we know when we're living our lives and when we're living the mission, especially if we can't even talk to each other about it?"

Slash let out a deep breath, closing his eyes. "I would never hurt you, *cara*. I'm sorry if I did. Your ignorance of the mission—any of my missions—directly correlates to your safety. But you're not the only one who's been thinking about this. I have as well. My simulation business in New York is doing quite well. In fact, better than well. The company is practically running it-self since I've entrusted it to a few handpicked program managers and scientists. Even if it weren't doing well, I could easily start another tech firm, including a cyber-security one. There are many things I could do to make a living. One thing I want you to know for certain, if it comes to a choice between the NSA and you—you're going to come out on top." He tightened his arm around me. "I won't ever let my work come between us. And if it does, it's gone. Just like that."

I closed my eyes, letting his reassurance wash over me. "I want you to know how much I appreciate you saying that. But let's be serious, Slash, this country needs you and your skills on the front line. We both know that. So, in turn, I want *you* to know something. If the strain becomes too great for you, for us, or the secrecy too burdensome for our relationship to manage, I'll come back to the NSA. I'll work for you, on your team, so the work isn't just yours, it's *ours*. Because if it comes down to a choice between you or X-Corp—you're going to come out on top."

"Mio Dio," he murmured. He wrapped both arms around me so we were chest to chest, heart to heart. "How do you do that, *cara*? Just like that, you make me feel like I can have what other people have."

"You *can* have that, Slash."

"Can I? Before you, I never saw that for myself. But with you, I am me, or more of me than I've ever been with any other person."

"Likewise." I studied his face, the stubble on his cheeks, the tiny scar over his left eyebrow. "Let's face it—neither one of us is ever going to be simple to live with. That's just who we are and what we do. But now

I see what we can make together, I'm not sure I could ever go back to being alone…or accepting less from someone else. Because without you, my world would be a narrowly defined space. You've shown me what it's like beyond that. So far, I like what I see."

After a pause, he laughed softly. "And the pupil becomes the teacher."

"What does that mean?" I asked.

"It means, I don't know what our future holds, *cara*, but as long as it holds you, I'm going to be okay."

NINETEEN

Bright and early, I headed into ComQuest in Baltimore to meet with Andy. The headquarters building was heavily guarded and I had to show my identification to the guard at a gate just to park. Another security guy picked me up in a golf cart from the parking lot. After checking my ID, he took me to the main building. There I had to provide my ID for the third time, but this time, they also took a digital thumbprint. Hi-tech companies like ComQuest were active targets of industrial espionage among just about every country in the world, not to mention fellow US competitors.

I was escorted right past Andy's executive assistant, directly into his office. Andy was on the phone, but he waved me into a chair. The security guard closed the door and I looked around as I sat down. As COO, Andy had a big corner office with lots of windows, which was great for natural light but awful if you had to peer at a computer screen all day. The furniture was a little too dark and pretentious for my taste, but the couch and armchairs in the sitting area behind me looked comfortable.

Andy hung up and stood, coming around the desk to take my hand. "Lexi. I'm glad you took this on for me. I appreciate it."

"Sure. I'm happy to help."

He walked over to a bookshelf. The top half had

shelves lined with books, the bottom half was a bar with a mini-fridge. He opened the door of the fridge and grabbed a bottle of iced tea. "Can I get you something to drink?" he asked over his shoulder.

"No. I'm fine, thanks."

He opened the bottle and took a drink, then left it on top of the mini-fridge. Reaching up, he pulled down a white box from the bookshelf and carried it over to me.

"This is a prototype of ComQuest's tricorder, but it should give you the basics on how it is operated." He lifted the lid and I peered at the contents. It contained a smartphone with a docking station, a couple of cords and several pulse oximeters. After he removed it from the box, I opened a couple of drawers on the side of the docking station that were filled with small medical items.

I lifted my gaze to Andy's. "That's it?"

"That's it. What were you expecting?" He looked amused.

"I don't know. Something more futuristic-looking, I guess. Something along the lines of the *Star Trek* tricorder. You know, kind of bulky and handheld. You wave it magically over a patient and, voilà, patient is diagnosed. I can definitively say I wasn't expecting to see a cell phone."

Grinning, he removed the smartphone and held it up. "It's not just a cell phone. It's a modified smartphone. See those sensors? They connect to the phone using Bluetooth. The pulse oximeters are attached to a patient to determine a myriad of issues, from skin cancer to a heart murmur. Right now, we are able to accurately diagnose about forty-six ailments."

"Forty-six? Are you kidding me? That's amazing."

"It is."

I pointed at some items in the drawer. "What are those?"

"The tricorder comes with blood-glucose and urine test modules, among other things. It's a thorough diagnostic device. I'm sorry to report, however, it doesn't hover over a patient like the tricorder in *Star Trek*. I'm afraid the patient needs to be connected for it to work."

I grinned, turning the smartphone over in my hand. "Still, this is way cool, Andy. Kudos to ComQuest. I had no idea we were so far along with such technology."

"It's still in the early testing phase, but it could change the way we diagnose illness, especially in areas where medical care is inaccessible."

"I believe that." I examined the cords, compared them to the docking station. "How is it charged?"

"The docking station can charge any of the devices. The station itself can be plugged into the wall or it can work off a special battery. Simple as that."

"Wow. You're really onto something here, Andy."

He smiled. "We are. We really are. So, we need to make sure that package is returned safe and sound to ComQuest."

"Andy, can I ask you a question? Why would you send a prototype somewhere else? Why aren't you working on it here in the lab?"

He tensed at my question, then smiled. "Sometimes we need expert advice conducted in a neutral location."

Personally, I would never risk a valuable prototype by sending it to someone else's lab. It seemed more prudent to have the experts come to ComQuest to work with it. But since I wasn't being paid to ask questions, I didn't say anything.

"You're to go to the hotel restaurant on Friday under reservations made in your name at precisely one thirty to meet the person who will give you the package," Andy was saying. "Understood?"

"I understand, Andy, but I'll be honest, it seems a little clandestine. I think the logical course of action would have been to put this on the shipping company. They should be the ones retrieving it for you."

He clasped me on the shoulder. "I know it seems a bit odd to you, but this is the way I prefer to do it. I don't want any more mistakes. I trust you to be efficient and discreet."

While discretion was *not* always my middle name, I plastered a smile on my face and nodded. "Sure, I'll do my best."

"Your best is exactly why I'm hiring you."

Eventually a security guard was called to escort me out. I ran into Elvis, who was just coming into the building as I was going out. He accompanied me back outside so we could talk.

"What are you doing here?" he asked.

"Ah…" I groped for an answer. "Stuff."

He frowned. "Stuff?"

"Yeah, I'm sorry, Elvis. I can't really talk about it."

"Oh."

He kind of looked hurt, but what could I do? Andy had been especially specific in mentioning that any discussion of my assignment was off-limits, especially to the Zimmerman twins, since Andy knew we were close friends.

"Okay. So, how are things?"

I dug my sunglasses out of my purse and put them on. "Good. You know, unpacking boxes. Moving is a pain."

I leaned closer and lowered my voice so the security guard couldn't hear. "Hear from any of the girls yet?"

He shook his head, his expression sad. "Crickets."

"I'm sorry. You any closer to deciding what to do?"

"I'm waiting for inspiration to strike. Do you think that's the right approach?"

"Heck if I know. But here is a small piece of advice. Stop being afraid of what you feel. Follow your heart, Elvis."

"Without defined parameters of what the heart wants, that isn't useful information."

I smiled, patted him on the shoulder. "You'll figure it out. I'm confident of that."

They weren't expecting me back at X-Corp, so I drove home to pack for the trip. Since I wouldn't be meeting with a client or anyone I had to impress, I threw a pair of jeans, a couple pairs of shorts, three T-shirts, a sweatshirt, undies, socks, suntan lotion, sandals and a floppy beach hat into my suitcase. I added my toiletry kit and snapped it shut. All under ten minutes.

"Well, that was easy," I said, lugging the suitcase downstairs and leaving it by the front door. I had only to pack up my laptop in the morning and that was that.

Since I had time, I changed and went down to the kitchen and started unpacking kitchen items. I washed them and stacked them to dry first, so it was tedious work. Today I put on music from the '90s and rocked it while waving around spatulas, pans and chopsticks. More time passed, then I realized I was starving and it was after six o'clock. I checked my phone and saw a text from Slash had arrived about thirty minutes prior.

Going to run very late tonight. Eat without me. Sorry.

I looked around the disaster of a kitchen. Every inch of counter was taken by drying dishes and utensils. The boxes and bubble wrap scattered everywhere. Good thing Slash was running late.

I dried the frying pan, plugged in the toaster and made a cheese omelet and toast. I ate standing up at the counter, then put my dishes in the dishwasher before tackling the items I'd already washed. When those were dried and put away in locations that made logical sense in a kitchen, I cleared the bubble wrap and lugged the boxes outside to the recycling pile.

I was just alphabetizing the few cans we had in the pantry when I heard him come in. I peeked my head out of the pantry. "You're home."

He set his briefcase by the door and swept me into his arms. "I'm sorry I'm late." He looked around the kitchen. "You…unpacked the kitchen."

"Mostly. I got off early, so I put it to good use. Are you hungry?"

He shook his head. "No. We had sandwiches and coffee brought in to the office. We encountered an unexpected penetration that was a little more complicated than originally expected."

"You took care of it?"

"Of course." He rested his chin on top of my head. "Crisis averted. You would have been very impressed."

"I'm sure. Glad to know the security of this country is in such good hands."

He loosened his tie and rolled his neck. "I'll change and be right back down. Time to unwind."

When he came back down, I was pouring hot milk from a saucepan into a cocoa mix. He joined me at the stove, his arms sliding around my waist. "You made me hot cocoa?"

"I did. I thought chocolate seemed right for the end of the day. Since we're currently out of peanut M&M's, I figured this was the next best thing." I popped in a couple of marshmallows and handed him the mug.

Grinning, he took it and headed for the living room. I picked up mine and followed him. Other than some stacked boxes, the only thing in the living room was a black couch from Slash's apartment, a coffee table from mine and a piano. He took a sip of the cocoa and sat it down on the coffee table, then took a piece of sheet music from the bench, propped it on the piano and sat on the bench. I headed for the couch, but he patted a spot next to him on the piano bench, so I joined him, carefully holding my cocoa and blowing on it before taking a sip.

He considered the music for a moment, then placed his long fingers on the piano and started playing. Although I was no music aficionado, I knew enough about the connection between music and math to understand his skill. The patterns, the cadence and the rhythm were good. Slash had technique, no question. But what made him interesting was that he also played with passion, which in my opinion, made the music far more accessible and meaningful to the average listener, like me.

I didn't recognize the music. Leaning over, I read the title of the song on the sheet music. *"Meraviglioso."* It sounded Italian to me, I couldn't be sure.

The melody seemed sad and haunting at first, but after the first part, the tempo began to pick up slightly. Then, to my astonishment, Slash began to sing...in Italian. While he clearly didn't have a trained voice, it still sounded nice. Way better than me in my car, singing along with the radio at the top of my lungs.

When he finished, he shifted on the bench so he faced me. "So, *cara*, what did you think?" He was smiling, but his eyes were melancholy.

"Wow. Just wow." I stared at him in awe. "It was beautiful. I didn't know you could sing."

He laughed. "That's because I *can't* sing. But when I play this song, I can't help but try. The lyrics are poetry."

"Really? What song is it? I've never heard that tune before."

"It's an Italian classic called 'Wonderful' or '*Meraviglioso*.'" He stood and retrieved his cocoa, taking a sip and bringing it back with him. "It's a song about a man who is standing on a bridge, looking at the dark water below and contemplating his life. Where he's been, what he's seen, what he's done. Trying to decide if life is worth living."

"Whoa." I held up a hand. "Before you go any further, this song has a happy ending, right? If I want to be depressed, I'll stream a French movie."

He sat down, chuckled. "Do you want to know the story or not?"

"Yes." I sighed. "Please continue."

He tapped the sheet music with his finger. "Someone comes along on the bridge behind him and says his name. Maybe it's a man, maybe it's a woman or maybe it's an angel. He turns around to see who it is, and the passerby asks him if he has reflected lately on the wonders of the world."

"That's kind of an unusual question. He doesn't freak out, right?"

"No, he doesn't. He takes the time to reflect exactly on that—the world that was created for him. He imagines the vastness of the sky, the first blush of morning light, the innocence of a child's face, the warm hug of a friend and the affection of a woman who loves only him."

"Then what happens?"

"He is humbled and realizes his life isn't as empty as he thinks. Like the wonders of the world, his future holds possibilities he can't yet fathom. Despite the pain, the regrets and the mistakes he's made—his life has a purpose."

I thought for a moment. "So, what does he do?"

"When he looks up, he realizes the night is over. He leaves the bridge and goes home, because even through the prism of pain, he realizes life is a gift and he shouldn't waste it. Life, with all its hardships, can be...wonderful."

"Wow." I leaned my head on his shoulder. "That's sad and beautiful at the same time."

"It is." We sat in silence for a moment before he picked up his cocoa and stood. "Shall we get unpacking?"

I put a hand on his arm. "Would you mind if we forgo the unpacking for tonight and stay here with the piano instead?"

He looked at me a bit surprised. "You want to hear more music?"

"I do, if you're not too tired." I grinned. "Will you sing again? Please?"

"Only if we're clear that I sing for you and for you only. Deal?"

"Deal."

He cocked his head, studied me thoughtfully. "So, what might the Piano Man expect in return for such a performance?"

"I have about fourteen dollars I could stuff into your proverbial jar."

"Regretfully, that's not enough."

"Hmmm…how about a kiss?"

He tugged my hair out of the ponytail. It fell loose around my shoulders. "And?"

"And what?" I narrowed my eyes. "A kiss isn't enough?"

"Piano playing and singing is hard work. Quid pro quo, yes?"

"Is that a thinly veiled request for additional sexual favors?"

His grin widened. "It might be."

"Fine." I blew out a breath. "You can consider your barter accepted."

"Such a negotiator, you are." He laughed and pressed a kiss on my cheek.

For the next hour, he enthusiastically played a variety of songs, some I knew, some I didn't. I tapped my foot in time, laughed, and sometimes tried to sing along. The longer he played, the more his hair got tousled, his eyes happier and his posture relaxed.

He was beautiful, and he was mine.

When he began to tire, I put my hand over his on the piano. He stilled and shifted on the bench. I slid my fingers between his as I leaned forward, my lips brushing his ear.

"Vuoi aiutarmi a sfare il letto?" I said softly.

His eyes flashed surprise before his generous, sexy

mouth curved into a smile. "Your Italian is getting better. Much better."

"I need more practice."

He·slid his hand beneath my hair, resting his fingers at the nape of my neck and drawing me closer until his mouth was a millimeter from mine. His breath was warm on my mouth as he traced my lips with his fingertip. "Then practice, we shall. To answer your question, *si*, let's go to bed, *cara. Ti voglio. Il mio cuore è solo tua.*"

"What did you say?" I whispered.

He pressed his mouth against mine and I could feel him smile against my lips. "Look it up tomorrow," he murmured. "Tonight, you're busy."

Yes, life was wonderful, indeed.

TWENTY

THE NEXT MORNING Slash insisted on taking me to the airport even though I told him I was perfectly capable of calling my own ride. I gave up when he put my suitcase in his SUV and told me to get in the car. The agents at the curb outside dutifully fell in behind us.

He pulled up to the curb at the airport and got out, taking my suitcase from the trunk. I slung my computer bag over my shoulder along with my purse. Drawing me into his arms, he murmured, "Be safe, *cara*."

I hugged him back and said, "I can't say where I'm going or what I'm doing, but I can say that it's a relatively safe assignment."

He pulled back, cupped my cheek, and looked at me with a mixture of amusement and affection. "Little black cloud, remember?"

"I remember. But I'll be careful. Okay?"

"Okay." He gave me a lingering kiss, then left.

My flight went directly from Washington to St. Thomas in the US Virgin Islands. I was then booked on a ferry to take me to Tortola in the British Virgin Islands. It was a double nightmare for me because I hated flying, but I hated being on the water even more. Ugh! I just hoped everything would go smoothly.

The flight went as well as could be expected despite the businessman seated next to me who fell asleep. He snored and his head lolled onto my shoulder more than once. Still, we didn't crash, no one hijacked the plane, and the weather was crystal clear, so I considered it a highly successful flight.

The ferry ride, however, was another story. The businessman who had sat next to me wasn't a businessman at all, but one of about thirty other proctologists heading for the World Proctology Conference, which just happened to be taking place in the British Virgin Islands. It didn't escape my notice there were no female proctologists. There had to be a joke in that, but believe me, if there was, I didn't want to know it.

Other than the crew, there appeared to be only two non-proctologists on the ferry, me and a young woman from Spain who told me she didn't speak much English. It sounded fine to me, and she certainly spoke English better than I spoke Spanish. She said her name was Camilla and she was headed to the island for a job interview.

We had to board the ferry about forty-five minutes before it departed, and while we waited on the boat, the businessmen wasted no time in visiting the open bar. For a bunch of supposedly smart and accomplished people, they were acting like idiots. They were tossing back shots like water, thumping chests, swearing, mooning us and each other (and whatever fish were unlucky enough to be swimming by), and making all kinds of rude body sounds. Apparently, this was what happened when proctologists went wild. They weren't all American, thank goodness, as I could hear various accents in the mix. But it wasn't shining a favorable light on their profession, if you know what I mean.

About five minutes before departure time, one of the doctors moseyed his way over to Camilla and me.

He looked about forty years old, was wearing a cowboy hat, reeked of rum and was not in any shape to perform surgery if anyone on the boat needed his or her colon examined.

"Hey there, little lady," he said in a drawl.

Apparently, when I'm sitting down I don't look five foot eleven. I pretended not to hear him.

He snapped his fingers in front of my face. "Hey. I'm just being friendly. I'm a doctor. That's MD, not PhD." He tipped his hat when I looked up at him. "How are you this afternoon, sweetheart?"

"Wishing we were already at the island so I wouldn't have to deal with this," I muttered.

He laughed. "Ah, so she speaks English after all. I'm available for a little partying if you and your friend are interested. On me. What do you say?"

I wrinkled my nose. "Honestly? I'd rather endure thirty-six colonoscopies performed by a chimpanzee than party with you."

He stared at me for a long moment, before turning hopefully at Camilla. "How about you?"

She replied in a stream of Spanish that didn't seem favorable to his proposition.

"Well, let me know if you ladies change your mind." He held up his paper cup. "Have a good trip." The liquid sloshed over his hand as he staggered back to his buddies.

Camilla and I rolled our eyes at each other. Guess that was a universal signal for moron, because it was clear across languages what we thought of him and his offer.

The ferry finally left the dock and began heading for the island. My stomach rolled queasily and I tried to ignore the sway of the boat and the fact that I was no longer on solid ground.

Not two minutes later a different doctor approached us. This one was younger, but chubbier, with thin hair and red cheeks. He, too, was holding a drink and looking hopeful.

"Hello, ladies. You look all lonely over here all by yourselves. How are you doing?"

"Go away," I said.

He laughed. "Ah, come on. We're just trying to have a little fun. No harm intended. I assume by now you probably know we are proctology surgeons." He pointed to his polo shirt that had a logo of a proctoscope. "Did you know that as a trainee, I had to work my way up from the bottom? The bottom? Get it? That was a joke. Ha, ha, ha!"

"Ugh. That was beyond awful."

"I've got more." He took a gulp of his drink. "Do you know the definition of a proctologist?"

"No." I held up my hands in a time-out sign. I began to envy Camilla who didn't understand English all that well or at least could pretend not to understand. "Would you just go away?"

"It's a doctor who puts in a hard day at the orifice." He burst into laughter and Camilla and I exchanged a disgusted glance. Apparently, her English was good enough to understand that stupidity. Ugh!

Luckily whatever the doctor was about to say next was drowned out by reggae music being blasted from another doctor's phone.

In fact, one of them had climbed up on a bench and started waving his hand back and forth above his head. He had something in one hand, but I couldn't tell exactly what it was. A drink? A phone?

Oh, dear God, no. It was a microphone.

Karaoke. He was going to sing karaoke. Someone just shoot me.

My stomach felt queasy so I stood and pushed my way past the surgeon, following the signs to the women's bathroom. If I knew how to swim, I would have jumped overboard and swam the rest of the way.

Seriously.

In fact, I was considering hiring someone in a motorboat to get me back to the US Virgin Islands once I retrieved the package for Andy, so I wouldn't have to take this ferry from hell again.

I splashed water on my face and stared at my pale reflection in the mirror, wishing the trash can wasn't bolted down so I could carry it with me back to the bench. I could hear the reggae music blaring, the screeching of a bunch of plowed surgeons singing, and the ship was rocking back and forth a lot more than I liked. I wasn't sure I could endure another forty-five minutes on this boat without losing it, and I meant that in more ways than one.

After about ten minutes, I felt bad about leaving Camilla out there alone with the doctors, so I wiped my face with a paper towel and left the bathroom. I was just coming back onto the deck when I heard people shouting and screaming.

I ran forward and saw the surgeons, Camilla and two crew members all crammed to one side of the boat. They were clutching each other and trying to press into a tiny space behind the benches. Then I saw the reason why.

Advancing on them was the biggest crocodile I'd ever seen.

TWENTY-ONE

HOLY REPTILE!

Many things flashed through my mind, but foremost were two things: first, I hoped someone was still driving the ferry, and two, I had no idea crocodiles even lived in the Caribbean. I skidded to a halt on the deck, my sneakers squeaking, not that anyone heard them over all the shrieking and yelling.

I quickly surveyed the situation. People were in a complete panic, throwing anything they could at the crocodile. Shoes, paper cups, brochures, wallets. The guy with a cowboy hat threw his boot. The croc slid his body to the side and with a lunge, snapped at it.

Chomp. The boot disappeared in a few bites.

For a moment, there was shocked silence as we all stared at the croc in horror before one of the doctors screamed.

About that time, the guys noticed me standing on the deck behind the croc and started shrieking for my help. I looked around for something—an axe, a gun, a rope, a crocodile handler—but saw nothing. Worse, the crocodile was on the move and less than ten feet from the group now. It didn't escape my notice that Camilla had somehow been maneuvered in front of the men like a human shield. She stood frozen in fear. I didn't like the way the crocodile suddenly seemed focused on her, a smaller, easier target.

I started to breathe fast, my heart racing. I couldn't let it just eat her, but I was without a weapon or a plan.

What would Slash do in this case? He wouldn't panic. He would think and strategize. I could almost hear him speaking to me, calmly and logically.

Start with the crocodile's weak spots. Just like in Krav Maga, the strategy is to injure to allow escape. Forget about your size and physical strength. Everyone has weaknesses.

My mind raced through everything I'd ever read about crocodiles. Where were its weak spots?

I suddenly knew what I had to do.

I slipped my purse and laptop bag off my shoulder and dropped them to the deck. "Hey, croc! Over here."

I whipped my T-shirt off over my head and advanced on the reptile from behind. He swung his head around to see me. I waved my shirt in the air like a lasso. "Shoo. Go away."

He regarded me for a moment and seemed to grin before turning his attention back to the group. Apparently, he didn't consider me much of a threat.

His mistake.

The most dangerous part of the operation came next. I had to approach the croc directly from behind. If I came at him from either side, his jaws could reach me and he'd be having shredded geek for a snack. Lucky for me, his attention was focused on another treat in front of him.

He was about five feet from Camilla now, his body stilled, his back legs tensing. Not a good sign at all. She closed her eyes, almost as if accepting her fate.

I was out of time.

The shouts from the men were splitting my ears.

Before I could change my mind, I ran in a straight line directly at the back of the crocodile. I leapt onto its back with my hands extended so my T-shirt fell directly across the crocodile's eyes, blinding him. I landed on his back with a hard jolt snapping his mouth shut. I put my hands on either side of its neck, exactly between the back of its jaws and the front legs, pushing with the weight of my body and every bit of strength I had in my arms to force the croc's head to the ground. My knees squeezed his flanks, pinning his back legs so he couldn't move.

It was pure physics. Since a crocodile jaw works in a similar way to humans', I knew that only the bottom jaw moved. Therefore, once his head was on the ground, the weight of my body and the force of my arms would be able to trap his bottom jaw shut between me and the boat. The croc thrashed wildly. I held on for dear life, thinking this hadn't been one of my better ideas. I just hoped physics didn't fail me.

Still gripping the bucking croc, I shouted at the group. "Run!"

I'd never seen grown men move so quickly in my entire life. Even Camilla snapped out of her trance and bolted across the deck. Thank God, everyone was safe. Except me.

Now came the difficult part. How the heck was I going to get off an extremely pissed crocodile?

Simple logic dictated the safest way to get off would be the same way I got on. That meant I had to stay behind it at all times. That was key. If I slipped to either side, he could bite me, even blinded.

Stay calm, Lexi, I urged myself. My breathing was coming so fast now, I feared I'd hyperventilate myself into unconsciousness if I didn't calm the heck down. I had to push aside the fact I was lying atop of a five-hundred-pound animal who wanted to eat me.

What had Slash said to me? *Injure to allow escape. You are not conquering, the strategy is to get away safely.*

I had to focus. Keeping my hands pressed firmly against the croc's head, I shifted my legs to get my feet under me so I was squatting over him. He felt me shift and tried to move his legs, but I squeezed my thighs together to keep his back legs pinned.

Now I needed to calculate my way to escape. The length of his head. The projected reach of his bite. The force at which I'd have to propel myself backwards to escape that reach. The odds I would make it out alive.

I didn't like those last set of odds, so I discarded them.

The crocodile was getting restless and I was tiring. It was now or never.

Three, two, one.

Inhaling, I pushed off the alligator's head with all my force and propelled myself backward. The fact my T-shirt still blinded him and he had to physically turn his body around to get a clear snap at me, gave me the precious few seconds I needed to scramble to my feet and run. I snatched my purse and laptop as I hightailed it below deck. It was completely empty.

Suddenly, the door to the concession stand opened. I bolted through it and someone slammed it behind me. Every proctologist on the boat, two crew members, me and Camilla were crammed into the small space.

There was a moment of silence before the entire room broke out in cheers and clapping. Camilla gave me a hug.

The guy with the cowboy hat slapped me on the shoulder. "Damn, girl, you didn't tell us you were a crocodile wrestler." Suddenly, the entire group of proctologists were chanting "Dundee, Dundee!"

Camilla gave me her sweater because there was no way in hell I was going back out there to get my T-shirt.

I turned to one of the crew members. "How did that crocodile get on the ferry?"

The crew member looked shaken. "I do not know."

"Poacher," another crew member muttered.

"A poacher?" I looked at him incredulously. "Someone brought a live crocodile on a boat crammed with people *on purpose*?"

"Well, I would think it wasn't supposed to be roaming around."

I still was having a hard time wrapping my head around this. "You've *got* to be kidding me. Whose brilliant idea was this?"

The crew members all pressed their lips shut. No one was ratting out anyone, which meant they were all probably in on it in some way or the other. Holy crap.

I sighed. "Does the captain even know the croc is on board?"

"He knows now." One crew member pointed to a walkie-talkie on his belt. "He's already called to shore. The authorities will meet us at the dock and get the crocodile off safely. No worries."

"How about getting *us* off safely?" one of the doctors demanded.

"Don't worry, man. Be happy." The crew member's mouth stretched into a wide grin. "You're safe and your money will most certainly be refunded. Happy Island

Ferry Service guarantees you safe passage to the island, and we've kept our word."

"Yeah, thanks to her," one of the doctors said, pointing at me.

The crew member's grin widened. "I suggest you all relax and forget about the crocodile. Let me be the first to welcome you to the British Virgin Islands."

TWENTY-TWO

THE WARM WELCOME didn't help. By the time the authorities captured the crocodile, released us from the tight quarters of the concession stand where I was way too close for way too long to the proctologists, and I finally arrived at the hotel, dragging my suitcase behind me, I was completely wiped out. Thankfully, my hotel was *not* the same place the doctors were holding their world conference to discuss whatever it was proctologists talked about.

Thankfully, this hotel was more like an über-exclusive resort and spa. At this point, I didn't care where I stayed. As long as it had a bed, a shower and *no* crocodiles, I didn't care.

I checked in and saw I'd been assigned to the thirteenth floor. I hoped that didn't signal bad luck. Holding my key card in front of me, I dragged my suitcase to the elevator. A few seconds later, one of the elevators arrived. Reggae music was playing. I winced, now forever ruined for reggae by a bunch of hammered proctologists.

I was pleasantly surprised by my room. It was nice and airy with a big bed and a shaded balcony overlooking the beach and ocean. The view of the water was pretty, especially if I didn't have to swim or sail in it. The decor was beachy—blues, yellows and brown. It was cheerful, simple and clean. The bathroom had exposed stone and a fancy coffeemaker. I could definitely live here for a couple of days.

I examined the welcome basket of fruit on the desk and took out an apple. After washing it in the bathroom sink, I took a bite and started to get my computer equipment set up. As soon as I could, I checked out the Wi-Fi speed. For a remote island, the speed was decent. I'd brought a Wi-Fi enhancer, and while the speed wouldn't be what I was used to, it would do.

I took my phone and a bottle of water and sat out on the balcony. I called Finn first to let him know I'd arrived.

"So, was the trip uneventful?" Finn asked.

"Ah… I wouldn't say uneventful, but I made it here alive, so that counts for something."

"Knowing you, it certainly does. How's the hotel?"

"It's prime. Andy booked me at some exclusive resort with a private beach, villas, a couple of infinity pools, a spa and the works. It's pretty sweet, even for someone like me who isn't a big fan of sand and sun."

"He said it was the last hotel room he could find available. Guess there is some kind of huge conference going on this week."

"Proctologists."

"Excuse me?"

"The proctologists of the world are having their big meeting here."

"Damn. Guess it has to happen somewhere."

"Right? But what are the odds it happens when I'm on the island?" I sighed. "Oh, well. At least they're not meeting at my hotel. I'm thankful for that. In fact, I'm considering an alternate route back to the US Virgin Islands. I'm not doing that ferry ride again."

"I'll have Glinda look into it. I do have a bit of interesting news for you, however. Guess who arrived at our office bright and early this morning?"

"Who?"

"The Executive Vice President of DPR Shipping."

"And that's interesting because…"

"Because he hired X-Corp to find out why all their packages are going astray. Some are being diverted, but other high-value packages are disappearing. Their computer system shows them as being delivered, but they are not making it to the correct destination. Some packages are mislabeled within the system and others are being re-routed. Obviously, their system has been compromised, but they can't find where and how. They hired an IT firm to check it out, but they couldn't crack the code. So, they've come to us. They're desperate to fix this, obviously."

"That is interesting. Do you happen to know if Andy was sending his package via DPR Shipping?"

"He was."

"Okay, that is *not* a coincidence. Can you shoot me the particulars on DPR's system? The Wi-Fi here isn't great, but it should suffice. I'd like to take a look of my own."

"Of course. I'll send everything your way by the end of the day."

"Appreciate it, Finn."

I called Slash, but his phone went straight to voice mail, so I left a message saying I'd arrived safely and was at the hotel.

In the meantime, I started an online investigation of DPR Shipping. The company was a full-service packaging converter and distributor. They were family-owned and had started in 1946 in Baltimore as an industrial packager, going nationwide in the '70s. In addition to shipping and mailing, they carried a wide array of stock boxes and packing supplies, including custom-made boxes. Admirably, they claimed ninety-six percent of their packaging and box materials were recyclable. They were small, but solid.

I did a quick run-through online regarding customer service, financial stability and reputation. All were good to excellent.

I did a scan of the leadership, but nothing jumped out at me. I read more on shipping companies, how they were structured and run, when my stomach started growling. I was hungry.

Since I hadn't yet received a call back from Slash or any files from Finn, I decided to check out the hotel restaurant. It was elegant, even swanky, with seating at a large outdoor terrace facing the ocean. There were tiny flickering candles on every table and pretty ocean blue tablecloths. I felt self-conscious in my jeans and a sweatshirt, but the host didn't mention the fact that I was woefully underdressed. Instead, he led me to a small table and handed me a menu. The breeze was light and felt good. Small lights were strung across the venue, sparkling and twinkling, like it was Christmas. There was live music, too, a six-man band playing island music. I appreciated the fact it wasn't loud, even if I didn't have anyone to talk to. When the waiter came to my table to take my drink order, I decided to live dangerously and order a piña colada. I'd wrestled a crocodile and survived, which, in my opinion, meant I was entitled to one.

After surveying the menu, I ordered the grilled bonefish, Johnny cakes—cornmeal-based flatbread popular in the Caribbean—and a salad. I sat sipping my drink and listening to the band. After a few minutes, the group went on break. Three guys, however, continued to play, walking around the tables and serenading the patrons. One guy played the guitar, the other, a small drum, and the third, some handheld shakers. Eventually they stopped at my table and started playing for me. Usually I loathe attention, but they were friendly, and the music was good. The piña colada was kicking in and I was feeling relaxed. At some point, the guy with the shakers handed me one and asked me to accompany them.

I didn't know the song, but I figured I could shake it. Laughing, they sped up the tempo and I enthusiastically shook along. That is, until, the shaker flew out of my hand and hit the back of the head of a man sitting by himself two tables over. I could hear the crack from where I sat.

The musicians abruptly stopped and we all stared in shock at the back of his head. Snapping out of my horror, I jumped out of my seat, rushing over to him, apologizing profusely. The man rubbed the back of his head, then turned around in his chair to see who had hit him.

Holy honeymoon! It was Xavier Zimmerman.

TWENTY-THREE

I took a step back, utterly flabbergasted. "Xavier?"

"Lexi?" He pushed his chair sideways to get away from me, nearly falling out of his seat. "What are you doing here?"

"Oh, God. Please tell me this is not your secret honeymoon destination."

"It's my *not*-so-secret-anymore honeymoon destination, apparently."

I closed my eyes, feeling sick. "Okay, this is beyond awkward, even for me."

"Why are you here?" A flash of panic crossed his face. "Elvis? My mom? Is everything okay back home?"

"Everything is fine, Xavier. I'm here for work."

The band, bored by our discussion and seeing that Xavier had no intention of hitting me back or suing me, moved away to sing and wiggle the shakers at someone else. I slipped into the chair across from Xavier to make way for the waiters.

"Where's Basia?"

"Getting dressed, of course. She could be here anywhere in the next two to forty-five minutes. It's hard to say."

"I've got to get out of here before she gets down here. Do *not*, under *any* circumstances, tell her I'm here. Technically, you never saw me. It's important to her that you two are alone without any outside influence. Erase me from your memory, okay?"

"It's too late for that, but I'll do my best. What work brings you here?"

"Sorry, I can't say. Nondisclosure agreement. No worries. I'll be gone by Friday night."

"How are you going to avoid running into us?"

"I'll hide in my room as much as possible and not loiter in public spots."

"What about your work?"

"Leave that to me. I'll figure out a way to deal with it."

I rose and walked behind him, touching the growing bump on the back of his head where it had collided with the shaker.

"I'm so sorry about your head. An ice pack might help."

At that exact moment, a guy with a camera around his neck started snapping photos of us.

"Congratulations to the happy couple!" he said, snapping us from all angles. Couples at the tables around us started clapping and cheering. "May you have decades of sweet love and happiness."

"No, no, no!" I waved my hands in horror. "Not a happy couple."

"Lexi, get out of here," Xavier said, panic on his face. "Basia's coming."

Holy crap.

"You didn't see me," I reminded him.

"Never," he agreed.

I dashed toward the beach, telling my startled waiter to charge the piña colada and whatever my dinner cost to my room. I hoped I hadn't been spotted, but the detour to the beach meant I had sand between my toes, which I hated. I took off my sandals and held them in one hand as I made my way back to the front of the hotel. I was going to have to be a hermit for the next few days. It was a small sacrifice to make to ensure I wouldn't be a third wheel on a honeymoon.

Since I knew Xavier and Basia were on the restaurant terrace, I swung by the hotel gift shop and bought a pair of oversized sunglasses to serve as a disguise. I also purchased a Diet Coke and a big bag of nacho-flavored Doritos for dinner. As I waited by the elevator, I noticed the signs and pictures I hadn't paid attention to before. Notifications for couple's massages, couple's tennis, couple's boat tours. There were photos of newlywed couples and congratulation messages.

Aaagh. Why the heck had Andy reserved me a room at a hotel for honeymooners? Oh, right, because apparently, proctologists were taking over the island.

Now I wished I would have asked Xavier for their schedule so I could make sure I didn't venture out when they might be around. Although, maybe there was no schedule on a honeymoon. Which didn't make sense because how would you know what to do next? But people were strange. Not operating on a schedule made me nervous, but maybe other people, like people on a honeymoon, liked that.

When I got back to my room, I immediately washed the sand off my feet, then checked my phone. I'd missed a call from Slash. I sat down in the chair on the balcony and called him back.

This time he answered. *"Cara."*

"Hey, Slash. How are you?" It was weird, but we hadn't even been apart twenty-four hours and I already missed him. How this was possible when just a year ago I didn't even *have* a social life mystified me.

"I'm good. The house feels empty without you."

"Well, it's a big house."

"That it is. How are things…wherever you are?"

"Do you want the good news or the bad news?"

"There's bad news already?"

I blew out a breath, figuring I might as well get it out of the way. "Well, I may or may not have discovered Basia and Xavier's secret honeymoon destination."

"What?"

"Pretty crazy, right? Xavier saw me, but Basia has no idea I'm here. We plan on keeping it that way. I no longer plan to leave my hotel room except to do what I came here for, which doesn't take place until Friday. The hotel is awesome, but I think it's primarily for honeymooners. I should have paid attention to the type of hotel it was when I came in, but I didn't. I mean, who reads signs and posters in a hotel anyway?" God, I was babbling. Like this was my fault, which it wasn't, except for the part where I brained Xavier with a musical instrument.

Slash finally spoke and, as usual, got straight to the heart of the matter. "Where was Xavier when you saw him?"

"At the hotel restaurant on the terrace. I went down for a quiet dinner and hit him in the back of head with a shaker."

"A what?"

"A shaker, you know the musical instrument you shake?"

"Are you talking about a maraca?"

"Yes, yes. A maraca. The band came over to serenade

me, maybe because I looked pathetic sitting all alone at a honeymoon hotel restaurant in my jeans, while everyone else was all fancied up and making googly eyes. The guy offered me his maraca. So, I shook it."

"And it magically hit Xavier's head how?"

"Well, the band was playing the music at a rather upbeat tempo, so I shook it a bit more enthusiastically than I should have, I guess."

He must have been thinking that over because it was at least a half minute before he asked, "How surprised was Xavier to see you?"

"Not as surprised as I was to see him, although I can say with one hundred percent certainty my presence came as a shock. Unfortunately, he now has a large lump on the back of his head. I suggested ice to keep the swelling down."

Another long silence.

"Slash?"

"I'm here, *cara*."

"Did you put me on mute? Are you laughing?"

"I'm not providing a verifiable response to that question."

I glared at the phone and huffed. "Fine. Go ahead. It's not funny."

"If you say so. How large is this resort?"

"It's huge. There are villas and apartments and God knows what else. I don't have a clue where Basia and Xavier are located."

"That's a good thing. If you avoid most of the public areas, you probably won't run into them."

"That's what I'm hoping." I uncapped the top of my water bottle and took a big swig. "It isn't the best day of my life, I can say that with certainty."

"What about your travel? How did it go?"

"Funny you ask. Well, the plane ride was okay, except for the guy who snored and used my shoulder as a headrest. But the ferry I had to take for the final leg of my destination was nothing short of hellish. First, you know how much I like the water. Not. I was seasick the entire time. Then a bunch of proctologists got hammered, sang karaoke, and propositioned me and my new friend Camilla. When I came out of the bathroom where I was hiding, trying not to hurl, I had to wrestle a giant crocodile to keep Camilla from being eaten. But it all worked out in the end. Hey, did you know Krav Maga techniques work on animals, too?"

This time there was a very, *very* long silence before he finally said, "Did you just say...crocodile?"

"I know, right? Honestly, I didn't even know they had crocodiles here, but apparently, they do. How the heck it got aboard the ferry is another story altogether. I guess there's an investigation underway as to how *that* happened. At least we'll get our money refunded for the ride, although I'm really not looking forward to the return trip. Finn is having Glinda look for an alternative route back to where I have to get to the airport."

Slash seemed to take forever to respond and I knew it was because he likes to process things before he speaks. But it was getting ridiculous, the long and longer pauses in this conversation.

"Slash?" I said.

"I'm sorry, *cara*, you're just going to have to start at the beginning. I'm not following you at all."

I gave him an abbreviated version of the events, letting him know how his explanation of the Krav Maga technique had helped me wrestle the croc into temporary submission. This time he spoke right away, muttering a few choice swear words in Italian.

"*Mio Dio*, I taught you those techniques to *protect* yourself, not put yourself in danger." He was angry.

"Don't get mad at me, Slash. If I didn't help her, who would?"

"How about any of the other dozens of passengers on the ship?"

"There were only about thirty passengers, and unless the crocodile needed his prostate examined, it wasn't going to happen."

He sighed. "Oh, *cara*, I wish I were there with you."

"I wish you were, too, Slash." *Crap.* Sleeping alone for the next couple of nights was going to stink.

We spoke for a bit more and then hung up. Seeing as how I didn't have anything else to do, I booted up my computer and opened the files Finn had sent me on DPR Shipping. I took extra time to secure my laptop and fine-tune my Wi-Fi speed before I got to work, examining DPR's system and the possible problems.

I worked for several hours while eating Doritos and drinking Diet Coke. After setting up some tests and running a couple of standard protocols, I started poking around in their system. I found no overt evidence of a hack, but someone was messing up things.

Foremost in my mind was an insider threat. I hated that these days it seemed the norm instead of the exception. I started scrolling through employees, shot our DPR contact a message asking for the names and information on any recently fired or disgruntled employees or anyone on probation or with a bad performance review. I also shot a couple of emails to my assistant,

Ken, asking him to check certain sectors within DPR's system and report back to me.

I had no idea how long I worked, but I fell asleep fully dressed, my face planted in the hotel bedspread.

When I woke, sun was streaming in through the balcony door I forgot to close. My laptop was still running on the bed next to me. I rolled over and did a quick check to make sure things were still progressing. Satisfied with the progress, I stood and stretched. I wandered onto the balcony and looked out at the water. The ocean was turquoise, which was quite different from the muddy blue water of Ocean City. Coupled with the shimmering rays of sunlight, it sparkled like a well-polished gem. While I could have stood there for some time admiring the view, I had work to do. I took a quick shower, ordered eggs, bacon and coffee from room service and got to work in front of my laptop.

I already had two emails from Ken with information I'd requested. After I reviewed those and answered some additional emails, my computer dinged to alert me it was finished with the routines I'd started with a search inside the DPR system.

It was a lot of material to go through, but I started methodically and worked my way through it. By three o'clock, I'd missed lunch, but I'd been able to follow the path of a diverted package and had traced it to an IP address.

"Got you," I murmured, flexing my fingers before doing a couple of neck rolls. I did a quick search on the address. When the results came back, I sat back, frowning.

"Okay, this really can't be a coincidence." The IP address was located here in the British Virgin Islands.

A few minutes later, I'd narrowed the IP address to a physical address. I pulled it up on Google Maps and saw where it was located—about a mile and a half from the resort where I was presently located.

After zooming in closer, I examined the structure. It was a beach house, similar to several others on the street, all facing the ocean. A quick view online of the public website stating who owned what property on the island garnered me a name—Mr. Atwater Burgess. A subsequent search of Mr. Burgess confirmed he was a retired accountant who lived in London. He owned the property in the British Virgin Islands, but listed it as a vacation house and rented it out when his family wasn't using it. After hacking into the top three rental companies on the island, I confirmed the house was currently rented to two Americans, a Jason Delgado and Richard Black.

I stood and lifted my arms above my head, trying to stretch out the muscles in my back. I needed to track down Delgado and Black, but breakfast had been hours ago and I needed a break. I could take a walk to check out the beach house in question and grab something to eat on the way.

I slung my purse over my shoulder, took my sun hat and sunglasses, before heading out of the room. Based on the rough estimate of how many hotel rooms and villas were at the resort, factoring in the number of restaurants and cafes on the grounds, and adding the fact that it was three o'clock—too late for lunch and too early for dinner—I figured the odds of running into Basia and Xavier were 659 to one. Despite my mathematical certainty and the odds in my favor, it didn't make me any less nervous.

The elevator doors opened. Thankfully, it wasn't

Basia and Xavier, but an elderly couple in bathing suits and robes, probably heading to the infinity pool. I nodded to them as I got on. The gentleman smiled at me.

"Are you enjoying your stay?" He spoke in a distinct British accent.

"Sure." I shrugged. "It's a nice hotel."

"Congratulations, dear," the woman said. "Marriage is a wonderful thing. A lot of hard work, but stay the course no matter how rough the water."

"Oooooo-kay." I looked at her in confusion. What the heck was that supposed to mean? Maybe she had me confused with someone else. Or maybe that was a regional phrase, like in the Deep South they often say, "Bless your heart," or in Wisconsin they say, "whoopen-socker," which means something extraordinary of its kind.

The elevator dinged. Perhaps the woman sensed my confusion, because as she got off, she smiled and tapped one of the flyers taped to the elevator wall.

As I took a step closer to look at it, my mouth dropped open. It was a photo of me standing behind Xavier, touching the back of his neck. At first glance, it looked like a tender moment between a couple. The photographer had even caught the spectacular scarlet and orange sunset blazing in the background. The caption read, in big bold letters beneath the photo: *Congratulations Basia and Xavier Zimmerman on your wedding.*

TWENTY-FOUR

HOLY CRAP!

Horrified, I ripped down the flyer and crammed it in my purse. I might have started hyperventilating, but it was too hard to hear my breathing over the reggae elevator music. I glanced at the other flyers, but the ones remaining were of other happy couples celebrating their honeymoons.

What the heck was wrong with this hotel? Who did this kind of cheesy thing to people on their honeymoon?

I tried to get off the elevator before I realized the elevator was already on its way back up. It opened on the fourth floor and I hopped off as a young couple got on. As soon as the door closed, I pushed the button and waited. I was now going to have to check every freaking elevator, not to mention every hallway, to make sure there were no more flyers of me and Xavier plastered around the resort. This was turning into a freaking nightmare.

A different elevator opened. Another young couple in shorts and T-shirts, holding hands and looking ridiculously happy, smiled at me as I got on. I might have snarled slightly before ripping down the flyer with Xavier and me.

They looked at me in surprise.

"I'm keeping it as a memento," I explained. "For my

memory book. Or hope chest. Or whatever the heck you are supposed to keep these kinds of things in."

They scooted away from me. Guess I couldn't blame them. I pulled the brim of my hat lower over my face.

It took me twenty-eight minutes to clear all six elevators of the offending flyers. I was totally pushing the odds of not running into Basia and Xavier, but the flyers had to go. The problem was I couldn't wander around aimlessly looking for them without fear of running into them. At this point I couldn't decide which would be worse—her seeing me in a poster with her new husband or actually running into them.

It was a no-win situation. Either way, I was screwed.

I was standing in the lobby, debating if I should check out the other parts of the hotel for any more stupid couple pictures when my phone rang. I decided I should go outside to take it, so I dug into my purse and answered it as I walked through the lobby toward the exit.

"Hello?" I said.

"Lexi?"

It was hard to hear the caller with the reggae music blasting over the hotel speakers, so I plugged one ear with finger. "Elvis? Is that you?"

"It's me. What's all that noise?"

"Music."

"I thought you were working."

"I *am* working." I exited the hotel and the absence of music was a welcome relief. The sun was hot on my shoulders, so I made a beeline for a couple of palm trees and sat down on a bench beneath them. "How's it going on the girl front?"

There was a silence and then he spoke. "Not very

well." Dejection filled his voice. "How's the work gig going?"

"Not all that great either."

"We're a pair. So, where are you at again?"

"I already told you I can't say."

"Oh, I forgot. What the heck is with all the secrecy these days? I don't know where you are. I don't know where Xavier and Basia are. My friends and family are, for all purposes, invisible to me. My two girlfriends are mad at me. It's like I'm operating in a vacuum."

"Hey, at least I'm talking to you, so that does not qualify as a total vacuum. Besides, Basia and Xavier are fine. Theoretically speaking, of course. It's not like I know firsthand about their location or anything. It's just a feeling."

Jeez. I was the worst liar in the world. The only saving grace was that Elvis couldn't see my non-poker face.

"Your voice sounds…funny," he said.

I'd never make a plausible spy. Ever. "It must be the connection," I lied. "I take it neither Bonnie nor Gwen is talking to you?"

"No. I'll be honest. It kind of sucks to be me right now."

"I'm sorry, Elvis." I wish I knew what to say to help him out, but I had nothing. "Have you researched the problem any further?"

"Of course, I have. According to the book *What to Do When You Piss Her Off*, I'm supposed to give her—or in this case, them—time to cool off. Do you think forty-eight hours is enough?"

I thought it over. "No idea. Doesn't the book offer specific parameters?"

"Unfortunately, it's not clear on that point."

"Hmmm…is there information on groveling?"

"Chapter Nine." He sighed. "Lexi, I messed this up badly. I wish I could make things go as smoothly as you and Slash."

"Whoa. Back up. There's no smooth sailing with Slash and me. It's hard work. Harder than anything I've ever done before, and that includes clearing the ninety-ninth level of 'Black Elixir.' Trust me, there's no scientific method to working out a relationship. It's all about emotions and feelings and reciprocity. It's messy, illogical and unpredictable. If you want to be in a relationship, you'd better get used to it. Have you tried extending an olive branch to cither of them?"

He was quiet for a long moment. "That's the problem. Lexi, I'm not sure I know what I want to do. How do I decide which woman is right for me, assuming either of them will ever speak to me again?"

"Make a pro and con list. That always seems to work for me." It wasn't the greatest advice, but it was all I had at the moment.

"I guess that could work. I do like them for different reasons. Do I go with the woman who *challenges* me to be more? Who motivates me, encourages me and helps me? Or do I go with the woman who makes me *feel* like I want to be more? Right. Now I sound like an idiot. That didn't even make sense."

"No, it did. Elvis, if you're asking me to tell you which woman to choose, I can't. What I do know is that the hardest decisions are between two positives. My advice is when you decide to make a commitment like this, lead with your heart. That's what Basia told me to do and it worked out for me. Now, that doesn't mean leave your brain behind—it just means do what feels right emotionally, *then* justify it with reasoning. And I can't even believe I just said that. Don't spread that around."

He chuckled. "I won't. Thanks, Lexi."

"Anytime, bud."

I hung up wondering when I'd become Dear Abby, and more importantly, whether I was getting any good at it.

TWENTY-FIVE

I DECIDED TO worry about any lingering flyers later and head for the beach house instead. I needed to get away from the hotel for a bit, get something to eat and clear my head. As I walked along underneath the brilliant sun, I was grateful for my floppy hat but wished I'd put suntan lotion on my arms, legs and face. According to the GPS on my cell phone, the house I was looking for was exactly a 1.7-mile walk from the hotel. After being cooped up all day, it felt good to get some fresh air and exercise, even if it felt hotter than a quantum circuit.

I stopped at a small bakery and bought a latte and a coconut bread pastry filled with warm egg and cheese. Both were delicious. After I ate that, I ordered two cherry tarts and considered a third before I made myself leave. The place smelled heavenly.

The walk, however, was just as heavenly, and it became even nicer the farther I moved away from the tourist areas and into the residential neighborhoods. I still had a killer view of the beach from the simple paved road I traveled. The flashes of turquoise from the ocean were pretty amid the swaying palm trees and brilliant cobalt sky. The air smelled like salt and brine, while the breeze offered a bit of relief from the heat of the sun. I strolled along, surprised at the number of people who waved cheerfully to me, despite not knowing me. No one seemed in a hurry. I decided to take a page from their book and ease up my speed, trying to mimic the languid pace of island life.

When I finally found the beach house with the suspect IP address, I stopped and studied it. It looked like every other beachfront home on the street—a two-storied weathered gray house with blue shutters and trim, large windows and a white wraparound porch. Two wooden rockers sat on the porch, but the paint looked as if it had seen better days. The blinds in the front windows, both downstairs and up, were closed. It looked deserted.

I decided to go around back. I walked between the house and the neighbor's place on my left to get to the beach. A sprawling deck and staircase were attached to the house. Beneath the deck, in the shade, was a beat-up picnic table.

I stood in the shade for a moment to cool off. Finally, I climbed the stairs of the wooden deck to try and see into the house. Lucky for me, the back entrance was a sliding glass balcony door without curtains. I couldn't see anything from the glare of the sun, so I cupped my hands on either side of my eyes and pressed my face against the glass to better see.

Directly in front of the sliding glass door was a round kitchen table with some papers and packets. To the right was a kitchen. The sink looked empty and no plants, food or dishes of any kind cluttered the countertops. Beyond that led into what I presumed was a living room. I'm not sure what I thought I would find, but it all looked rather ordinary.

"Hey, what are you doing?"

I jumped, whirling around to see two large guys standing on the deck. They were both pretty muscular, which was easy to see since they both wore sleeveless T-shirts and shorts. The one on the right had black hair and a beard with legs as thick as tree trunks. The guy on the left was thinner, but had a barrel chest and a thick gold chain around his neck. I had no idea how two guys that big had managed to climb the wooden steps without me hearing them. Both were wearing sunglasses, so I couldn't read their expressions well. Regardless, it wasn't as if they were oozing friendliness.

"I'm sorry. Is this your house?" My heart was galloping like I'd just drank six Red Bulls.

"What if it was?" The accent was Jersey, but the attitude was mean.

"Well, I'm considering renting a house just like this one. It looked deserted, so I thought I would peek inside, you know, to see if the interior was what I had in mind."

"There's no rental sign on this property."

"I know. I just wanted to get a feel for the layout of the house. I thought this one was empty, so I checked. Guess I'll be going now."

Jersey Guy held up a hand, stopping me in my tracks. "How about you answer a couple of questions first?"

"Like what?"

"Like, do you know the guys who live here?"

"Why would I know that?"

He jerked a meaty thumb at his chest. "We're asking the questions here. You got a key?"

"What? Of course not. I just told you, I'm looking for a vacation rental."

Jersey Guy exchanged a glance with the guy with the gold chain. A message must have passed between them because they both abruptly stepped aside and pointed to the stairs.

"Fine. After you," Jersey Guy said.

I hated having to pass by them so closely, but I didn't see any other way off the deck. I slid past without managing to touch them and took the stairs two at a time, jumping to the bottom. I began to walk as quickly as I could back to the hotel.

It was an ominous sign that they followed me and didn't even try to hide it. Thankfully, once I got to the hotel, I lost them in the lobby. They didn't know my name, so hopefully, they wouldn't be able to track me. Just in case, as soon as I got back to my room, I locked the door, bolted it and wedged a chair underneath the doorknob.

I immediately called Finn.

Glinda answered. Oh, great. Better hope she was in an accommodating mood, although who was I kidding? She was *never* in an accommodating mood when it came to me.

"Hey, Glinda, is Finn around?" I tried to keep my voice light, casual.

"Maybe."

I swallowed my annoyance. "Look, I need to talk to Finn. It's important. Can you please have him call me when he's available?"

"Of course I can." She hung up.

Usually I wouldn't let her antics bother me, but I really did need to talk to Finn. I went to my laptop and shot him an email anyway, asking him to call me as soon as he was available. Just in case Glinda "forgot" to tell him.

I didn't know who those two thugs were and why they were hanging around the house with the IP in question, but my best guess was that someone on their team had possibly lost a package and done their own trace back to that house. There were too many coincidences piling up about the mixed-up packages. My best guess is that they wanted to know what I knew, which at this point, wasn't much.

I needed to see what information I could find on the renters of that house, Delgado and Black, as soon as possible. It took me about forty minutes of dedicated searching to discover that the two guys were bogus.

"I guess that's no surprise." I sat back in my chair and stretched my arms over my head. I drained the last of the water bottle and grabbed the room service menu. Unfortunately, hamburgers weren't on the menu of this high-end resort, so I decided to live dangerously. I ordered a crabmeat salad, conch fritters and fried bananas for dessert. After I ordered, I sat on my bed thinking how proud Slash would be of me for being adventurous food-wise, then feeling sad he wasn't here to share it with me.

Just then my phone rang. I picked it up off the bed where I had tossed it.

"Lexi, it's me, Finn. I'm sorry I was tied up in a meeting all afternoon. How are things?"

"Hey, Finn. Thanks for calling back." I quickly updated him on my findings inside the DPR Shipping system and how I'd traced it back to an IP address right here in the British Virgin Islands.

Finn whistled. "That can't be a coincidence."

My thoughts exactly. "Even better. I found a signature in the hack. It was Beach Bum."

"Beach Bum? What does that mean?"

"It means I've got a hacker on my hands who has cornflakes for brains. Here's my initial analysis. I have a feeling Andy's package isn't the only one that has been diverted here. I also think it's directly related to the problems DPR Shipping is having with their system."

"What about the package mix-up at Basia's wedding?"

"My gut tells me they're connected. I think DPR has an insider threat, but whoever they are working with doesn't have this diversion thing down to a science yet."

Finn considered. "Or the package mix-ups are to cause confusion over the ones they actually divert."

"Possibly. I don't know what IT firm DPR hired originally, but they were no good. I found and pulled the diversion thread in less than twenty-four hours with slow Wi-Fi and no fancy equipment. My gut feeling is whoever is doing this is an amateur."

"So, you're thinking inside threat with a little hacking on the outside?"

"That's what I'm thinking."

"Okay. What's the next step?"

"Get Ken working on the list of employees and tell him to scrub it and go deep. Look for disgruntled employees, employees that may be in debt, and cross-reference it with anyone at the company with known ties to the British Virgin Islands. I'm working the rental agreement of the house. So far, I've confirmed the two individuals on the renter's agreement are ghosts. However, the rent is paid on time every month. I went by this afternoon and checked out the house. It didn't look lived in, but there were packages and papers on the kitchen table when I peeked in through the back window. It's possible the location may serve as a depository of some kind."

"That's very interesting."

"It is, indeed. Even more interesting were the two

guys who were *also* checking out the house." I gave him a brief rundown on what had happened.

"My God, Lexi. Were you in danger?"

"I don't think so. Why should I be? But still, they followed me back to the hotel which was creepy. I lost them in the lobby. They don't have my name or know who I am, but they may be watching for me, so I have to be careful, just in case."

"Who do you think they are and why were they at the house?"

"My guess is they traced the IP address there, too. Which is another reason this smacks of an amateur."

"Wow. Suddenly, I don't like this situation at all."

"I wouldn't worry about it too much. I don't have any reason to leave the hotel. I intend to stay put until Friday afternoon when I'm scheduled to accept the package for Andy. All I need to do is accept and check Andy's device and ensure it's working—all from the safety of my hotel. Then I get the heck off this island. End of story."

"So, why does this whole thing make me bloody nervous?"

"Because I'm involved?"

"Exactly."

I didn't want to tell him, but he was boss and was entitled to know all aspects of the current job environment. "Well, in the spirit of full disclosure, there may be another indirect issue affecting my work here."

"Such as?" His voice sounded wary. I didn't blame him.

I sighed. "Such as…this happens to be Basia and Xavier's secret honeymoon destination."

"What?"

"Even worse, Xavier spotted me. Luckily Basia

hasn't, and we plan to keep it that way. Unfortunately, the idiot hotel photographer got a picture of Xavier and me the one minute we were together. Now the hotel is plastering it around, congratulating us on our marriage. I've been going all secret agent and ripping them down as fast as they go up. It's a nightmare. Trust me, being a third wheel on someone's honeymoon is *not* my idea of fun."

"Are you bloody *kidding* me?"

"Would I kid you about something like this?" I pressed a hand to my forehead, hoping the faint headache brewing there would not transform into a raging migraine. "Anyway, it does give me extra incentive to stay in my room and venture out as little as possible."

He let out a loud breath and then fell silent. "One more day, right? What could possibly happen in one day?"

"Exactly. I'd have to calculate the odds to be exact, but I'm certain the chance of anything happening, if I don't leave the hotel, are going to be extremely low."

"Good. Keep it that way."

"Trust me. I don't plan on going *anywhere* until I have that package in my hands. Until then, thankfully, I'll have plenty of time to continue to review the DPR Shipping case. At this point I'll be doing the most logical thing—following the rent money. Hopefully that will lead me right to whoever Delgado and Black really are."

"Just be careful, okay, Lexi?"

"Sure, Finn. You don't have to tell me twice. It's at the top of my agenda."

"It better be."

About ten minutes later room service brought me my food and several bottles of water. I ate dinner while working on my computer. I'd just finished the main course when my phone rang.

I pounced on it happily. "Hey, Slash."

"*Cara*, how are things?"

"Okay, thanks." I couldn't believe how happy I was to hear from him.

"Work is okay?" I could hear the smile in his voice. "Boring, safe and uneventful, right?"

"Well, about that…"

"You didn't encounter any more crocodiles, did you?" he asked.

"No crocodiles, thank goodness." I didn't offer more, I couldn't without giving away proprietary information. Unfortunately, that was probably enough to set off alarm bells with him.

He hesitated, probably trying to figure out what he could ask and what I could answer. "You'd tell me if you felt you were in danger, right?"

"I would, Slash. At this exact moment, here safely in the hotel—the location I plan to stay for the next twenty-four hours—I do not feel like I am in any danger."

He fell silent. I think for the first time, he was seeing his life through someone else's perspective. "Just don't take any unnecessary risks, *cara*."

"I never take unnecessary risks. I don't even like risk."

That seemed to lighten the mood a bit. We talked for a few more minutes before we hung up. I was leaving him with an uneasy feeling about my safety and I felt bad about that, but somehow that was becoming the norm for us.

I ate my dessert, while starting my search on Delgado and Black. A relatively easy hack into the real estate brokerage handling the rent payments for Mr. Burgess and I had a copy of a cancelled check with a routing number, which was all I needed to get going. I was neck-deep into the hack of the bank when the hotel phone rang.

Puzzled, I stood and picked up the receiver. "Hello?"

"Lexi?"

"Xavier?" I was more than surprised. "Why are you calling me? What's wrong?"

"The hotel lobby." His whisper was panicked. "It has a huge poster board of you and me at dinner the other night. I managed to steer Basia away from it, but you've got to take it down, *right now,* before Basia sees it."

"*What?* What's *wrong* with this hotel?"

"Just do it and fast." He clicked off.

"Holy crap." I shoved my feet into my tennis shoes, grabbed my key card and raced to the elevator. Stepping off the elevator, I took a cautious look around. There were a lot of people milling about, but I didn't see Basia or Xavier loitering anywhere.

I headed toward the registration desk and saw a large gold easel on which the picture of Xavier and me that had been enlarged and pasted on a huge poster board, above which was a sign that identified us as the Featured Couple of the Day.

"For crying out loud," I muttered. "Is this really necessary?"

I sidled up as inconspicuously as possible to the poster board. Seeing as how there was no quick and subtle way to do this, I snatched it off the easel and tucked it under my arm.

"Hey," one of the receptionists behind the registration desk yelled at me. "What are you doing?"

Uh, oh.

"Nothing, really," I said. "It's flawed. The lighting is all wrong. No worries. I'll take care of it for you."

"You have to ask the manager first," the receptionist said.

"No time. I'll bring it back as soon as I adjust it." I started to walk away.

"Hey! Come back."

A sideways glance indicated a security guard was headed my way. Oh, great. This was *not* going as planned.

I pushed my way through the lobby with several people gasping and shouting at my rudeness, and pulled open a door adjacent to the elevators. I ran down the corridor of what looked like the spa section. Several of the walls had built-in fountains with running water over earth-toned tiles and soft lighting. It smelled of candles and incense. Soft music was being piped into the corridor.

The door crashed open behind me with the security guard hot on my heels.

"Hey, you, stop!" he shouted in a British-accented voice. "Stop right there."

I ran to the door at the end of the corridor and burst in, surprising a group of people sitting around in white towels drinking wine with green goop caked on their face.

"Sorry." I dashed past them and out a door. Darting down another hallway, I skidded to a halt at a glass door that led to the huge outdoor infinity pool. I could hear the pounding footsteps behind me, so I yanked the door open and walked as casually as I could onto the pool deck.

I did not want to attract undue attention, although I

was the only person fully dressed and carrying a large poster board under my arm. Not like I had a choice. The hot, humid air assaulted me as I hoofed it around the pool and a crowded hot tub of staring people, heading for a side gate exit.

"You! Come back here." The security guard shouted something else as I pushed open the pool gate and ran, hearing it clank shut behind me.

Once out of sight of the pool, I cranked up the speed. I dashed around the side of the building toward the front of the hotel. I saw a Dumpster pushed up against the side of the hotel, so I snapped the poster board in half over my knee and tossed it inside.

"Good riddance," I muttered.

I resumed running and had just turned the corner, heading toward the front entrance of the hotel, when I ran into a brick wall. I took a couple steps to the side, rubbing my forehead. When I looked up, I realized I'd run right into one of the thugs from the beach house this afternoon.

Jersey Guy.

"You?" I suddenly got a bad feeling. "What are you doing here?"

He looked as surprised as me before his mouth stretched into a slow grin. "Lexi Carmichael? We were just coming to get you. Looks like you saved us the trip."

TWENTY-SIX

I DIDN'T HAVE time to worry how he knew my name, because the security guard rounded the corner at that exact moment. He nearly crashed into Jersey Guy like I'd done. This time, however, the big guy deftly stepped aside, causing the security guard to screech to a halt when he saw me.

"You!" The security guard pointed an accusing finger at me. He was breathing so heavily I worried that he might have a heart attack. Guess hotel security guard training didn't put special emphasis on the physical fitness part. "Why are you running? Why did you take that poster?"

Jersey Guy looked at me curiously. "What poster?"

"It's a long story." My cheeks heated.

Before I could utter a warning, the second thug standing behind the guard pulled out a gun from beneath his Hawaiian shirt and he hit the security guard in the back of the neck. The guard went down hard, sprawling on the pavement.

"Why the heck did you do that?" I screeched.

"He got in our way." Jersey Guy grabbed my arm. "Let's go."

"Oh, heck no. I'm not going anywhere with you. Thanks for the offer, but I've got work to do."

"Yes, you do," he agreed.

Before I could enact my Krav Maga move for getting

out of a front arm hold, Jersey Guy stabbed something into the fleshy part of my upper arm.

Pain sliced through me while a weird cold sensation shot down my arm. "Ouch." I yanked my arm away. "Why did you do that? Have you lost your mind?"

"Nope, I haven't." He laughed as my legs collapsed and the black rushed up to greet me.

I WOKE UP in a room I didn't recognize, with a pounding headache and a mouth that felt as if it were filled with cotton balls.

I coughed a couple of times, then blinked until my surroundings came into focus. I wanted to rub my eyes, but my hands refused to move. I was handcuffed to a chair in a room with a four-poster bed made of dark wood, a dresser with a flat screen television and a balcony that looked out onto the ocean. The balcony door was closed, so I wasn't confident that yelling would bring any passersby to my rescue.

I'd been drugged, kidnapped and handcuffed. More entries for my "Little Black Cloud" spreadsheet. Why did this keep happening to me?

I couldn't stress out about that now. I had to get out of here—wherever *here* was. I wiggled my feet, dismayed when I discovered my ankles were bound together, too. They weren't taking any chances. Regardless, I tried to hop with the chair toward the balcony to get a better idea of my bearings. I hadn't got far when the door opened. Jersey Guy strolled in.

"Nice to see you're awake, Sleeping Beauty. Thought you were out for the rest of the evening."

"You do realize you're not funny, right? How do you know my name?"

"I know a lot of things."

My arm ached where he'd stabbed me with a needle. "What did you give me?"

"A little sleeping potion."

"Why?"

"I'm not a fan of screaming and struggling women. That shot was mostly for me. You're welcome. Come on. The boss wants to talk to you."

"What boss?"

He didn't answer and instead unlocked my handcuffs, untied my ankles and hauled me to my feet. My knees were wobbly, I had a headache and my vision was blurry. "Can I have some water?"

"Later." Jersey Guy took me by the arm and half-led, half-dragged me out of the room.

When we got to the corridor, I realized we were in a house. The bannister was old and wooden. I held on with one hand as we went down. At the bottom, we went left into a large living room. Seated in a large armchair with a book on his lap and a cup of coffee or tea on the small round table next to him was a heavyset man with short dark hair peppered with gray, piercing brown eyes and a short neck. He was dressed in dark pants, a blue dress shirt and more bling around his neck and on his fingers than six supermodels combined.

Jersey Guy yanked me forward until I stood in front of him and then stepped to the side, leaving me alone to face him.

For a moment, we stared at each other without saying a word. I spoke first. "Who are you?"

"You may call me The Father."

His voice was thick with an accent. Possibly New Jersey or New York or Italian. Perhaps a mixture of all three. It was hard to tell. One thing was certain, I wasn't calling him that.

"Why did you bring me here?" I asked.

"Because I figure it's in our best interest to help each other."

"I don't see how drugging and kidnapping me is in my best interest at all."

For a moment, the room was deadly silent. Then The Father laughed—a deep bellyache laugh. As if on cue, everyone else in the room started laughing, too.

"I like you," he said, slapping his thigh and wiping an eye. "You've got spunk."

I didn't get why everyone was laughing, so I remained silent.

After the laughing died down The Father studied me. "Miss Carmichael. We know you are here to pick up a package on behalf of ComQuest. That package was deliberately diverted here, just like an important package of ours was."

I wasn't going to confirm or deny anything to these whack jobs, so I didn't say anything.

"I also know you traced the IP address to the British Virgin Islands, to that house where you were this morning, just like I did."

I lifted an eyebrow in disbelief. "*You* traced it?"

The Father snapped his fingers. A kid, maybe sixteen years old on a good day, stepped into the room. He was thin with shaggy black hair and dressed in dark jeans and a black T-shirt.

"I traced it," the kid said. "I know who you are. My name is Carlos. I had the pleasure of gaming against you in an online tournament of 'Hollow Realm' just over a year ago. My moniker was TheOtherJackal. Your name was GirlCodeBoss. Am I right?"

I studied the kid. "Maybe."

"Well, when they—" Carlos pointed at Jersey Guy and his pal "—said they'd caught you at the beach house and passed on your photo to me—"

"Wait. You took a photo of me?" I narrowed my eyes at Jersey Guy.

He shrugged and lifted the lapel on his shirt. "Mini-camera, built in."

I shook my head as Carlos continued. "Anyway, once we had your picture, I cross-referenced it with your passport, which was registered when you came onto the island. Just like that I had your name and, wow, was I surprised. Lexi Carmichael? Gamer girl extraordinaire? Plus, I saw you on that reality show. That was prime. After that, it was an easy hack into the hotel database to get your room number."

"Yeah, and we didn't even have to go into the hotel to get her," Jersey Guy said with a snicker. "She ran right into my arms. Girls do that a lot."

"Ugh." I rolled my eyes.

"Anyway, when I realized you were you, I couldn't believe my luck," Carlos continued. "You're pretty well-known in certain circles, you know. It's pretty exciting to have a chance to meet you in person."

This was getting creepier by the minute and I still wasn't sure where it was headed. "I don't understand what you guys want from me."

"Someone stole from us. One package is irretrievable, unfortunately, but one package is still available. You're going to help us get it."

"Me? What do I have to do with any of this?"

The Father leaned forward in his chair, his gold necklaces swinging forward on his chest. "I think you know. We are *not* going to pay a ransom for what is rightfully ours."

"Whoa? Did you say ransom? Your package is being ransomed?"

The surprise on my face must have been genuine, because The Father looked carefully at me. "You didn't know?" He seemed surprised by the possibility of my ignorance.

I didn't. Andy hadn't mentioned being coerced to get his package back. If it were true, and he'd hidden this from me, it changed things. Many things. For one, if a ransom was involved, Andy should have gone straight to the FBI. That possibility troubled me because he was far too much an experienced businessman *not* to know that.

If Andy's package *was* being ransomed and he hadn't told me, that could only mean there was something in the package Andy didn't want the authorities to see. Now that I considered his unusual insistence that I personally pick up the package and sign a nondisclosure agreement, in addition to giving him my personal guarantee I wouldn't mention it to the Zimmerman twins, maybe there *was* something he was hiding, even from his closest employees at ComQuest.

"Miss Carmichael?"

The Father had been talking to me and I'd completely missed it.

"Sorry." I blinked a couple of times. "I'm still a bit fuzzy from whatever your guys shot me up with. Can I have some water?"

The Father jerked his thumb impatiently and someone scuttled off. In a few seconds, I had a full glass of water with ice. I drank it and wiped my mouth with the back of my hand, my mind still racing in all kinds of different directions.

Someone took the glass from me and The Father clasped his hands in his lap. "Better?"

"Marginally. Look, I don't know anything about a ransom. I'm here to pick up a package and that's it."

"No, that's not it." The Father seemed annoyed with me now. "In case you really don't know, your client, ComQuest, has already paid the ransom or, at least, a good chunk of it. In fact, they paid more to have it personally delivered to you at the hotel restaurant where you are staying, at precisely one thirty."

I blinked. "Whoa. How do you know that?"

"I have my ways." He sat back and regarded me as he chewed on one end of a straw. "Just so we're clear—we don't care what's in your package. What we care about is who delivers it to you."

"Why?"

"That's none of your business."

I thought it was definitely my business, but the way The Father and the guys were glaring at me, I didn't particularly feel like arguing.

Still, there was a big picture here that I was missing. There were a lot of potentially connected parts and I needed to figure them out. "You said one of your packages was irretrievable. Was it under ransom, too?"

The Father shook his head. "Unfortunately, it was mixed up with another package and sent to a hotel where a wedding was being held. It was confiscated by police before we could retrieve it."

My eyes opened wide. "Wait, this didn't happen, like, at a beach hotel in Ocean City last weekend, did it?" I thought of the Mandrax package and the thugs that had accosted Basia and me.

The Father narrowed his eyes. "What do you know about that?"

"Not much. Look, how exactly do I fit in here?"

"You're going to help us get these guys."

"How am I supposed to do that? You kidnapped me. I don't have my phone, computer or purse. My boss will worry when I don't check in with him. I'm supposed to meet my contact tomorrow afternoon at the hotel restaurant to get our package. I don't see how kidnapping me helps you."

The Father dropped his half-chewed straw to the table. The guy standing next to him immediately whipped out a new straw from his jacket pocket and slipped it into his boss's hand. The Father started chewing on it again. "You don't have to see anything. You only need to do as we say. We'll retrieve your phone for you and make sure you have an opportunity to connect with your boss…on our terms. The rest of your things stay at the hotel. You're not touching a computer. We're fully aware of your capability, Miss Carmichael. You don't get to be left alone with your toys."

Carlos looked at me and shrugged. It was perfectly clear who'd given The Father the scoop on me.

"And if I refuse?" I figured it was better to know all my options.

"The ocean is a big place." The Father studied his fingernails. "A very big place. And I have a lot of boats that can go way, *way*, out to the deepest spots."

I gulped. "Well, if you put it like that."

"I thought you'd see it my way." He smiled and stood. "Let me be clear. If we catch you trying to send out a message for help, if you try to escape or sabotage our plan in any way, trust me—we'll do more than just get rid of you."

"What more do I have to lose than my life?"

"I'm glad you asked. I do believe your friends are honeymooning at the same resort as you. It would be such a shame for their married life to be cut so short."

I closed my eyes, feeling sick. "What do you want me to do?"

TWENTY-SEVEN

THEY TOLD ME I'd be helping Carlos. Instead of taking me back to the room where I'd awoken, one of the men escorted me to what looked like a converted den. A couch, a couple of armchairs and a large screen television were unimaginatively arranged, but someone had pulled in a beat-up dining room table and set it up with several laptops, a printer and two large-screen monitors. My fingers itched to touch the keyboard, *any* keyboard, but instead I was led to a hard dining room chair in the corner and handcuffed to it, my arms behind my back.

Carlos came into the room and sat down across from me.

"I know all about you," he said.

"Okay. What do you know?"

"You're Lexi Carmichael, Director of IT Services at X-Corp Global Intelligence and Security in Crystal City, Virginia. You were the chick who helped put away those terrorists at the high school in DC. That was totally sick, Lexi. I saw you on the news. Plus, I already told you how much I liked that reality television show you were on. You were way better than the girls who came before and after you."

Ugh. I hated any mention of that television show and my appearance on it. "Uh, thanks, I guess."

"I also know you used to work at the NSA and you have a boyfriend that works there, too. I couldn't find any information on him except for his nickname, Slash. Is that short for backslash?"

"It is. Not bad work, kid." A little flattery could go a long way, especially when it was geek to geek.

He grinned. "Is Slash any good at computers?"

"He's okay," I said.

"Well, just so we're clear, all of that means I'm fully aware of your capability at the keyboard. I may be a kid, but I'm not going to underestimate you. Are we clear on that?"

I hoped I'd adequately suppressed the eye roll at his attitude. "Crystal."

"Good." He sat down at one of the laptops and started working. "I may ask for your thoughts on certain things as I work, so stand by."

Jersey Guy came in and sat down in an empty armchair. He turned on the television to a fake wrestling match, then jacked up the volume.

Double ugh.

I squinted, trying to get a look at Carlos's screen. "What are you doing?"

"Well, I tracked those guys' rental checks from the beach house to what looks like a fake company." He took a swig from a bottle of Coke, an actual glass bottle. It reminded me that I was still thirsty, but there was no way Jersey Guy would unlock my hand so I could drink.

"You mean a shell company?" He looked confused. "That's a front for another business, usually illegal."

"Yeah, I guess that's what you'd call it."

"Good for you. I hadn't got that far yet. What did you find out about it?"

"Well, the shell company is called Beach Bums, which I think is supposed to be a stab at humor."

"From where I'm sitting, that's not really funny."

"I see your point. Anyway, I haven't been able to figure out how to track the money from Beach Bums to an actual pocket. It's an offshore account."

"Yeah, those are tough to figure out. But the key will be to look at the inside data of the shell company." I wiggled my arms. "Can you move me closer? I might be able to walk you through it."

Carlos stood up and tried to maneuver my chair closer. Unfortunately, I was heavy and the chair didn't move much. Jersey Guy finally noticed what we were doing. He stood and glared at us. "What do you think you're doing, kid?"

"She's going to help me figure something out."

"Like hell, she is."

"She is," Carlos insisted. "The Father said she could assist as long as she didn't touch anything. Don't worry, she's not going to manipulate me. I'm not that stupid. That's part of the reason she's here, okay?"

Jersey Guy walked over and dragged my chair closer to the laptop, but not too close. His jerky movements put strain on my neck and shoulders.

I yelped in pain. "Hey!"

He bent down and stuck his nose in my face. "If we catch you doing anything dumb, you're dead."

He gave the chair a final kick and returned to his seat, jacking up the volume. I rolled my neck, trying to get the kinks out.

"Sorry about that," Carlos said. "He can be a jerk."

"It's okay."

Carlos sat back down in his chair. "So, can you help me find that data?"

"I can. But let me ask you something first, Carlos." I

glanced over my shoulder at Jersey Guy. He was laughing and pointing at the wrestling match. "How old are you?"

"Sixteen. Almost seventeen."

"Why are you hanging out with these guys? You're obviously a smart kid with a bright future."

He sighed. "The Father is my grandfather."

"Oh." I digested that for a moment. "Wait. You call your grandfather The Father?"

"Everyone calls him The Father. Even *my* father."

"Well, he's not being fair with you. You do realize that by simply being here, he's made you an accessory to kidnapping, assault and potential murder. Add the hacking to that and it's a pretty serious list of felonies, and I didn't even cover everything."

"I'm sixteen. What choice do I have? The Family owns me."

I felt sorry for him, I really did. But my life, along with those of my friends, were on the line. "I don't know what to tell you, Carlos, except sometimes you have to stand up to what's wrong, even if it's in your own family."

"Forget it. I'm not going to help you get away. He'll kill me, even if I am one of his grandsons."

"I understand. Don't worry. I'm going to help you get what he wants. You don't have anything to worry about with me."

"I really hope you mean that. So, let's stop talking and start working, okay? I warn you, don't try to trick me. I'm not stupid. Plus, if I mess up, The Father will hurt me."

Unfortunately, I believed him. "You're not going to mess up and I won't trick you. Let's just start at the beginning. Take me to where you are inside the shell company and we'll start from there."

"You sure you can do this?"

If he only knew all the things I could do. But right now, I had to be careful. "Seeing as how our lives depend on it, I'm sure. Just put your fingers on the keyboard and we'll figure this out together."

TWENTY-EIGHT

It took us two hours to find the information we needed.

During that time, I was uncuffed and permitted to eat a couple of cold pieces of pizza and drink some bottled water. Jersey Guy also brought me my phone.

"What's the password?" he said, holding it up.

"It's biometric."

"Huh?"

I wiggled my hands behind my back. "It reads my thumb."

Carlos sighed and took my phone from the guy, pressing the button to my thumb. My phone opened and Carlos turned off the protection before he handed it back. "Give it to The Father."

Jersey Guy nodded and disappeared. Other than being permitted to go to the bathroom twice, we worked. Each time I went to the bathroom, my hands would be freed, so I'd spent most of my time in the bathroom, stretching them and getting the circulation back, which hurt like crazy. I checked, but found nothing I could use as a weapon to protect myself, unless I wanted to throw toilet paper or hand soap at someone.

On the bright side, Carlos was much smarter than I'd expected and had caught on to what I wanted him to do without any problem. I walked him through a hack on the shell corporation, because finding out who was running this scam was at the top of my list, and I didn't see any harm in moving things along on that front.

I'd also carefully directed Carlos into an area where I knew I could send Slash a message. It wouldn't really be a message—more of a single ping—but it was an account not many people knew of, and if Slash suspected I was in trouble, he'd trace it. If he traced it, it would lead him here. That was the plan anyway.

I'd masked the path to Slash's secret account within the search of the shell company's financial data I was helping Carlos trace. So far, Carlos hadn't spotted the incongruence, probably because I'd been careful to do nothing to raise his suspicions, and also because he'd never hacked into a shell company before. Both worked in my favor.

I'd had him just where I wanted him—within one keystroke of a ping to Slash, when he paused his finger poised over the key. I held my breath as he glanced at me, hoping I looked casual, almost bored, when inside my heart was beating like a bongo drum.

"I don't get how this sector is connected," he said, peering at the string of code.

"It's connected to the financial data."

He lowered his finger from the keyboard and stared. "No. Something's not right. You're trying to trick me."

"There is no trick." I hoped my expression was one of innocence or boredom. "We're just poking around. You know that's eighty-five percent of hacking."

"Liar." His eyes narrowed to slits. "And to think I admired you." He closed his laptop and left the room.

"Carlos, wait," I called out and then sighed. Crap. The kid was too smart for his own good.

I waited for nearly an hour, but he didn't return. I finally bugged Jersey Guy to let me go to the bathroom again. He finally acquiesced after a half hour of asking.

When I came out of the bathroom, The Father was waiting for me. I shrieked and took two steps backward into the doorjamb. "Jeez, you scared me. Do you always lurk around bathroom doors?"

He was scowling. "You tried to trick my grandson."

"I didn't. He just didn't understand what I was trying to do."

"He understood perfectly and so do I. Do you think I'm stupid? Do you really think I didn't have someone else watching every keystroke he took to make sure you weren't trying to pull one over on him?"

"You have someone watching your own grandson?"

"I have someone watching *everyone* I know. You tried to trick him, which means you need to be punished."

"Whoa, no." I spread out my hands, my pulse jumping. "Look, I wasn't trying to trick him. Hacking is complicated and I'm pretty good at it, that's all. Yes, it was an unconventional move, but that's standard for me. You've got this all wrong. You can have whoever you want follow the road I was on and see what's there. I was exploring, looking around. That's what hackers do."

"We'll see. For now, let's go talk to your boss and confirm your appointment for tomorrow. If I get the faintest wisp of deception, I assure you, you'll sincerely regret it."

At least he wasn't talking about immediate punishment and he hadn't mentioned Basia or Xavier by name. If something happened to them, I'd never forgive myself.

When we got back to the dining room, the television was off and Jersey Guy stood near the table, holding my phone.

I glanced at The Father.

He gave a brief nod. "You may call, but put it on speaker. Think very carefully before you speak. Remember what I said about your friends being at risk. Right now, they're enjoying a late-evening dip in the resort hot tub. Let's not make it their last. *Capesh?*" He gestured with a slicing movement across his neck.

I swallowed hard. "Understood. But it's eleven o'clock at night. That's kind of late to check in with the boss."

"What? He has a bedtime? Call the damn number."

"Fine." I took my phone and pressed Finn's number.

After a few rings, he answered. "Lexi, where the hell have you been? I've been trying to reach you all day."

My eyes met The Father's. "Uh, sorry to call so late. I was, um, enjoying the scenery because, ah, it's so scenic here. Anyway, Finn, can you confirm I'm to accept the package tomorrow afternoon at one thirty local time at the hotel restaurant? Last I heard, I'm to sit at a reserved table for two with the name of Carmichael."

"That hasn't changed as far as I know. Have you heard anything contrary from Andy?"

The Father shook his head, which I presumed meant he, or someone else, had already gone through the email on my phone.

"No. I haven't received any emails from Andy or anyone else saying anything to the contrary. Just making sure."

He paused. "Lexi, are you sure everything is okay? You sound funny."

"I do? Too much sun, I guess. You know how I love

island living—the beach, sand and sun. Look, I've got to go, Finn. I'll talk to you later."

"Wait, don't hang up. Did you make any progress on the DPR situation? I wondered whether you had any thoughts as to the purpose of the diversion?"

I knew full well what the purpose was—ransom. But I wasn't sure how much I was allowed to say, so I played it safe. "I'm still working on that. You got anything else for me?"

"Well, Ken's been going through the list of DPR employees and has it narrowed to a few possibilities as the insider threat. Disgruntled employees, a few employees consistently working late, etc. I'll shoot the list your way in the morning."

"I'd appreciate it."

"So, what's next, Lexi?"

The Father made a slicing motion across his neck indicating it was time for me to end this call.

"Uh, I'll give you more details tomorrow after I get Andy's package. I've got to go now. Talk to you soon."

I clicked off before Finn could say anything else. Jersey Guy took my phone and pocketed it.

The Father seemed satisfied with my efforts. "Much better, Miss Carmichael. Despite your pathetic attempt at tricking my grandson, Carlos reported you helped him penetrate the shell company. As a result, we believe we know where the insider threat sits."

"See, I told you I was helpful," I said. "It wasn't that hard. Your package was routed through Baltimore, right?"

"Right."

"So was ours. It's logical to assume geographic location had something to do with the problem. Carlos and

I narrowed it down that way. The way I see it, someone at that Baltimore location, most likely someone in a managerial position, is either doing the hacking or letting the hacker in. I need more time to narrow that down and figure out how the British Virgin Islands plays into that."

"Not tonight. You have a more important job to worry about tomorrow."

He was right—I was finished. My eyes were gritty with exhaustion and my head pounded. I was disappointed I hadn't got my message to Slash. Besides, getting kidnapped, drugged and dangled as fish bait did wear a person out. Overall, my day had sucked. I didn't even want to think about all the entries I'd have to add to my "Little Black Cloud" spreadsheet after this…provided I survived.

Jersey Guy indicated I was to go in front of him up the stairs. He took me to the same bedroom I'd awoken from when I'd first been brought here. Without a word, he led me to the corner of the bed and told me to sit. I sat, and he snapped the handcuffs onto my wrist and then around the bedpost.

He pulled on the handcuffs a couple of times to test their strength and then strode across the room, flipping off the light.

"Hey," I yelled. "I didn't get to brush my teeth."

My answer was a slamming door. Letting out a breath, I leaned back against the headboard, swinging my feet onto the bed. I tried several times to pull on the handcuffs to try and break the wood, but it was strong and solid. After working a solid thirty or forty minutes, I also discovered I couldn't slip my wrist out of the cuffs either. I had big hands for a woman, which was great when you were a hacker and not so great when you were trying to escape from handcuffs. Finally, I closed my eyes and thought of Slash.

In the brief look I'd had at my phone before pushing Finn's number, I saw I'd missed two calls from him. I wasn't sure whether he'd be alarmed or just figured I was busy. We hadn't really set up any specific phone-calling parameters such as I-call-you-and-you-call-me-back-right-away or If-I-call-you-twice-and-you-don't-call-back-I'm-in-trouble. This absence of parameters meant there was no logical reason for him to assume I hadn't called him back because I'd been kidnapped by the mob.

Finn hadn't seemed to notice anything was off either, even though I'd thrown in that bit about loving island living, which was a total lie. But at least I could hope Basia and Xavier were safe for the time being. The best thing I could do at this point was cooperate and hope they would let me go. I didn't want to examine the lack of logic in that assumption too closely, because I really did need to rest, so I had a clear head for tomorrow.

Even though I was sitting up and in the uncomfortable position of having my arm chained to a bedpost, sleep claimed me instantly.

TWENTY-NINE

I AWOKE TO a stiff neck and blinding sun streaming in through the window. Before I remembered where I was, I tried to rub my eyes and was surprised when one hand only went so far before coming to an abrupt halt.

I blinked and massaged my neck and shoulders the best I could with one hand. Now that it was light, I studied the handcuffs and the bedpost to see if I could determine a weakness. I didn't see one and a couple of hard yanks confirmed I wasn't going anywhere. I didn't try too hard. Now wasn't the right time for escape. I'd just have to stay on alert and figure it out as I went along.

Another twenty minutes or so passed before someone finally came to check on me. It was a guy I hadn't seen before. He didn't knock, just stuck his head in the door and then yelled to someone, "She's awake."

Someone replied, but I couldn't hear what was being said. The guy disappeared and then returned minutes later with the key to my handcuffs. He unlocked me and I rolled my sore shoulder, wincing as it seized up.

He grabbed my arm. "Come on."

"May I at least go to the bathroom and wash my face?"

"Make it fast." He led me down the hall, checked in the bathroom to make sure no one had left any guns or knives lying around before letting me do my duty in peace. When I was done, we went downstairs. This time, instead of going into the converted den, I was led into the kitchen.

"Good morning, Miss Carmichael." The Father sat at a round table eating eggs and bacon. He had a white napkin tucked into the front of his shirt and different gold bling around his neck and on his fingers. Jersey Guy stood behind him.

The Father motioned to an empty chair across from him. "Sit down, please. Won't you join me?"

Although I was starving, I didn't sit. Jersey Guy came around, put his hands on both of my shoulders and forced me into the chair. A plate was set before me along with coffee and orange juice.

"Eat up." The Father dabbed the corner of his mouth with a napkin. "We've got a busy day ahead of us."

I was thirsty, so I drank the orange juice and then nibbled on a piece of bacon. "What are we going to do before I have to be at the hotel at one thirty?"

"Oh, we've got a lot of things going on. You're going to be a good girl and cooperate while you get decked out with a wire."

"A wire?"

"Of course. We have to make sure you're following directions." He snapped his fingers and Jersey Guy instantly placed my phone in the palm of his hand. He swiped across the phone and slid it across the table to me. There was a picture of Basia and Xavier having dinner out on the terrace, smiling happily, not realizing some deranged mobster had just snapped their photo with my phone.

"I know what I have to do," I said, pushing the phone away.

"Good. Then sit tight. You'll be summoned when we are ready for you."

The rest of the morning, I sat around watching wrestling with Jersey Guy until I wanted to hurl myself out the window. Grown men, dressed in barely-there thong-style tights, pretending to smack each other down was one of the dumbest things I'd ever seen. I suggested changing the channel once, but he threatened to strangle me, so I dropped it.

Carlos was missing in action. I had no idea where he was and no one seemed to care. Apparently, I'd burned that bridge, although I didn't blame myself for trying. At some point, a guy with glasses and a briefcase showed up. Jersey Guy took my handcuffs off after warning me not to try anything or else.

The guy with glasses opened his briefcase and pulled out a ballpoint pen. "Here you go."

I took it, examined it. "I'm going to be writing a letter?"

He rolled his eyes. "It's your wire—digital. We'll be able to hear what you and anyone around you is saying and record it as well."

"My wire is a pen?"

"The tip of the pen, to be exact."

I examined it, flipped it over in my hand. The tech part had me intrigued. "How does it work?"

"Put it in your pocket. Speak naturally. The digital microphone will easily pick up your voice, and those around you, even through your clothes."

I had a million questions.

"The pen part actually works," he said. "You can use it, but don't chew it, step on it or get the tip wet. Understood?"

"Understood."

He tested it briefly and then took the pen from me.

"Gabe, keep this safe and don't give it to her until she needs it. Boss's orders." He tossed the pen to Jersey Guy—Gabe—who caught it with one meaty fist and didn't even take his eyes off the fake wrestling match.

"Hey, don't you think we should test it further?" I asked.

"We will soon."

He closed his briefcase and walked out of the room without another word. I wondered how often he gave strange women recording devices and then left not knowing or caring who they were or why they were wearing handcuffs. Guess that was the mob for you.

The Father himself showed up at one o'clock wearing a hat, a light coat and a black long-sleeved shirt. In my opinion, he looked ready for tea with the Queen instead of the beach.

"You do know it's hot out, right?" I asked. "Tropical island and all."

"I have no intention of getting skin cancer. Are you ready?"

I'd been watching so many hours of wrestling I was ready to throw myself off a bridge screaming. At this point, picking up a package and pretending I wasn't being coerced while wearing a wire for the mob seemed like a reasonable activity.

Jersey Guy removed my cuffs and let me go to the bathroom before bringing me back to the living room.

The guy with the briefcase came back. As promised, he did a more thorough testing this time around, probably because we had an audience. It occurred to me that he probably knew full well the wire would work flawlessly, so the show was for The Father.

I had to count to ten about twenty times with the

pen in various locations such as my pocket, holding it in my hand and even sticking it behind my ear. Finally, the tech guy gave me a thumbs-up.

"She's ready."

I *wasn't* ready. I needed a shower, a good meal and six years of sleep without handcuffs or The Family. But I didn't see any of that in my immediate future, so I went with it.

They dropped me off at the hotel after multiple warnings about what would happen to Basia and Xavier if I didn't stick exactly to the plan. So, without a purse, phone or plan of my own, I walked into the hotel and headed straight for the restaurant.

I told the maître d' my name and she led me onto the terrace to a table for two overlooking the beach. I sat down, immediately drank the entire glass of water, then picked up the menu. I sincerely hoped we could eat because, life-threatening danger notwithstanding, I was starving.

I was deciding between the crab cakes and the co-conut shrimp when the waiter approached. "Are you Lexi Carmichael?"

I lowered the menu. How many waiters knew their customer's names? "Yes?"

"Your date has asked me to give this to you." He handed me a cell phone. "Sounds like he has something more intimate planned than a hotel restaurant rendez-vous." The waiter winked at me before giving me a quick tip of his head and moving away.

"A cell phone?" I said for the benefit of those listening in. It was a cheap burner phone, but I was starting to see how this was going to go down and I didn't like it. I'd just turned the cell over in my hand when it rang. I nearly jumped out of my chair.

Steadying myself, I answered it. "Hello?"

"Lexi Carmichael?" a male voice said in a clipped British accent.

"The one and only."

"You're prompt. I like that."

I looked around the restaurant, wondering if the caller could see me. All I saw were a lot of people I didn't know, and most of them seeming to be enjoying their lunches, unlike me.

"What was the name of your fourth-grade teacher?"

"What?"

"What was the name of your fourth-grade teacher? You have ten seconds."

"Miss Marquis. But why—"

"That's correct," he interrupted before I could finish. "What was the name of your professor at George Washington University for the computer science course Pseudorandomness?"

"Whoa. Who are you and why are we playing Fifty Questions?"

"You allegedly have a photographic memory. I'm testing that. You have ten seconds."

"Okay, but a photographic memory is different than instant memory recall. Just so we're clear on that."

"Five seconds."

"It was Professor Harding, and it was Georgetown University, not George Washington University."

There was silence and then, "Go to the marina. Boat slip six. Climb onto the boat and await my instructions. You have fifteen minutes."

"Wait? Are you kidding me? A boat? Look, I don't

do well on boats. I get seasick, sailor's legs and my vision gets blurry. Plus, I don't have a hat and I'd need to put on more sunscreen before I go out on the water. Can we choose another venue?"

"Come alone. If you're followed, the deal is off and I keep the package. Do you understand?"

"I understand, but the boat—"

Click.

I put the phone on the table and sighed. "This day just keeps getting better and better. I wonder if I can get some food to go."

THIRTY

I DIDN'T HAVE TIME, of course. Plus, I was afraid if I ate anything I'd hurl as soon as I got onto the boat.

One thing was certain. If this had happened and I'd been blissfully unaware of The Family, The Father, and the threat to Basia and Xavier, I would have immediately called Andy and told him where he could stick his package. No way would I go out on a boat, alone, without knowing where I was going and to what end.

No package was worth that.

But seeing as how I wasn't unaware, didn't have my cell phone, and my every move was being watched and listened to by the mob who was threatening my best friends on their honeymoon, I didn't have that option.

But, for crying out loud. Did it have to be a boat? Again?

Since I didn't know how long it would take me to walk to the marina—and the clock was ticking—I stood and stuck the cell phone in my pocket.

"Off to boat slip six, I guess."

I hoped I'd said it loud enough for everyone to hear, and by everyone, I meant whoever was listening to the pen in my back pocket. I left the hotel and headed downhill toward the marina. The sun was hot on my shoulders and I worried my nose would get sunburned out on the water, although if I really thought about it, that was the least of my problems.

I walked briskly toward the marina, mentioning boat slip six a couple more times to make sure everyone knew where I was headed. I wasn't sure exactly how much time had passed, but I calculated it was close to ten minutes by the time I reached the docks. The sea sparkled like a blue gem, though I knew it was just random reflection of light off the gently moving saltwater molecules. Motorboats, commercial vessels, kayaks and sailboats with assorted styles and color of sails dotted the horizon.

Fishermen and tourists strolled along the wooden dock. The fishermen carried buckets of fresh fish and grinned as I walked past crinkling my nose. The smell of salt, brine and fish was strong.

"Excuse me." I stopped one of the fishermen as he started to pass me. "Do you know where boat slip six is?"

"End of the dock," he said, pointing at the far end of the marina.

"Thanks." I broke into a jog.

I sidestepped empty pails, fishing poles, life vests and tourists with cameras as I made my way to the end of the dock. Slips four and five were empty. Slip six held a small white motorboat called *Beach Bum One*.

Sensing a pattern here.

I shaded my eyes from the sun and looked around, but there was no one near this end of the marina. While I could see some people in the distance, it was impossible to tell if anyone was watching, yet I was a hundred percent certain I was being watched.

"Okay, *Beach Bum One*," I said eyeing the motorboat mistrustfully. "Time to get on board."

There was no one to help me. I was so scared I'd

fall in the water instead of the boat, I was shaking. Somehow, I managed to half-jump, half-fall into the boat. Once on board, I crouched in terror as the small boat rocked wildly from my jump. I took several small breaths before summoning the courage to stand. When I got upright, I pulled the cell phone out of my pocket. It didn't ring, so I decided to look around. The boat continued swaying—a lot—which made me nauseous, but I fought it down. My knowledge of human anatomy assured me I couldn't get sick that quickly from just the swaying, so it had to be nerves more than anything.

There wasn't much to the boat. It was an open, air-powered skiff, perhaps twelve feet long with a single motor in the back. A wheel, and what I suspected was a throttle, were attached to a dashboard that had a small space underneath it where items like life vests would normally be stored.

Unfortunately, it was empty.

Crudely taped to the dashboard was an electronic device that had a small screen and keyboard. I guess that was where I would enter the coordinates. There wasn't a key in the ignition next to the steering wheel on the dash.

As I finished my brief survey, I wondered what to do next. I was clearly out of my depth. My knowledge of boat operations rivaled my understanding of wedding dress fashion, which equaled zip.

The cell in my hand rang and I lifted it to my ear.

"Hello?"

"Go to the third bench from the bow, lift it up and inside you'll find a key. Start the boat and set these coordinates using the dashboard instrument." He rattled off some numbers.

"Whoa. Slow down. I've never driven a boat before."

"I'll tell you one more time. Listen carefully. These are the coordinates." He said them slowly. I committed them to memory even as my blood pressure rose exponentially.

When he was done, I repeated them back to make sure I had them right.

"Good. You have fifteen minutes to arrive at those coordinates. If you try to make any type of communication from this phone or the boat, the deal is off."

"So, I just put the key in the engine and it starts like a car?"

A pause. "You're a geek and you don't know how to start a boat?"

"Hey, just because I'm a geek doesn't mean I know everything about everything."

"You should. Figure it out. Okay?"

"Wait, wait!" I shouted. "I honestly have no idea how to start the engine and I'm terrified of the water. Plus, I don't see any life vests on the boat. That violates the rules of safe sea travel. Where can I find them?"

He sighed. "Put the bloody key in the ignition. Pump the throttle forward and back a few times to prime the motor. It's been run today so you won't need to check the kill switch or set the choke."

Wait…what? Kill switch? Choke? I didn't like where this was going.

"Now move the throttle to the neutral position and turn the key," he continued, oblivious to my terror. "Push the throttle up to go forward. You won't need reverse as that is used for docking. Got it? Now get moving, as you don't have much time."

Click.

I was so busy trying to assimilate the instructions that it wasn't until a little later I picked up on the statement I wouldn't have a need for docking. Even as I reran all the instructions through my mind, my subconscious was debating as to whether this constituted one or two new columns in my "Little Black Cloud" spreadsheet and just how they should be labeled.

I jammed the phone in my front jeans pocket. Things were not going well. I would have to figure out how to drive a boat, suppress seasickness and hope I didn't get thrown overboard without a life vest. I had no idea how far out on the water I'd have to go or how the mob intended to keep track of me if the wire no longer worked on the open sea.

Not my problem. I was doing my part.

I inserted the key into the ignition, wiggled the throttle as instructed and left it next to a faded "N" setting, hoping that was neutral. I turned the key. After a short pause, the motor sputtered and turned over. Okay, one problem solved.

"Now I just push the throttle up and off I go, riding the waves like a freaking surfer," I muttered.

"Hello, there. You need me to untether you?"

I covered my eyes from the sun and peered up on deck where an older gentleman in a cap and shorts stood. It was the fisherman I'd asked about the location of the boat slip. Holy crap, it occurred to me I had almost tried to leave the dock while still being attached.

Epic sailor fail…and I hadn't even left the dock yet.

"Ah, thanks." I smiled weakly.

He grinned and tossed the rope into the boat before walking away. I tried not to panic now I was officially disconnected from solid ground. Fear seized me by the throat, but I put my hands on the wheel and opened the throttle slowly.

I was moving. Anchors away!

As I puttered away from the deck, I said loudly, "I hope I'll still be able to get cell phone reception or any kind of reception once I get out on the water. If I can't, that's not my fault." I hoped The Family could hear me and not blame me if their listening device went dead. The technician had said the wire had about a half-mile range, and the way things were currently looking, there was a good chance I'd go outside that range on the open water.

I clutched the wheel with both hands in a death grip, my stomach lurching. I started to relax a bit when I realized driving a boat was a lot like driving a car. There was something to be said about the exhilarating rush of wind in my face. If I tried hard enough, I might be able to convince myself I was in my Miata convertible instead of a motorboat on the open sea.

I was so caught up with driving the boat I suddenly realized I had no idea where I was going. I hadn't entered the coordinates into the GPS device. Bringing the throttle back toward idle, I shifted my attention to the small electronic device. It was simple, fortunately, and within my natural skill set, thank God.

Within a few moments, I had it turned on and the coordinates loaded. When I selected the "navigate" button, I received a directional arrow on the screen and a distance and time to go readout. It pointed out of the harbor and toward the open ocean.

Gulp.

With the listening device in my pocket and the one in the boat guiding me, I was uncomfortably aware that everyone knew where I was except me. As I turned my boat to follow the arrow, and carefully accelerated, I was conscious there were a lot of boats in the harbor. I cautiously maneuvered around them, leaving lots of leeway.

The cell phone rang.

"Luigi's Pizza Palace," I said. "Do you want pineapple or anchovies on your pizza?"

"Very funny. You're moving slower than my grandmum trying to upload her phone photos. Put your foot on the bloody gas."

"Look, there are a lot of boats out here. I've never driven a boat or navigated a harbor before. Plus, I don't have a life vest. I'm just being careful."

"Go faster or I'm gone…with the package." He hung up.

Sighing, I opened the throttle a bit more. The boat leapt forward and the bow rose higher out of the water. The throttle wasn't all the way forward, but I was moving as fast as I dared. Even though I felt like I was going fast, the scenery seemed to crawl as I slid out of the harbor into open water.

I was beginning to find the salt air and gentle waves almost relaxing until my brain kicked in and I started calculating how far I was from the nearest piece of land should the boat start leaking. Shortly thereafter, the theme song from *Jaws* started playing in my head. I began hyperventilating, so I quickly partitioned my brain so those fears could run around in an unused part of my head without interrupting what I needed to focus on to get the package.

I was well out into the open water before the phone rang again. Guess reception wasn't so bad out here, although by this time, the pen was surely no longer transmitting. It probably didn't matter since I presumed The Family had already heard the original coordinates of where I was headed and could figure it out for themselves.

"See that island to your right?" the voice on the phone asked.

I looked to my right and saw a small dark green lump rising above the horizon. "Yeah, I see it."

"Good. Head that direction and wait for further instructions."

He clicked off before I could ask if that meant I was to no longer follow the GPS device. Guessing so, I stuck the phone in my pocket and turned toward the island.

About three minutes later I saw two motorboats headed in my direction from the island. I slowed down and waited. Two guys with shaggy blond hair wearing T-shirts and swim trunks pulled up beside me. I cut the engine as the one wearing a backpack and a blue T-shirt that said Beach Bum hopped aboard. The other boat moved off several hundred feet, perhaps in case I was going to try something funny, which was so laughable an idea it bordered on pathetic.

"Lexi Carmichael?" the guy asked me in a British accent.

"That's me. Are you the guys with the package?"

"Yes." He shrugged out of the backpack, putting it on the floor.

"Did we really have to do this on a boat?" I asked in exasperation. "I can't swim and I'm seconds from hurling. You're lucky I didn't crash this thing."

He shook a finger at me. "You'd better not toss up

on my boat or I'll throw you overboard. Just inspect the package, okay?"

He reached to unzip the backpack when his eyes widened at something over my shoulder. "Who the hell is following you?"

"Someone is following me?" I hoped I adequately faked surprise.

I turned and saw a larger, commercial boat in the near distance coming directly at us from the harbor. The guy reached under the dashboard and withdrew a pair of binoculars.

"You know that boat?" he asked.

"Let me see." I took the binoculars from him and quickly found that staring through binoculars while on a rocking boat accentuates the sensation of nausea. I fought past it. Once I got the hang of focusing the binoculars on the horizon and finding the ship I could see a guy standing on the bow.

It was Jersey Guy.

"Yep," I said. "We've got trouble."

"What kind of trouble?"

"The bad kind."

"Seriously?" He snatched the binoculars back and motioned to the other boat, then pointed at our pursuers. "Gary, come get me. We've got company."

Gary glanced over his shoulder at the yacht and frowned. "No time. They're coming too fast. Follow me. I'll see you at the dock." He quickly peeled away, heading for the island.

My driver started the engine and immediately shoved the throttle full open. Our boat shot forward. I fell back against one of the plastic benches, knocking my elbow hard.

"Ouch," I shouted in indignation.

He glared at me. "You let the cops follow you? How stupid can you be?"

"Those aren't cops," I said. "They're worse."

"What's worse than cops?"

I rubbed my elbow, where a bruise was starting to form. "The mob."

THIRTY-ONE

"THE MOB?" THE kid looked at me as if I'd lost my mind. "As in Al Pacino, Marlon Brando, godfather mob? Are you kidding me?"

"I'd never kid about the mob. And those aren't actors. Those guys are the real deal."

"How is that possible? I thought the mob only existed in Italy, American movies and really bad Japanese flicks."

"You thought wrong. They are alive and well. Unfortunately for us, they have a strong interest in something you took from them."

Cursing, he hunched over, trying to reduce the wind resistance and pushing on the throttle as if he could coax more speed out of it. Hair slashed my cheeks, the sound of the motor roared in my ears, and a fine spray of water lashed us as we bounced off every wave. I had to take off my sunglasses and hook them to the front of my shirt, because the scenery was looking a lot like a laptop with the video card on the fritz.

The kid kept looking over his shoulder through the binoculars, as if he expected Marlon Brando to appear on the deck. I was amazed at how he could keep them steady. I was also a little nervous he wasn't looking ahead to where we were going, even if we were on the open sea.

"Why the hell is the mob following you?" he shouted at me, lowering the binoculars.

"They are following *us*," I shouted back. "You, because you stole their package. Me, because I could lead them to you."

"Bollocks." He lifted the binoculars and looked through them again as if our pursuers might magically disappear. "Now there's a couple more boats behind them. If the mob is in the first boat, who's following them?"

I shrugged, thinking he was being paranoid. Not that I blamed him. Once you have the mob on your tail, it isn't a leap to imagine every boat in the universe is chasing you. I just couldn't imagine why the mob would need more than one set of hired killers. Two beach bums and a geek. How hard could that be?

Even as I was doubting him, he tossed me the binoculars. I only caught them because they hit me in the chin and fell into my lap. It took some practice and patience to train and focus the binoculars as the boat jarred up and down. But sure enough, as the binoculars swung between the waves and the sky, I caught glimpses of two more boats behind the mob. I had no idea who else would be following us. The nearer of the two new chasers was a smaller motorboat skimming the wave tops and gaining steadily on the mob craft. I could barely see a dark-haired figure behind the wheel. Behind that boat was a much larger craft that had to be at a much greater distance given the comparative size. It, too, was headed our way.

Holy armada. It was a freaking caravan.

I adjusted my position on the slippery seat and felt something hard press against my thigh.

The cell phone.

I'd forgotten I still had it in my pocket. I glanced furtively at the kid driving the boat. He was now singularly focused on outrunning the armada. The island was still some distance, but closing rapidly, so I decided to take a risk. I slipped the phone out of my pocket and turned so my back was to him. I hoped the noise of the engine, combined with the regular thump of the waves, would muffle the sounds of me talking. Or at least, I hoped so.

Taking a breath, I dialed Slash's number, praying he would pick up.

He did.

"Slash?"

There was a lot of background noise and static before I heard him say, *"Cara?"*

I didn't have any time to waste, so I spoke as quickly as I could. "I'm in the British Virgin Islands on a boat with some kid who is taking me to a nearby island to get a package for ComQuest. Finn knows the details. I was kidnapped by the mob. They're trying to track down who diverted and held their package for ransom. I connected the hackers to an IP address right here on the island. Basia and Xavier are in grave danger. The mob is threatening to harm them so I'll cooperate."

"I know. I'm two boats behind you. Can you get the driver to turn back my way?"

I froze. "You're...*where*?"

"Get the—"

I didn't hear the rest of his sentence because the phone was suddenly slapped from my hand. It flew through the air and disappeared into the water.

Rough hands grabbed my shoulder and squeezed. "What in the bloody hell do you think you're doing?"

I lifted my chin. "I'm trying to get us help, okay? Believe me, I'd rather face the cops than The Family. They kidnapped me to get to you. Unfortunately, I'm pretty sure I've outlived my usefulness."

"Just shut up and sit down or you're next to go overboard."

He returned to the wheel. I figured he had the boat going as fast as it could, but the mob and the other boats were gaining on us. We'd get to the island first, but we wouldn't have much of a lead on them. If this powerhouse of a craft I was sitting in was any indication of the resources these guys had at their disposal, my stay on the island was likely to be a short one.

I tried to see the small boat behind the yacht, but it was frequently obscured by the first boat. Was that Slash back there or had I become delusional in the throes of danger? And who in the heck was behind him? The police? More of The Family? Tourists? It was hard to say at this distance.

It was also worth considering that if those boats were chasing the mob, perhaps they didn't know we were here. I wondered if the mob even knew they were being followed. If so, they didn't seem too concerned. So, what the heck did that mean?

I didn't have much time to worry because we were coming in fast to the dock. The other young man, Gary, had already docked and was waiting for us.

"Hurry up, Travis," he shouted at my driver. "Bring her in fast."

Travis aimed the boat in alongside the dock, then slammed the throttle into reverse at the last moment, throwing me forward and facedown on his feet. He grabbed me by the shoulder pushing me aside even as he cut the engine and tossed Gary a rope. Gary grabbed it, tethering us. Before I could say a word, Travis snatched the backpack and leapt onto the dock.

"Good luck," he yelled.

"Hey," I shouted. "Wait for me."

Neither of them slowed as they ran toward the forest.

I clumsily reached for the dock and hauled myself out of the boat. I heard shouting and the crack of a gun behind me. That energized me. I leapt to my feet and ran after them.

"Stop," I shrieked, even as my brain noted one more tally for the spreadsheet. I was going to have a serious discussion with myself about personal protection whenever things slowed down. This was getting ridiculous. Although, if I didn't get moving and stop talking to myself, I might not have a chance for that conversation.

Surprisingly, the kids turned to see what I was doing, which gave me the edge I needed to catch up.

"Why are you following us?" Gary said in surprise as I reached them.

"I want the package. Plus, they're going to kill me if I stay behind."

"Why would they kill you? You're working for them."

"I'm *not* working for them. I agreed to help them because they threatened to kill me and my friends if I didn't."

"*We* could kill you."

"No offense, but I'm more afraid of the mob than you."

Gary sighed, but at least he didn't try to take me down. He turned and plunged into a grove of trees and dense brush along a well-trod path. Travis and I followed him. They seemed like they knew where they were going, so I stuck with them. At this point, my best hope of survival was to stick with the guys, even if there was a chance they might kill me, too. The island was perhaps a mile long. It had a rocky shoreline that rose a hundred feet or more toward a central, densely forested ridge that ran its length. We climbed steeply, slipping occasionally on the wet rocks and stepping in and over frequent puddles.

Sounds of pursuit came from below and behind us now. I thought that was a little surprising since my impression of mob killers was that they were the strong silent type. Jersey Guy had done nothing to date to dispel that notion. I suspected they were just trying to frighten us into doing something stupid. Must be they had determined that with me in tow, the two guys were likely to make a mistake.

Nevertheless, the sounds added an urgency to our steps. Though the hill we were climbing wasn't all that high, the path we followed alternated with relatively flat areas. Trails periodically diverged from the main path, with most running back toward the water. I wondered why we weren't following any of those to throw our pursuers off our trail. I concluded that Gary and Travis had a hiding place in mind or the other possible paths would serve to slow our pursuers, as they had to investigate them or split up to find us.

As we neared the crest of the ridge, a side trail from the beach below intersected with the main path. Alongside the path were half-height wooden telephone poles like those often used for running just power lines. I wondered where they led. It quickly became apparent when we came upon a small wildlife station. As we ran past, we had to divert off the path due to a wide puddle that ran from behind the station across the path. We trod carefully, not wanting to leave any muddy prints, and continued down the trail. It looked unoccupied, although the exterior light was on, meaning someone was paying the power bill.

As we started down the backside of the hill, we slowed our pace. The trails narrowed and our footing became more treacherous. After several twists and turns, my lungs and legs burned. I was falling behind. The sounds of pursuit had been absent for some time and looking back and seeing me struggle, the guys finally stopped. Travis dropped the backpack and leaned against a tree to catch his breath.

"Oh, thank goodness," I said, panting. I was dripping sweat. I bent at the waist, breathing hard. "If I had known I was going on a five-mile run in an island forest, I would have put more deodorant on."

Travis rolled his eyes but was breathing too hard to comment.

I wiped my damp forehead with the back of my hand. "So, guys, what's the plan? Do you have a secret hideout? A cache of weapons we can use to defend ourselves?"

Gary looked at me in disbelief, his face red from the heat and exertion of running. "You want to know the plan? Our plan?"

"That would be helpful."

"The plan is for you to stop bloody following us." He looked seriously pissed. "You put the mob onto us."

"I did nothing of the sort." I braced one arm against the tree trunk. "You take all the credit for that. And, by the way, not following you is *not* a plan. Do either of you have a weapon?"

"I've got a screwdriver." Travis patted his backpack.

"I've got my fists," Gary said.

That wasn't exactly what I was hoping to hear. I tried to picture the scenario where we faced down the hit men with our highly lethal screwdriver and told them to drop their guns, or else. While I considered what to do next, it started to sprinkle. A few fat raindrops quickly turned into a deluge, all in the span of about fifteen seconds.

"Oh, great," I said, wiping the water from my face. "This day just keeps getting better and better. What in the heck were you guys thinking? Hacking, diverting packages and holding some of them for ransom? Surely you had to know it was only a matter of time before you got caught. Didn't you consider the consequences?"

Gary snorted. "Who are you—my priest?"

"You know who I am. You were the ones who asked me who my fourth-grade teacher was."

"Yeah, but that was easy to find out," Travis said. "I did some searching about you online and came across a fan site called the Lexicons. Imagine my surprise when it was all about you. Since it was open to anyone, even internationally, I joined."

I looked at him incredulously. "You joined...the Lexicons?"

"Hell, yeah. Who knew you had a fan club? It was good reading, by the way. I had no idea you were on the telly or credited your fourth-grade teacher for helping you succeed in math and science because she told you those subjects were for boys. You are a cheeky one, aren't you?"

My face heated. That Lexicon fan site dedicated to my adventures, and run by Gwen's younger sister, Angel, was going to be the end of me. Literally.

"Forget the fan site." I scowled. "This isn't about me. This is about *you*. You guys got in way over your heads."

"Why are you putting this on us?" Gary pushed wet strands of blond hair out of his eyes. "How do you know we're the hackers?"

"It's not that hard to put the pieces together. The boat we were just on was called the *Beach Bum One*, Travis's shirt says Beach Bum, and the signature in the hack says Beach Bum."

Gary glared at Travis. "You put a signature in the hack?"

Travis jutted his chin out, the rain plastering his hair to his skull. "Every cool hacker has a signature."

"You're such a dumbass." Gary sighed and lifted his face to the rain.

I swiped the water from my cheeks. "Anyway, since I'm keeping it real, your hacking sucks. Newsflash— it's not exactly hacking when you have someone on the inside helping you out."

"Hey, there was hacking involved," Travis insisted. "Some."

"Minimal," I said. "Dude, a sixteen-year-old kid working for the mob traced your IP address to the beach house."

"Really?" Travis seemed surprised. Apparently, his ego was a lot bigger than his brain. "Are you sure?"

"I'm sure. I tracked it, too, and it took me less than a few hours and that was on a regular laptop without any of my special equipment or software."

"So, again I ask, who are you?" Gary narrowed his eyes. "Some kind of cop?"

"Nope. I really just came here to get the package for a friend."

"We never intended to steal from the mob." Gary lifted his hands. "I mean, how could we have known who belongs to what package? It was totally random."

"Like the mob cares whether it was intentional or accidental," I said. "You don't piss off the mob and expect to walk away clean. Remember, they think extortion is their exclusive business line. Haven't you watched enough movies to know what happens to people who try and cut in on mob business?"

Both guys went a little green.

I drove my point home. "I suspect your buddy, who gave you inside access at DPR, will not only lose his job, but he'll go to jail. Bet he never had any idea *that* would happen when he agreed to help you. I sure hope you're paying him well."

"Look, if you're really a hacker, you know it's a lot of work," Travis protested.

"Let's be clear, I'm an excellent hacker, and even *I'm* not sure what you're doing. Are you diverting high-value packages here so you can resell them or are you stealing them so you can ransom them?"

"Both," Gary said, shrugging. "Whatever works. We're flexible like that. Sometimes, packages don't end up where we intended them to go, but that's a temporary kink in our operation. Those kinds of things are expected when you start a business."

I put my hands on my hips and glared at them. "One of your *kinks* caused a mix-up of packages at a wedding I was attending. Some thugs from the mob held me and the bride-to-be hostage while they tried to get their package back. Luckily their attempt failed, they were arrested and the package was confiscated. There were drugs inside that package. We could have been seriously hurt or killed."

Gary held up a hand. "Again, you can't blame us. It was a random situation. Look, we're not into reselling drugs, guns and the like. So, if we, by chance, intercept one of those packages, we offer the senders a chance to buy their merchandise back. It's a win-win for everyone."

I rolled my eyes. "Wow. I can't decide if you guys are naive or just plain stupid."

"Hey," Gary said, frowning. "We're not the world's moral compass here. We're just doing what everyone else is doing and trying to get ahead."

"Not *everyone* gets ahead by engaging in criminal activity." I ground my teeth. "Your little enterprise is having far-reaching consequences and now you're paying for it. And, unfortunately, so am I." Rain dripped from my chin. "But all is not lost. If you don't have any more of a plan, I do. I think I can save us."

"You?" Gary looked at me in disbelief. "How exactly do you intend to do that?"

"My boyfriend is in one of those boats that was following us."

"Your boyfriend?"

"Yes. If I can contact him, he can bring his boat around to the other side of the island and pick us up before the mob can find us."

"Why should we trust you?" Gary asked.

"At this point, it's either me or the mob. Your choice."

I heard someone yelling in the distance. Our pursuers were getting closer, though it was difficult to judge distance and direction in the trees and rain. I could see the indecision in their eyes.

"They're going to kill us," I said, crossing my arms against my chest. "Decide quickly, unless you have another plan."

Travis and Gary exchanged a glance. Finally, Gary turned to me. "How would you let your boyfriend know where to go?"

"You got a cell phone?"

Gary reached into his pocket and pulled out a cell phone. He hunched over it to protect it from the rain, tapped on the screen and handed it to me. I saw there were bars, so I quickly dialed Slash's number.

He answered immediately. "Who is this?"

"Slash, it's me. Are you really in that boat or am I dreaming?"

"I'm here—but I am still about five minutes out from the island. I got delayed. Where are you?"

"On the island and on the run with two guys. No time to explain. The mob is here and they're after us. Instead of landing where we did, as that might be guarded, can you change course and drive around to the other side of the island and pick us up?"

"That would take me at least twenty minutes. Can you evade for that long?"

"We'll have to."

I turned to Gary, hunching close and lowering my voice. "Is there a place I can tell him to rendezvous with us that he can identify from the water?"

Gary thought and then nodded. "Tell him to look for the small rock island with two dead trees that form a large V. There are typically hundreds of seabirds perching and flying around the trees. We will meet them at the shore, just to the right of those trees."

"Slash, did you get that?"

"I did. Two dead trees in a V. Lots of birds. To the right of it."

"Perfect. Just hurry."

"I will. Be careful, *cara*."

"It's at the top of my list of things to do."

I clicked off and handed Gary back his phone. "It will take him twenty minutes to get there. We're going to have to stay ahead of the mob and hopefully lead them astray at the same time."

"How do we do that?" Travis asked.

I straightened. "For now, we run. Let's see if we can lead them away from our rendezvous point."

THIRTY-TWO

TRAVIS AND GARY guided us, moving along the ridge and away from our ultimate destination. I figured we had an advantage because the guys knew the island. But the mob guys would be methodical. If they split up, they could be watching the trails from anywhere and waiting for us to appear.

It was tough going since the underbrush was thick and not well traveled. We debated briefly about making more noise so we could more easily lead our pursuers astray. But the guys wanted no part of it. They were terrified, not that I blamed them. Besides, they assured me that the spot we were going to rendezvous was not an easy place to reach, and it wasn't likely the mob would follow.

We hung on to limbs to keep from sliding down a rain-swollen path. We came out on the shore on the other side, now looping back toward the dead V trees. I could see them as we walked through the trees and the rain, as I scanned the horizon for Slash's boat. My tennis shoes squished with every step. The rain made my vision blurry and I tripped more times than I could count.

Then, as quickly as it had started, the deluge stopped. We paused and listened for sounds of pursuit. All I could hear was water dripping from the trees and the trickling water at our feet. Shrugging, Gary set off again. Now we were following only the faintest of paths.

It was mostly rocks, uneven, slick and sharp. My attention narrowed to where to put my foot for the next step. My body ached from the stress and concentration.

"How much farther?" I asked, panting when Gary and Travis pulled up short.

"We're here," Travis said.

I stared at him in astonishment. "Already?" Slash should be here by now. I peered over Gary's shoulder and saw we were indeed at the edge of the forest. A rocky shoreline punctuated with boulders lapped with gentle waves was in front of us.

"There," Gary said, excitedly pointing in the distance to a boat out on the water. "A yacht is coming. Is that your boyfriend?"

I saw the yacht on the horizon, but was confused. It wasn't the boat that had been tailing the mob. Nor was it The Family's boat. It might have been the yacht that was last in line, but I couldn't be sure. I hadn't had a good look and my recallable personal database of ship types had fewer entries than AOL had five-star reviews. But since it was the only boat in the near vicinity, I went with it.

"Yes. That's him."

The boat was moving cautiously as it approached our location.

"There must be shoals out there the captain is trying to avoid," Travis noted. "Look at the waterline, it's low tide. I doubt a boat that big will be able to make it to shore."

We quickly made our way down the shore, staying in the trees to avoid being seen. Gary told us to wait while he darted out to the waterline to alert Slash of our location.

Travis huddled next to me, shivering. "We're in a lot of trouble, right?"

"Right." I sighed. "Why did you do it, Travis? You seem like a nice guy."

"It was easy money. Besides, hacking doesn't hurt anyone. Not really. Most businesses have insurance, right?"

I rolled my eyes. "So, hacking is an anonymous crime unless it happens to you? Well, now the results of said hacking are happening to you."

"I know and it sucks."

"It really does. So, how did you guys make the leap from hacking to stealing to ransom?"

"The ransom thing was Gary's idea," Travis said with a sigh. "I'm more the computer guy." He looked down at his hands. "The ransom thing does pay pretty well, though."

"Look where it's got you now. You're not going to be alive long enough to enjoy it."

"Yeah, I get it. This is a definite setback. I hope there are no hard feelings. Nobody was supposed to get hurt."

"That's the problem, Travis, a lot of people got hurt. Aside from the hacking, stealing and economical harm to a small business—those mobsters kidnapped me, shot me up with a mystery drug, threatened my best friends who are here on their honeymoon, and said they would make me fish bait if I didn't cooperate with them. Epic fail on that front."

"Those were totally unforeseen consequences," he said.

"There are a *lot* of consequences you guys didn't think about, but that's a discussion for another time. Here comes Gary."

Gary dashed back to us, alarm on his face. "The yacht saw me. They waved. But we've got a problem."

"What kind of problem?" I asked.

"They can't get much closer. The water is too shallow for that large a boat. There are a lot of unmarked rocks, too."

"Is there another place they can go?" I asked.

He shook his head. "Not really. Not within a mile or so. I wasn't counting on a big yacht. The only dock and true beach on this island is where we landed. We're going to have to swim out to the boat."

"What?" My heart dropped. "I can't swim."

"No better time to learn than when your life is in mortal danger."

"That's not funny, Gary," I said.

He shrugged. "Die here. Die there. Better to at least give swimming a shot."

"A yacht that big should have a lifeboat," Travis said. "Maybe they can bring it out to us."

"Will we have time?" I asked.

"Guess we'll find out," Gary said. "Let's go."

The yacht appeared to have come as close as it dared. We dashed out from the safety of the trees. When we got to the water, I saw why the yacht had to stop. In the clear water, I could see a jumble of rocks and sand only a few feet under the surface. Hopes that I might be able to walk out to the yacht were dashed as I also noted gaps and scoops in the sea floor where depths surely plunged to more than ten feet.

Whoever was on the yacht had realized my plight. Even as they were dropping anchor, a small boat tethered to the side was being lowered.

Sounds of shouting came from our right. About a

half mile up the beach were Jersey Guy and some other thug I didn't recognize. They were pointing at the yacht. Then they saw us and started shouting and running our way.

"How did they find us?" Gary waded into the water to his waist. He intended to swim. "Hurry your arses up."

I didn't move. There was no way I could make it. Travis looked between Gary and me, clearly indecisive. Finally, he shook his head. "I won't leave you here alone. No one was supposed to get hurt."

"Hurry up," Gary shouted, waving his arms wildly and urging us to follow.

"No, man. She can't swim," Travis yelled. "I'm not going to leave her."

Gary looked out at the yacht and then at the guys running toward us. Cursing, he turned and climbed out of the water. "You're such a stupid, softhearted fool, Travis."

Personally, I was grateful. As soon as Gary reached us again, we left the shore and headed back into the forest again. This was getting intolerable. After a few minutes and another couple of twists and turns on various paths, we paused for a quick rest and review of our current situation.

Travis wiped his brow. "Do you think your boyfriend called the authorities for help?"

"I do. I'm also one hundred percent certain he will personally try and rescue me, assuming he can get ashore. But he may not be in time. We need to stop thinking we'll be rescued and come up with a plan of our own to handle this."

"How? They keep finding us so quickly." Gary

slammed the heel of his hand against the bole of a large, smooth-barked tree trunk. "It's not that big of an island, but they're tracking us a bloody lot faster than they should."

Crappola.

I pulled the ballpoint pen out of my pocket and held it up. The guys looked at it, then me, and shrugged. Holding a finger to my lips, I darted into the forest, left the pen on a stump and returned.

"What the hell was that all about?" Gary looked at me as if I'd lost my mind. Maybe I had. I hadn't been thinking clearly from the moment I had climbed onto the boat. It was hard for me to admit I'd had a serious lapse of mental acuity.

"While I was getting shot at and running for my life, I completely forgot the mob had planted a listening device on me. It wasn't working while we were out on the water, but when they joined us on the island, given their proximity, I bet it activated again. I suspect it has a GPS tracking device as well."

"You've got to be kidding," Gary said. "A listening device in a ballpoint pen? I hope you buried it."

"Not yet. We may be able to use it to our advantage, especially if they are using it to follow us. What else is on this island?"

"Just the dock, the trails we've been roaming, a frigate bird rookery on the north end and the small wildlife station we passed earlier," Travis said. "Why?"

"Which way is the station?"

"That way." He pointed uphill through the trees. "Away from rescue and a boat, I might add."

I paused, my mind racing. "Travis, what else is in your backpack besides a screwdriver?"

"I already told you I don't have any weapons."

"I know. Just tell me what you *do* have."

"Your package, some assorted bolts, my cell phone, a sandwich and a bottle of water. What can we do with that?"

My eyes narrowed. "Set a trap."

THIRTY-THREE

"Whoa. What kind of trap?" Gary asked.

"I'm not sure yet," I said. "But we have to move fast and we're going to use the GPS to draw them to us. Once I pick up the pen again, don't say anything you don't want overheard."

"What?" Gary's expression was one of disbelief. "You *want* them to come to us and you don't even have a plan?"

"Yet."

Gary looked at me as if I had lost my mind. "You're bloody, raving mad. You want us to take on the mob with a screwdriver?"

"I wish you had brought a few more tools, but that will have to do. You got any better ideas?"

"Yeah, take my chances back at the boat."

"No one is stopping you."

I darted back into the woods, picked up the ballpoint pen and stuck it in my pocket. I returned to the guys. "Whoever is with me, let's go. Now."

Travis looked at Gary, who frowned but blew out a breath and shrugged. Picking up the backpack, Travis pointed into the woods. "Follow me."

Even running hard, it took us ten minutes to reach the wildlife station. I swore that if I survived this nightmare, I was going to use our home gym every single day to work on my stamina.

The station was a small, concrete and wood building. It had one door and window in the front and a small window on each side. Around the back, a power line running from a pole stretched to the station and had wires running down the roof and into a junction box on the outside wall. An exterior light hung off the power pole.

Approaching the station, we splashed through the large puddle we had so carefully avoided last time. It was about four inches deep and was further swollen by the recent deluge. It ran from under the pole and around the back of the house to completely cover the path we had just come up.

"Keep an eye out for visitors," I instructed Gary.

My mouth was parched from fear and all the running. I desperately wished I had something to drink. It didn't seem fair that every part of me was wet except for my dry throat.

I froze. That thought triggered an idea. Dry…wet. Possibilities ran rampant through my head, most of which I reviewed and discarded, until suddenly I had a plan.

I dashed back through the puddle and left the ballpoint pen on a tree trunk a good fifty feet down the path we had just come from the wildlife station. Close enough to track us, but not close enough to hear what we were doing.

I tried the front door, but it was locked. I peered into the barred window and saw the station had no appliances and only a couple of overhead lights. That meant the station would likely only use 110 volts.

I walked around the back, following the wire to the

building's power box. I tried to open it but it was rusted stuck.

"What are you doing?" Travis asked, coming around the back with me.

"Plotting. Give me the screwdriver."

He rummaged around in the backpack and handed it over. I wedged it in the metal crack on the box, prying it open. Inside was surprisingly dry and dusty, populated by the expected collection of spider nests and the wire junctions I was hoping to find.

Ugh. Spiders. Why did it have to be spiders?

Travis peered over my shoulder. "Why are you looking at those wires?"

"They're an integral part of my plan."

"What plan?" Travis asked.

"No time to explain. But I have an important mission for you, okay?"

I quickly told him what I needed and he ran off to do it, while I got my section of the plan underway.

First, I had to clear out the spiderwebs. That freaked me out so much, I almost passed out from hyperventilating. In the end, I got the box clean without technically seeing or touching any spiders, thank God.

Spreading my legs so I straddled the puddle, I carefully loosened the wire nuts that joined the wires coming from the house with those coming from the pole. As I loosened each wire running from the pole, I slid it out of the box and recapped it so I didn't electrocute myself. The pole light remained on, so I was confident that the wires were still hot, but I didn't have a good way to confirm that assumption.

I stretched the wires toward the puddle, but they

came up about a foot short. I swore in frustration. I couldn't catch a break.

Frowning, I followed the wires with my eyes and saw they ran from the pole facing the roof to drop down to the junction box. The wire was nailed into the roof edge by U-shaped nails. I tugged to try and pull them loose. While they wiggled under my weight, they wouldn't release. I needed more muscle.

"I've got that for you, Lexi," Travis said. He must have come around the side of the house to watch me. The two of us managed to release the wires by pulling them free.

"Thanks," I said.

Just then Gary dashed around the corner of the station. "Someone's coming," he hissed.

I inhaled a deep breath. "Okay, this is it guys. We have one chance to get this right. We must get whoever's out there to step into this puddle that runs from here around to the front. The minute he's in, I'm going to stick these wires in the water and shock them senseless. Just make sure neither of you are standing in it. If they stop short of the puddle, Gary, you're going to have to go out there and convince him to move into the puddle to come to you."

"*Me?* Are you mad? He doesn't need to get me. He'll shoot me on sight."

"Not on sight," I clarified. "Hopefully."

"Hopefully?" Gary repeated.

"Well, logically, he shouldn't because he needs information from you. So, just stay calm and make him come to you. Tell him you have more of the Mandrax."

"What the hell is Mandrax?"

"It's what was in one of the packages you mistakenly

sent to the hotel wedding location. It's a synthetic drug worth millions on the street. My guess is that you're holding a twin package for ransom. The mob wants it back. Bottom line, if the guy out there doesn't walk into the water by himself, you're going to have to lure him in by surrendering where you stand and offering him a backpack full of drugs."

Gary stared at me, incredulous. "That's the plan? Lure him into water by promising drugs I don't have and hope he doesn't shoot me? Why don't you just ask him to stick his fingers in a socket or request nicely that he gives us his bloody gun?"

I lifted my hands, still holding the wires. "You're going to have to trust me on this. We're out of time."

"She's right, Gary," Travis said. "No time for another plan."

Gary looked between us like he couldn't believe we were considering this an actual plan. After a moment, he threw up his hands. "Fine, but we're all going to die."

"Not if I can help it," I said.

"What do you want me to do?" Travis asked.

"You'll keep watch from the other side of the station and let me know if the guy steps into the puddle from that side," I said. "As soon as he has one foot in, I'll stick these two wires into the water and hold them there until he's incapacitated. It shouldn't take long for him to go down."

"What then?" Travis asked.

"We'll cross that bridge when we get to it," I said. "Let's just focus on the operational need of the moment." I blinked in surprise as soon as the words left my mouth. Wow. I sounded a lot like Slash. When the heck did that happen?

"They're getting closer. I hear something." Travis pressed himself against the wall and slid down it, peering around the side of the house. Gary did the same, but with a view from the opposite side of the structure. I knelt by the giant puddle with a wire in each hand, ready to plunge them into the water as needed.

Gary caught sight of them first. He lifted his arm pointing to the front, holding up two fingers.

Two? If there were two of them, that changed the plan. We had to get both men in the water at the same time or we were out of luck.

Gary peered around the edge again, then snapped his head back. He pointed at his eyes, then at his chest, indicating they'd seen him.

Crap. Things were going south already.

"Is he in the water?" I mouthed.

Gary looked and shook his head, his face etched with worry.

From the front of the house Jersey Guy's voice rang out authoritatively. "We know you're back there. Come on out and no one gets hurt."

"How do we know you won't hurt us?" Gary surprised me by replying.

I looked at him, unsure what he was doing. Was he going to reveal my plan and sell us out? Or perhaps he'd try and cut a deal for himself and Travis. It was hard to say at this point.

"Isn't my word good enough?" Jersey Guy said.

"Not really," Gary replied. "But I may have something you want. The Mandrax. I'll tell you where I have it, if you don't hurt me."

There was silence, then Jersey Guy said, "Okay.

Come out with your hands up and we talk. Otherwise, I'll come back there and shoot you dead."

Gary knelt beside me, murmuring. "When you hear me yell Travis's name, spring the trap." With that he stood up, hoisted the backpack on his shoulder and stepped slowly around the side of the station, his arms up in the air.

"Man, we're sorry about your package," I heard him say. "It was a total mix-up. We can work something out, right?"

I squeezed my eyes shut, bracing for the crack of a gun, but it didn't come. I breathed a sigh of relief. There was a moment of silence before Jersey Guy spoke. "Where are the others?"

"They're running back toward the dock," Gary said. "They're going to try and take a boat to escape."

"Why did you stay behind?"

"I figured you were smart enough to have someone guarding the boats. I hoped it might be easier to reason with you here than after you started shooting at me. Look I'm sorry. Real sorry. We'll do whatever you want to make it right."

"You think you can cross the mob and then ask for a deal?" Jersey Guy asked.

"We didn't mean to cross the mob. Totally not planned. We won't do it again. As a gesture of good faith, I've got some Mandrax right here in my backpack. And there's more where that came from."

He was promising too much and his nervousness was making him sound unbelievable, but I had other things to worry about. Travis had turned to me with one finger up, waving his hand frantically at his side of the station.

I took that to mean the other guy was coming around to check out things.

I should have figured they wouldn't take Gary at his word.

To my great relief, however, I heard splashing. That likely meant Jersey Guy was walking through the puddle toward Gary. That was the good news. The bad news was the other guy wasn't in the water. My plan wouldn't work if I only took out one mobster. It had to be both or we were dead.

I motioned for Travis to approach me. He practically tripped over his feet coming toward me. When he knelt next to me, I thrust the wires into his hands.

"When you hear either me or Gary shout your name, stick the wires into the water," I murmured. "Got it?"

He nodded, fear shining in his eyes. His Adam's apple was bobbing and his hands were trembling. I understood exactly how he felt.

Ignoring my own terror, I crept to the edge of the wall and peeked around, promptly colliding with the other mobster coming around the corner.

Yikes!

We'd both been taken by surprise. As he was better trained, I only had time to gulp before he twisted me into a choke hold from behind.

I clawed at his arms, certain he'd snap my neck. Then he abruptly relaxed his hold.

"Oh, it's you. The girl."

He wasn't worried or scared. Hadn't even raised his voice. *That* pissed me off. I wasn't just a girl. I was a girl who knew Krav Maga *and* had tested it on a crocodile. *That's* who I was.

Just as he noticed Travis kneeling by the puddle, I

bent at the waist, dropping one shoulder and thrusting my butt into his stomach to get his body off-balance. It worked. Once I had the space I needed, I elbowed him in the groin with all my strength, which was a lot more than usual considering I was in fear of my life and hyped on adrenaline.

The air went out of him with something between an *oomph* and a grunt. He was totally unprepared for my ferocity, which meant I got the rest of the space I needed. I turned ninety degrees inside the hold and brought my knee up again in the exact same place, except with even more force and pressure.

"Oooogh," he gurgled, releasing his hold on me. I chopped at the arm holding the gun and it landed in the water. He tried to take a step toward me, but grimaced in agony, clutching his privates with his hands, his face contorted in pain. I slipped behind him, giving him a hard kick in the butt, causing him to drop forward, knees-first, into the puddle.

Slash had been right. Self-defense was all about timing, physics and the belief you could do whatever you needed to survive, regardless of size or weight.

"Travis. Now!" I hissed, hoping Jersey Guy was still in the water out front.

If he weren't, we were totally screwed.

THIRTY-FOUR

TRAVIS THRUST THE wires into the water without hesitation. The mobster in the puddle began to shake uncontrollably and twitch.

It was working!

I held my breath, watching his body jerk spastically until I snapped out of it.

"Brilliant!" Gary yelled from the front. "You did it. Crack, sizzle, pop!"

I ran over to Travis, yanking the wires from his hands and out of the water. "We just want to disable them. Not kill them."

Travis closed his eyes. "Thank God. That was bloody stressful."

"Welcome to my life," I said.

I retrieved the gun from the ground where the mobster had dropped it, then carefully pressed a finger to the pulse in his neck. I was relieved when I felt it throbbing. He was alive, but unconscious. Weirdly, his eyes were open, but unfocused. His face was not underwater, so he was not in danger of drowning or suffocating. I patted him down for more weapons, a wallet or cell phone, but only found a bottle of water.

I kept the gun as Travis and I went around the station to the front. Gary was kneeling beside Jersey Guy. The big lug had fallen forward so only his legs were in the water. He was out cold, too, but thankfully, his eyes were closed.

"He's alive," Gary informed me. "Damn, that was cool."

"Electrocution isn't cool. But it may have saved our lives."

As Gary stood, I saw he had already retrieved Jersey Guy's gun and held it in his hand. I froze, realizing I had no idea how this would play out.

Gary blinked and looked down at his hand and then at me. After a moment, he thrust the gun at me, handle first. "Here you go."

I blew out a breath of relief, checked to make sure the safety was on, then tucked the gun in the waistband of my jeans. As I'd done for the mobster I'd just fought, I patted Jersey Guy down, trying to find ID or any other weapons. Unlike the guy in the back, Jersey Guy had a knife, a coil of wire, brass knuckles and a cell phone. No wallet, however. Guess it was part of thug code for none of them to carry a wallet.

I glanced over my shoulder at Travis. "Where'd you set up the cell phone?"

He pointed to a corner of the front window of the station. I rose from Jersey Guy's side and retrieved it. The video was still running. I turned it off and played it back a bit. The video was grainy from the distance, but the mobsters were clearly visible at one point or the other. The audio was perfect.

Evidence in the bag, so to say.

"You did it," I said with a smile. "Good work, Travis. You, too, Gary."

Travis pumped his fists and danced around the front of the station liked he'd just scored a touchdown. Gary gave him a chest bump and they started whooping, grunting and high-fiving each other.

"Stop making so much noise," I scolded. "We don't know how many more bad guys are out there, all of whom are probably on their way here, now that we've so effectively alerted them to our position."

I'd barely finished that sentence when a voice rang out from the forest behind us. "Freeze. Now."

We'd been celebrating too early.

I slipped the gun I held in my hand underneath my shirt as I slowly turned around. My fear turned to relief when I saw Slash, crouched in a firing position, a gun trained on Gary and Travis, who were frozen in a silly embrace from celebrating.

"Slash!" After an initial moment of shock, I dashed toward him. "You made it. How did you find us?"

"How couldn't I with all this shouting?" He wore dark mirrored sunglasses, a black muscle shirt and black jeans. He hugged me tight with one arm while keeping the gun trained on Travis and Gary. "Are you okay, *cara*?"

"I'm fine, but we have to be careful. I think there are more mobsters on the island. Here are two of their weapons." I handed Slash the guns, happy to be rid of them. He took one, but made me keep the other just in case.

There was a loud cracking sound, like a foot stepping on a branch, in the trees to the left of us. "Incoming," a voice said.

I jumped as a guy I'd never seen walked out of the trees directly toward us. He had a gun in his hand. Strangely, he wasn't pointing it at us, but instead had it aimed at Travis and Gary.

"Slash!" I said in alarm, tugging on his arm.

"It's okay, *cara*." Slash patted my hand. "He's with me. Secret Service."

The agent passed by, tipping his head at me, while moving closer to Gary and Travis. "Ma'am. I'm agent Dan Orlowski."

I exhaled a relieved breath. "Oh, hey, Dan. Nice to meet you, although I wish it were under different circumstances."

"Likewise." He spoke over his shoulder to Slash. "Ricollo and I rounded up three others. He's with them now. I think we got them all, but we must be prepared in case we missed someone. The authorities have been alerted to our position and intend to do a thorough sweep of their own."

I looked at Slash. "Isn't the Secret Service supposed to be protecting you?"

"They are." Slash jerked his head at Dan. "See, the agent has his gun out and it's pointed at the bad guys."

I rolled my eyes. "How long until the authorities get here?"

"In about twenty minutes, or so they say. Who's the guy in the water and who are those guys Dan's got covered?"

"The one in the water is a mobster," I said. "Those two blond-haired guys in T-shirts and swimsuits are hackers. There's one more mobster around back who is also unconscious."

Slash glanced at me in surprise. "There's *another* one?"

"Yep. He's out cold, too."

"I'll go check on him," Slash said.

Slash jogged quickly around the station while Dan

kept watch on the kids. I was surprised their attention was on me and not the gun.

"Hey, that guy's your boyfriend?" Travis asked jerking his head at the spot where Slash had disappeared around the station.

"Yep. That's him."

"You said you weren't a cop."

"I'm *not* a cop."

"But he's a cop." Travis pointed at Dan.

"He is not a cop either. He's Secret Service."

Both kids' mouths fell open. They exchanged a glance before looking back at me. "Secret Service?" Travis repeated. "Like, you're the president's daughter or something?"

"I'm not the president's daughter or a cop or a secret agent. I'm just a computer geek."

Travis shook his head. "I don't believe that. You went all James Bond back there and did some serious moves on that guy."

"Those moves are called Krav Maga and you don't need to be Bond to do it," I said. "The method is quite logical and based primarily on physics."

"Right," Gary said. I could see neither believed me, but there wasn't much I could do about it.

Slash came into view, dragging the unconscious mobster by the arms. He dropped him on the ground next to Jersey Guy, who Dan had already pulled out of the water.

"You got ties?" Slash asked Dan.

"Two." Dan reached into his pocket and pulled out two plastic cuffs.

"They're coming around," Slash said, pointing at Jersey Guy with his boot. "Cuff them."

"What about them?" Dan asked, jerking his head at Travis and Gary.

"I'll take care of them."

Dan rolled over Jersey Guy and started cuffing him. "So, how did you disable them, *cara*?" Slash asked. I *really* liked how he assumed I was the one who had masterminded the takedown…because I had.

"Electrocution," I explained. "The station had power and the deluge made a huge puddle, so all we had to do was get them to step into the water."

Slash looked at the power line and then down to the water. A smile touched his lips. "Clever."

"It wasn't just clever, it was bloody brilliant," Travis spoke up excitedly. "She came up with a plan and ordered us about like a buggering general. Then, she takes on a guy two times her size and knees him in the knockers before booting him into the puddle. I stuck the wires in the water, and *boom*, two grown men are down for the count, twitching and sizzling. Hell of a thing, really. She didn't even break a sweat."

He was wrong. I had broken into a sweat, but he just couldn't tell because I was already wet and sweaty from the running and the rain.

"Krav Maga?" Slash asked.

"Yep. I'm going to have to keep training with you."

"Not a problem. There's a lot more I can teach you. You're an excellent pupil."

"She had perfect timing," said Gary giving me a thumbs-up. "Perfect execution."

"Not really," I said. "I got lucky."

"No way. You were one badass woman," Travis said.

"Who would have thought? I mean, her?" Gary said. The two of them laughed again.

Slash wasn't amused. His frown turned into a scowl as he strode toward them, his expression getting darker with every step.

Their laughter ceased as they eyed him uneasily.

"Hey, man, take it easy." Gary spread his hands. "We're on your side."

Slash's eyes narrowed. "Get on your knees with your hands locked behind your head. Both of you."

Travis and Gary obeyed without hesitation. I could see a spark of fear in their eyes and understood why. Slash had suddenly morphed into a man seriously pissed off and wanting to hurt something.

I felt a twinge of alarm. "Hey, Slash, they're okay. Just a couple of hackers gone wrong."

Gary nodded vigorously, looking at me. "Yeah, what she said. We're good, right, man? Just let me get up and explain." He started to rise, but Slash leveled his gun at him.

"Give me a reason to shoot you."

"Whoa, whoa. No reason whatsoever." Gary sunk slowly back to his knees. "I swear, we didn't hurt her. We *helped* her. Tell them, Lexi."

I sighed. "Slash, this is Gary and Travis. They may have done some stupid things, but they aren't killers. They thought they'd found an easy way to hack and live as beach bums before they got in over their heads. They did help me disable the mobsters."

Slash's expression didn't change one iota, nor did he lower the gun. "You put her in harm's way, and that's enough reason for me to shoot you."

His voice was hard and unforgiving. In fact, it was cold enough that I glanced at Dan, hoping he might intervene. To my dismay, Dan was making no move to do so. Clearly, he saw this as Slash's show. If Slash decided to shoot them, he wasn't going to stop it.

Holy crap. Right now, Slash looked angry enough to do it.

"Please, sir, listen to what she said." Travis's voice squeaked. "We're not killers. We just made some bad decisions. Very bad decisions. But not in a bad-that-we'd-hurt-anyone-on-purpose kind of decision. We stayed with you, right, Lexi? When you didn't want to swim."

"You did," I agreed.

Slash took a step forward, looming over Travis. The kid squeezed his eyes shut, his lips quivering. "Please, don't kill me. I'm begging for mercy. I'm only twenty-three. I'm too young to die."

Slash dropped a hand on his shoulder and my breath caught in my throat. "Slash, I think—" I started to say.

"No!" Travis screamed. "I want to live!"

Slash grabbed a fistful of Travis's shirt. With one hard yank, he ripped the T-shirt off the kid's chest. While Dan kept Gary covered with his gun, Slash tore Travis's T-shirt into strips and tied the kid's hands firmly behind his back.

I blew out a breath I hadn't realized I was holding. That had been a little too close for my taste.

"That was my favorite T-shirt," Travis moaned.

"Be glad I didn't shoot you," Slash said grimly.

"Right, then. Good point."

Slash ripped off Gary's shirt, too, until both men were secured with their hands behind their backs. He returned to me, holding out a hand. I took it and he squeezed gently.

"You weren't really going to shoot them, right?" I said.

He lifted an eyebrow, but didn't answer my question. "You're sure you're okay, *cara*?"

"I'm fine. The question is—are *you* okay? You look really pissed."

"I *am* really pissed. You could have been hurt. I assure you, nothing in this world makes me angrier."

"I know." I leaned my head against his shoulder and sighed. "But all's well that ends well."

"*Si*, there's that." He put an arm around my shoulder and pulled me closer, pressing a kiss to my forehead. "Thank God."

I took a moment to lean against his warmth and strength. "So, what do we do now?"

"We sit tight. The authorities are on their way."

"Good to know. By the way, I have video and audio evidence of the mobster's attack on us. We filmed it." I handed over my cell phone.

"Good thinking, *cara*. I'll—"

He was interrupted by a crashing in the trees. Both Dan and Slash whirled around, guns at the ready.

"Lexi!"

I gaped in astonishment. Basia and Xavier, their faces red from sweat and exertion, were running straight at me.

Slash waved Dan back and lowered his gun, swearing under his breath.

"Basia? Xavier?" I blinked. My brain couldn't process why the two of them would be here with me, Slash, two hacker idiots and a bunch of mob thugs. "What the—"

Before I could finish, Basia threw herself in my arms, nearly knocking me over. She gave me a big, squeezy hug that had me wincing. "Oh, God, Lexi. I'm glad you're okay. I was so worried about you."

I was having a hard time breathing. Who knew that someone so petite could squeeze that hard? I really needed to ask her about her weight-lifting routine because it was painfully obvious it was ten times better than what I was doing. Of course, I wasn't doing anything, so that was beside the point, but clearly, I needed to review my fitness routine.

"What…are you guys doing here?" I managed to wiggle out of the hug. "It's dangerous. The mob is here chasing me. You could get hurt."

"We know. Slash filled us in. Oh, Lexi. I'm so thankful you're safe."

We were hardly out of danger, but with Slash and Dan nearby, I did feel exponentially safer than I had a half hour ago. "What do you mean Slash filled you in?" I looked between her, Xavier and Slash. "What's going on?"

Slash didn't speak and kept his attention on the tree line, presumably keeping an eye out for any additional unannounced visitors.

"We came with him, of course," Basia said, as if that explained everything. Which it did not.

"You came with Slash?" I repeated. "Here? Why?"

"To rescue you." Basia looked around at the mobsters and the kids, competently trussed up. "Although it looks like we're too late."

"We were *all* too late," Slash said shortly. "She handled it without us."

There was a hint of pride in his voice, but also something else. Anger, perhaps. Anger that he'd been late, or maybe that he might have been *too* late.

Basia pushed her damp hair off her forehead before

pointing at Slash. "He came to find you and we came along to help."

"Let's be clear. I did *not* bring them here." A scowl crossed Slash's face. "Not on purpose. And you both were supposed to wait on the boat."

I rubbed my forehead where a throbbing had started behind my eyes. The adrenaline of being chased by gun-wielding maniacs was wearing off, reminding me that I was exhausted, dehydrated and hungry. It was a miracle I could even think straight.

"Okay, guys, start at the beginning." I crossed my arms against my chest and surveyed the group. "Let's start with how you knew I was on the boat headed for this island."

Basia and Xavier pointedly looked at Slash.

Silence stretched on until Slash realized we were looking at him. Realizing he was on the spot, he sighed. "Fine. But we'll have to go back a bit further. Finn called me after you and he spoke. He didn't like the fact he hadn't been able to reach you for a long stretch before that, which coincided with my inability to reach you as well. When you finally called him, he thought your tone was wrong. Plus, the fact you were babbling about how much you were enjoying the sun, sand and island life raised a significant red flag. Then, when my subsequent calls to you remained unanswered, it concerned me even more."

"So, Finn *did* get that something was off," I exclaimed. "I wasn't sure he understood what I was trying to convey."

"He did. He immediately called me and told me your location, as well as updated me on what had happened with the two guys at the beach house."

"Really." That surprised me, especially since Finn was a lawyer. "What about the nondisclosure agreement?"

"When lives are at stake, the agreement becomes defunct. He was worried for your safety and that was far more important to both of us than an agreement. Regardless, I know how to be discreet."

"That you do," I agreed.

Over Slash's shoulder, I saw Jersey Guy awake and trying to struggle into a sitting position. His hands were cuffed and his limbs likely still felt like jelly, so he wasn't having any success. Poor guy, he probably had no idea what had happened.

The guy I'd kicked into the puddle still wasn't moving. Even though he might have killed me, a part of me hoped he was okay. I didn't want to be responsible for anyone's death.

"I called Xavier, since I knew he was at the same resort as you," Slash was saying. "He was worried about you, too. He said the last time he'd seen you, you were being chased through the hotel lobby by a security guard."

My cheeks heated. "So much for my stealthy operation to remove the poster."

"What poster?" Slash asked, frowning.

"That's a story for later," I said. "Please continue."

Slash rolled his neck, rubbed the muscles at the back. "Well, when Xavier confirmed your location, I caught a flight here immediately."

"I'm following you so far, but how did you get on the boat behind The Family?"

"I may have had a bit of help from a kid named Carlos."

"What?" I blinked in surprise. "Carlos? Really? He helped you out?"

"He did. Sent a message, blind, to one of my dormant accounts. I traced it back to him. He caught me up on events, so to say."

"Wow, I'm pretty shocked about that. He turned me over to the mob when I was *that* close to pinging you."

"I know. He said he was being watched. It was the only way he could protect you and himself."

"I *knew* he was a good kid," I said. "He was being coerced, Slash. We should help him out."

"We will."

"Lexi, how did you get mixed up with the mob?" Xavier interrupted. "Was that part of your work?"

"Not exactly. It's a long story, Xavier. First, I want to know how you guys knew which boat to follow."

Slash looked up at the sky which was darkening. I sincerely hoped it wouldn't rain again. My feet were damp and the humidity already made me feel as if I were a vegetable in a steam cooker.

"Carlos appraised me of what was happening by listening in on your wire and transmitting the information to me in real time."

"Wow. In exchange for…?"

"Immunity."

I considered that for a moment. "Smart kid and not a bad deal. Did you give it to him?"

"Not fully. He'll have to complete some classes regarding the dangers of hacking and he'll be on probation for a bit. But essentially, yes."

Basia squeezed a corner of her blouse to try and wring it out. "The past twenty-four hours have been crazy, Lexi. Everything happened so fast. Xavier and I met Slash and his entourage at the airport and brought him to the hotel. Apparently, we'd just missed you at the hotel and you were already headed down to the marina. Slash wanted to alert the authorities, but we didn't know enough yet."

"You had to wait, just like I did, for the kids to give me the coordinates."

"Si," Slash said.

Basia glanced over her shoulder at Dan. "Neither Slash nor the Secret Service agents wanted us to get involved, but you're our friend, too, Lexi. They couldn't stop us from following them—it's a free country, after all. And, in the end, it's a darn good thing we did."

I was touched more than I could say by their loyalty. I cleared my throat. "I don't know what to say, guys. Thank you for caring. But Slash was right. You shouldn't have put yourself in that kind of danger, and certainly not over me."

"Well, he did try pretty hard to prevent us from coming." Basia narrowed her eyes at Slash. "But we had already booked a private boat tour for the afternoon, and so off to the marina we went."

I glanced over at Slash who had pushed his sunglasses to the top of his head and he was frowning. I figured he wasn't happy that Basia and Xavier had put themselves in danger's way and there wasn't much he could do about it.

"Okay, so, you got a boat and you followed me based on the coordinates Carlos gave you in real time," I said.

"No." Basia shook her head. "They did not *get* a boat. They went all secret agent and flashed their badges before *commandeering* a boat. Just like in the movies."

Slash shook his head, but Basia lifted an eyebrow.

"Tell me I'm wrong, Slash." When he didn't respond, she laughed. "See, told you."

I held up a hand. "So, Slash, you and the agents commandeered a boat, and as soon as Carlos relayed the coordinates, you headed out."

"Correct," he confirmed. "It didn't take us long to spot your boat. It was moving pretty slowly."

"Okay, that explains how *you* found me." I looked at Basia and Xavier. "So, how did *you* guys find me?"

"Easy." Xavier shrugged. "We offered our tour guide an extra two hundred dollars to follow Slash's boat. And it was a good thing we did, too."

"Why?"

"Because their motorboat ran out of gas right about the time you were boarded," Xavier explained.

I looked at Slash in astonishment. "Your boat ran out of gas?"

Was it my imagination or did his face flush slightly? He nodded. "Unfortunately, that's true. We didn't check the fuel level when we, ah, acquired the boat."

Basia was nearly bubbling with excitement. "So, get this, Lexi. We rescued Slash *and* the Secret Service. They had to come aboard our boat and commandeer *it* so they could continue to follow you. How cool is that? For once, we saved the day, and it was on our honeymoon, too."

"It was pretty cool," Xavier added. "Slash pushed our poor tour driver to open the throttle all the way, maxing out the speed of the yacht to catch up with you. At one point, the yacht was shaking so hard, I thought the boat might fall apart."

"I was terrified the entire time." Basia's whole face lit up. "But there we were, chasing you across the ocean like we were in some kind of Bond movie. It was quite thrilling."

I wasn't understanding the whole excitement vibe about going a zillion miles an hour in a yacht while chasing after me and the mob, but I didn't think it would be polite to point that out.

"Anyway, before we stalled, I got your first call," Slash said. "I received the second call, where you requested we move to the other side of the island, once I'd boarded Xavier and Basia's tour boat."

I nodded. "*Now* I understand why you came to the rescue in the yacht and not the motorboat I thought you were on originally."

Slash nodded. "That's why. Unfortunately, there was no place for us to dock, so we had to anchor and come in using the lifeboat. Lost another ten years of my life when I saw those guys chasing you up the beach."

I sniffled. "So, you guys came for me. All of you. And you two—" I pointed at Basia and Xavier "—interrupted your honeymoon to save me. I don't know what to say except I have the best friends ever."

Slash put an arm around me and kissed the top of my head. "The thing is, you didn't need saving, *cara*. You saved yourself, little black cloud notwithstanding."

I leaned my head against his chest. "I've totally got to add all of this to my spreadsheet as soon as possible. In fact, I think it's time to run an analysis. I'd be happy to share the conclusions with everyone, if you're interested."

"What's it going to tell me?" Basia asked.

"It will tell you that Lexi is a trouble magnet," Xavier said. "Like duh, right?"

"Right." I smiled. "But there are patterns, algorithms

and peripheral information to consider, all of which play a role in the quantifiable proof of the existence of a little black cloud. However, just so we're clear, it's not just about the existence of the cloud. It's about the *meaning* of it. The spreadsheet will hopefully give me a clearer picture of myself. Because if there's one thing I'm sure of in all the craziness that has become my life—the data never lies."

THIRTY-FIVE

SLASH WAS OFF by ten minutes. The authorities arrived about a half hour later. Shortly before they reached us, I retrieved Travis's backpack and took out Andy's package. I sat down on a tree stump and began carefully examining the packaging on the outside of it.

While I was doing that, Slash joined me. I scooted sideways on the stump so he could sit next to me.

"Is that Andy's package?" he asked.

"It is." I examined the markings. "But it's strange. I thought it was a package coming *to* ComQuest. Instead, it looks like it was sent *from* ComQuest, but it never made it to its original destination. It was diverted right out of Baltimore."

Slash leaned over. "This is even more interesting. The package is addressed to Gaffar Maloof in the United Arab Emirates."

"Who's Gaffar Maloof?" I asked.

"He's the CEO of the largest tech firm in the UAE—Emeer Data."

I lifted an eyebrow. "And you knew that how?"

"Because my New York simulation company does occasional business with them."

"Okay, then why is it interesting? ComQuest is a big tech firm. It's not out of the ordinary that they would do business together, right?"

"Maybe." He studied the package for a minute. "But

it wasn't mailed from ComQuest. It's got Andy's home as the return address. That's odd."

"Why is that odd? Maybe he just mailed it from home for convenience's sake."

"Maybe." Slash fell silent. "But that would be highly unusual for a COO."

I got the impression he was thinking it was something else. Since he didn't offer what that might be, I began to pull apart the paper on the box. "I'm supposed to open it and check that the device is in there and working."

"Might as well," Slash said. "The authorities will certainly open it."

Slash lent me his pocket knife so I could tear through the tape on the box. Once the tape had been removed, I opened the box and pulled out yet another box and a single, sealed white envelope with a name, Gaffar Maloof on it.

Slash held the envelope, while I opened the second box and pulled out the tricorder, placing it carefully in my lap. It looked identical to the one Andy had shown me.

Slash whistled. "What's that?"

"A medical device. A tricorder, for lack of a better word. You know, like the device in *Star Trek*. You wave it over the body and it can diagnose certain illnesses."

He leaned on my shoulder, studying it. "Fascinating."

A shadow blocked our light, so we both looked up.

"Where did you get that?" Xavier had his hands on his hips, looking in surprise at the tricorder in my lap. "I helped design a part of the microchip in that device. It's proprietary to ComQuest. Why do you have it on a deserted island in the middle of the British Virgin Islands?"

"It's a long story, Xavier, but suffice it to say, I'm working for ComQuest."

"Oh." He digested that for a moment. "Why did you bring it here?"

"She didn't bring it anywhere," Slash said. "The package was diverted, much like the mix-up with your wedding presents. Andy's package, which was sent from his home address, not ComQuest's, was headed to the United Arab Emirates to Gaffar Maloof, the CEO of Emeer Data."

He and Xavier exchanged a long glance before Xavier held out a hand. "May I see the device?"

I gave it to him. He turned it over in his hands, examining it closely.

"It's an earlier prototype, but still contains most of the important technology."

"How many prototypes are there?" Slash asked.

"Three that I know of. My best guess is that this is number two."

"Why would Andy be sending a prototype of the medical device to the UAE?" I asked.

"I don't know." Xavier lifted his gaze from the device and looked at me. "We haven't even gotten it approved by the Food and Drug Administration yet."

Slash's face turned thoughtful. "Perhaps Andy was hoping for an early foothold in the Middle Eastern market."

"That's possible, but extremely unlikely." Xavier frowned. "Look, it's not like I'm at the top of the food chain at the company or privy to the highest decisions, but even if that *were* the case, Andy shouldn't be send-

ing him the actual prototype. Not at this stage. Not unless…" He let the sentence trail off, a pained expression
crossing his face.

"…unless he's bribing them," Slash finished for him.
He pulled out his phone and began swiping at his screen.

"Bribing?" I looked between Slash and Xavier not
understanding. "Bribing who for what?"

Xavier's expression looked pained. "Slash means
ComQuest may be trying to smooth the way for our
device to be quickly approved in the UAE market, but
without going through normal government channels. I
just can't see how this could happen, though. This kind
of secret negotiation never would have been approved
by the Board."

"Perhaps he did it without the Board's permission,"
Slash suggested.

"That's impossible," Xavier spluttered. "Why would
Andy do such a thing?"

"Maybe there's something in it for him."

I held up a hand. "Whoa. Slash, this is Andy we're
talking about." Regardless of my protest, there was a
sinking feeling in my stomach. A lot of things were
starting to make sense, and not in a good way. Andy's
insistence on keeping my trip highly confidential, his
avoidance of using anyone from ComQuest to retrieve
the package, the fact he didn't mention the ransom, and
his insistence on using me to carry out the mission and
keeping it quiet.

Me.

He'd used me.

"That would be…unethical," I finished.

"It's not just unethical, *cara*," Slash said quietly. "It's
illegal to bribe others in official positions in the US and

abroad. Violating the Foreign Corrupt Practices Act is a serious crime in the US. And, just so you know, Maloof's brother is the Minister of Health in the UAE." He held up his cell phone, showing me a picture of some guy. "This isn't looking good for Andy. Especially if there's something incriminating in that envelope. But it's not up to us to evaluate the evidence or determine guilt. This is a complex issue."

"What's in that letter?" Xavier asked, pointing to the envelope on Slash's lap.

"It's confidential," I said. "Andy specifically told me not to read it and to let him know if it had been tampered with or opened. I can't read it. I promised."

"It's lucky I didn't make any promises or sign any nondisclosure agreements." Xavier snatched the envelope. "Guess you'll have to tell Andy it was opened." Before I could say a word, he tore open the envelope and pulled out a single sheet of paper. It was a short, handwritten note.

Slash and I watched for a minute as Xavier read it. The way his expression changed—from disappointment to hurt to anger—indicated whatever he was reading was more than just a little incriminating.

Still I had to know for sure. "Xavier?"

He lifted his eyes from the note. "Andy expressed appreciation for the anticipated and expedited actions of Mr. Maloof and a promise of delivery of a certain number of devices, at an agreed-to rate, with a special profit margin for Mr. Maloof and his brother."

"Oh, crap," I said. "Seriously?"

"Furthermore, Andy praised Mr. Maloof's efforts to date, especially those clearing the way for the approval of the device," Xavier continued. "He also thanked Mr.

Maloof for his continuing discretion as to their agreement."

My headache throbbed with increasing intensity. "Oh, Andy," I murmured. "What were you thinking? I just don't get it. Why would he do this?"

Slash rubbed his unshaven chin. "It's an insanely big risk for him and the company. ComQuest is publically traded, so any kind of bribe would be subject to severe federal penalties by the Securities and Exchange Commission, not to mention prison time for Andy, if it were ever discovered."

"Would ComQuest be in trouble, even if they weren't in on it?" I asked.

"Most likely there would still be penalties leveraged against the company," Slash said. "Andy would certainly be fired and probably be charged with a myriad of offenses. My only thought is there would have to be something really valuable in it for him to make it worth this kind of risk."

"How about a potential market opportunity worth hundreds of millions of dollars?" Xavier said, his voice hard.

Slash and I both looked up at Xavier in surprise.

"Explain," I said. It was weird. I wanted to know and yet I didn't want to know. Every revelation was making me feel sicker.

"This medical device is going to be a game changer, Lexi," Xavier explained. "The potential market value of this device in the Middle East is worth at least that, if not more. It would be a game changer for ComQuest and could quite possibly make Andy a billionaire."

Slash nodded, following Xavier's train of thought. "True. Andy would also be seen as a groundbreaker who figured out how to succeed in this lucrative, but exceptionally difficult market. His reputation would skyrocket, as would company stock. A game changer is a good way to put it, Xavier."

I didn't know what to say. This situation totally sucked. I put my chin on my hand and sighed. "So, now what?"

"We presume Andy's innocence until proven guilty," Slash said. "That's only fair. But I won't lie, *cara*. It doesn't look good for him."

It made me feel marginally better that Slash refused to publicly jump to conclusions. But I could see by the upset expression on both of their faces, they already thought him guilty.

"I'm sorry, Xavier," I said. "I know Andy's a friend. He's my friend, too. Maybe this will all be explained away."

"Maybe." I could see he didn't believe it. Xavier glanced over his shoulder to where Basia was talking to Dan. "Until then, let's keep this from her, okay?"

"Of course," I said, and Slash gave a single nod of his head.

Without another word, I repacked the tricorder and put it back in the box, along with the letter.

The British Virgin Island authorities arrived shortly thereafter. We all traipsed back to the dock and loaded onto police boats. Ricollo, the other Secret Service agent, was reunited with Slash. The mobsters and the kids were taken into custody. Before they left, I told Gary and Travis I'd put in a good word for them. Not like it would help a lot, but I figured any little bit would be appreciated.

Basia and Xavier's tour yacht driver was also

rounded up and we were all taken back to the mainland for questioning.

We sat in a small police station for several hours, drinking coffee that was just as bad as it was in American police stations. Our situation quickly became an international event, with the Secret Service, the NSA, a US embassy official and the FBI all being summoned to sort things out.

We were interviewed separately. My lead interviewer was a policewoman from the British Virgin Islands. An embassy official and an FBI agent sat with us. The FBI woman took notes and was permitted to occasionally ask me questions. As promised, I emphasized how the kids had helped me defeat the mobsters. I kind of hoped they were doing okay.

The police kindly plied me with food, water and stale coffee as I told my story from the beginning, not leaving anything out. About halfway through, the FBI agent told me Andy and Finn had been brought in for questioning. I sincerely hoped my instincts were wrong and Andy would be cleared of any wrongdoing. But Slash was right. It wasn't our job to figure that out.

By the time the questioning ended, it was late and the police dropped us off at the hotel. We had promised to be available in case the authorities had any questions over the weekend, so they helped me extend my reservation at the resort through the weekend, which also gave Slash and me time to arrange our tickets home.

"No offense, guys, but we're going off on our own for the rest of our honeymoon," Xavier said as the four of us stood in the hotel lobby.

"By all means," I said with genuine sincerity. "Being a third wheel on someone's honeymoon is an experience I hope to *never* have again. In fact, I insist you enjoy the rest of your honeymoon without me. And Basia, if you see any flyers or posters around the resort, I beg you to just ignore them."

After hugs all around, we headed to our respective rooms.

Slash and I were both so tired, we took showers and crawled into bed. He gathered me in his arms, holding me tight and not saying anything. I lay there safe in his embrace, my ear pressed against his chest, listening to his heartbeat. I liked snuggling like this, feeling his heart thud hard and fast beneath my ear. I'd missed it these past few days. I'd missed *him*. A lot.

"So, you flew all the way to the British Virgin Islands to save me?" I made a circle on his chest with my fingertip.

"You doubted I would?"

"No. I did not. Not even for a moment."

"Good." He swept a hand down my hair. "You didn't need me, though. In some ways those kids were right. You're turning into a badass woman. *My* badass woman."

A chuckle slipped past my lips. "That's so not true. I was terrified the entire time—more afraid of the water than the mob. That hardly qualifies me as badass. But those moves you taught me, Slash, they weren't pretty, but they worked. He underestimated me, thinking because I was female, he could easily handle me. He was wrong. Thank you for teaching me Krav Maga and making me believe that in matters of self-defense, size doesn't matter. Logic and action do."

He smiled and squeezed me. "You're welcome."

I lifted my head from his chest. "And you're wrong about something else. I *do* need you. I need you more than I ever thought I would. Not necessarily to save me, although when you do, I sincerely appreciate it. What I need is us. I miss you when you're not with me. Does that make sense?"

"It does." He lifted my hand to his lips and kissed it, before pressing it against his cheek. "We're two of a kind, *cara*, in more ways than one. So, what do you want to do tomorrow on our little impromptu vacation?"

"Honestly? I want to sleep in, order room service and stuff my face with a lot of food, sit on the balcony and enjoy the weather, and drink lots of fruity, tropical drinks with little umbrellas. As far as I'm concerned, we don't ever have to leave our room."

He pressed his chin against the top of my head, tightening his arms around me. "Sounds like a perfect day."

THIRTY-SIX

WE SPENT THE next day doing exactly that. We laughed, talked, made love, watched old movies and even danced on the balcony to some soft music on Slash's phone. As the day passed and the evening arrived, Slash suggested we try a local restaurant for dinner.

"Sounds good," I said. "I need a shower first."

"Likewise. While you're in the shower, I'll go talk to the concierge and get a recommendation for a nice place to go to dinner. As I didn't have time to pack, I'll also buy myself a few supplies. I'll be back in a bit."

I took my shower and had just finished drying my hair when my cell phone rang. I picked it up, my face breaking into a smile when I saw who was calling.

"Hey, Elvis, how are you doing?"

"Hey, Lexi. I'm doing fine. But I just got off the phone with Xavier. He filled me in on what happened. So, you crashed my brother's honeymoon and put my boss in jail, all in the span of a few days?"

I sighed. "It really sounds bad when you put it that way. But, yeah, that's about right. But Andy isn't in jail. Is he?"

"He was taken into custody last night."

"Oh, no. That's awful. I'm so sorry. How are things at ComQuest?"

"I don't know. It's the weekend and no one has issued a press release yet. I'll keep you posted."

"Please do. I hope Andy makes bail and that he has a good explanation for this."

"The only explanation I see isn't a good one," Elvis said. "It sucks for everyone."

"It sure does."

"You are going to fill me in on what happened, right?" Elvis said. "Xavier was stingy with the details."

"I will. But when I return. Trust me. The whole story will require a lot of pizza and multiple beers."

"Well, at least you know I'm good for it."

"Yes, you are. The good news is everyone's okay, and Basia and Xavier intend to continue their honeymoon without me. Slash and I are coming home on Sunday night. He's out now getting us some supplies."

"I really can't wait to hear the details."

"I bet." I wrapped the towel tighter around my middle and ran the brush through my hair a couple of times. "So, how are *you* doing, Elvis? You okay?"

"Yeah, I'm good. Finally."

He was. I'd noticed a new tone in his voice. He sounded relaxed, confident, more assured. I sat down on the edge of the bed, placing the brush in my lap. "What happened?"

"I figured it out, Lexi. I figured out *me*."

"Wow." I paused to consider the significance of that. "That's certainly an accomplishment to be proud of."

"It is." He laughed. "Well, I don't have me all figured out, but I'm making progress. I owe it all to you, though. I thought a long time about what you said— that the hardest decisions are between two positives."

"It's true."

"I agree. And, while this isn't a comfortable question for me to ask, I hope you'll answer anyway. How did you come to that conclusion? Do you mind me asking if it was from personal experience?"

I closed my eyes. Heat rushed to my cheeks. I knew what he was asking. I'd considered a lot of things before I'd decided to date Slash, and one of them had been sorting out my feelings for Elvis. He deserved to know the truth, although I suspected he already knew the answer.

"Honestly, Elvis…yes."

I heard him exhale slowly. "I wondered. I appreciate you being honest with me."

"Honesty has always been the way between us."

"Yes, it has," he confirmed. "So, keeping that in mind, I thought hard about Gwen and Bonnie and what I should do."

"And?"

"And… I followed my heart like you suggested. Once I realized there was no right or wrong answer, I went with it. I *felt* it, Lexi, as crazy as that sounds. Both Bonnie and Gwen are great women. Highly intelligent, independent, thoughtful and kind. Either one of them could have made me happy, but in different ways. I knew, however, that only one made me feel comfortable with my true self."

I hesitated, then said, "Gwen?"

"You knew." He sounded surprised.

"No, but I suspected." I began brushing my hair again. The repetitive motion soothed me. "You changed in ways I'd never seen before when you were with her. You became more decisive, more courageous, more like the man I know you are. I like her, Elvis. She's a little kooky sometimes, but I think she's good for you."

"That means a lot to hear you say that, Lexi. It's a bit uncanny. We're into the same stuff—science, computers, comic books, old movies—we really sync up on those things." He sounded happy, *really* happy, and it made my heart soften. "More importantly, she makes me feel like I can do anything—she *believes* I'm able to do those things. It's like I could take on the world with her by my side. Plus, she makes me laugh. That's important to me."

"It should be. Life is hard without laughter."

He paused, maybe thinking through how to tell me what happened with Bonnie. After all, she was my friend, too, and I think he wanted to respect that.

"I didn't want to break it off with either of them, but it had to be done," he finally said. "It was hard. Excruciatingly hard."

"I'm sure it was."

There was something in his tone, a seriousness, a maturity, I'd never heard before. Matters of the heart, as agonizing and miraculous as they were, caused a person to grow in unexpected ways. I was finding that out for myself.

"The final decision came for me when I realized while I could break up with Bonnie, I didn't have it in me to hurt Gwen that way." He sighed and I could hear how difficult it was for him to admit it.

"Sounds like you made the right choice, then."

"Bonnie cried. She said she loved me. That damn near killed me, Lexi. But she deserved to know the truth regarding my feelings, and I respected her enough to break it to her as kindly and honestly as I could."

"You don't have to convince me of that, Elvis. I know you have a good heart and that you sincerely cared for Bonnie."

"It still hurts like hell. Maybe it always will. I'm just not sure what's going to happen with that relationship.

Does it fade away? It makes me sad to think I might lose her friendship."

"You might. You might not. I don't have an answer to that. Bonnie holds the cards. But you know, as well as I, that sometimes love and friendship can work together in mysterious ways."

"Yeah, it does." I could hear the smile in his voice. "You know, Gwen came to me exactly at the right time in my life. I was ready for her, thanks to Bonnie. Timing in love is really important, isn't it?"

"It is, Elvis. It really is."

He paused for a moment. "Well, whatever happens, I have a feeling I'm in for a wild ride with an awfully cute redhead."

A smile touched my lips. "I take it that means Gwen was happy to hear the news and didn't boot you to the curb?"

"Happy might be an overstatement." He chuckled. "She made me grovel first. A lot. I should have told her about Bonnie. I should have been honest about my feelings from the start, and so on. I hurt her, too, Lexi, and I hated that part the worst."

"But she forgave you?"

"She forgave me. And, if you don't mind me sharing, the makeup sex was mind-blowing."

"Elvis! Oh, jeez." I winced, wrinkling my nose. "That was *way* too much information."

He laughed, a good strong laugh that made me happy. "Just saying."

"Ugh. I'll see you soon. Just make sure the pizza and beer is ready when I get back. Apparently, we've got a lot to talk about…minus certain details, mind you."

He laughed again. "We sure do."

THIRTY-SEVEN

I HUNG UP the phone and tossed it on the bed just as Slash came in. He had a few shopping bags over his arm.

"The restaurant downstairs was booked for the evening, so I got us reservations at a smaller place on the ocean a couple of blocks down," he said. "It requires something other than jeans or shorts, so I picked up a dress for you. There weren't a lot of options in your size. I hope this will do."

He pulled a blue sundress and a soft white sweater out of one of the bags. They were simple and exactly my style.

"They're perfect. Thanks, Slash."

He gave me a kiss on the cheek before hanging up a short-sleeved shirt and pair of dark slacks in the closet. Before he took his shower, I updated him on what Elvis had told me about Andy. He didn't seem surprised, but sad. While he showered, I put on the dress and sweater combo. They fit well and my pair of plain white sandals worked with the outfit.

While Slash was shaving, a towel wrapped around his waist, I sat in front of the laptop and worked on my spreadsheet, adding the events of the past few days. When he was dressed, he kissed me on the top of the head. He smelled good and was easy on the eyes. How he could so effortlessly, carelessly, look *so* handsome remained a scientific mystery to me.

"Ready?" he asked.

"I sure am." I saved my work on the spreadsheet and stood. "You look really nice, Slash. As always."

"And you, *cara*, are a vision of loveliness. Kick-ass loveliness," he amended.

We held hands when we got outside. The Secret Service agents, dressed in oversized shirts and dark pants, fell in behind us, discreetly following on the other side of the street. Tonight, I didn't even care. Dusk was falling, the breeze was warm, and the lights on the ocean twinkled. Soft sounds of island music played from some of the shops and eateries as we passed. I walked hand-in-hand with the man I loved. Nothing could ruin my evening.

"Where, exactly, are we going?" I asked.

"The restaurant is just a few more blocks."

"You don't need the GPS?" I asked.

He grinned. "I do not."

We found the little place tucked away behind a few surfing shops. It was packed with people milling around outside. There were strings of cute white lights in front of the restaurant. Slash took my elbow as we stepped inside. The place looked cute from the outside, but inside, it was elegant, with crisp white tablecloths and all the servers dressed in tuxedos. I almost felt underdressed in the sundress, but no one paid us any attention. I thought we would have to wait for a table, but the maître d' whisked us to a table for two on the outdoor terrace with a perfect view of the ocean. A candle flickered on the table and the silverware gleamed. The way the table was situated, slightly at the corner of the terrace, it was almost like our own private space. That thought was dispelled when the maître d' seated the two Secret Service agents a few tables away, but it didn't dampen my mood. I waved and they waved back.

Guess I was getting used to the fishbowl.

Our waiter appeared immediately with a bucket of pink champagne on ice and two flutes. He popped the top and poured the champagne. Slash took a sip and nodded before the waiter disappeared.

"What's the occasion?" I asked.

Slash smiled, lifting his glass. "It's always an occasion when I'm with you."

"That's a good thing, right?" I reached for my flute and held it up.

"Right." His eyes softened as we clinked glasses. "To us."

"To us," I agreed. "May we always have the opportunity for such occasions."

Dinner involved excellently cooked fish and vegetables. Slash and I talked about everything and nothing as the warm breeze swept over us and the sounds of the ocean accompanied our meal. The Secret Service agents seemed to be enjoying their dinner as well.

"Shall we ask for the check?" I finally said. We'd already been at the restaurant for more than two hours. Strangely, I hadn't minded one bit. It had been one of the most romantic dinners we'd ever shared, and it hadn't even been planned.

"I already ordered dessert for us," Slash said. "It should be out in a few minutes."

"Okay." I finished off the rest of our champagne. "Guess I'll just have to figure out where to put it."

Slash stood. "I'll be right back." He headed for the men's room.

A moment later, our waiter appeared with dessert,

a delicious-looking chocolate mousse. He also brought us a carafe of decaf coffee and fresh glasses of bubbly champagne. I was feeling totally spoiled.

"Where's your date?" he asked looking at Slash's empty chair.

Wow. Did he think we were going to skip out on the check or something? "He's in the restroom. He'll be right back."

He gave me a slight bow and left.

I poured myself a cup of decaf while eyeing my chocolate mousse. It looked amazing. It was served in a gorgeous light blue and white dish with a handle. Chocolate shavings were scattered across a swirl of whipped cream and a few fat raspberries topped it. Even though just moments ago I was completely stuffed, my mouth started to water.

I figured I could sneak a bite while waiting for Slash. I scooped up a spoonful and slipped it in my mouth.

As I swallowed, two things happened simultaneously. First, the taste of orgasmic chocolate exploded on my tongue. And when I say orgasmic, I mean toe-curling, amazing, OMG-that-was-incredibly-good orgasmic. Second, a large raspberry slid to the back of my throat and lodged there. I dropped my spoon, pounded on my chest and tried to cough, but it would not dislodge. Panicked, I gripped my throat and stood, gagging.

It took me about ten seconds to realize I was suffocating. The raspberry had blocked my airway.

I staggered a couple of steps toward the waiter, gagging and clawing at the outside of my throat. Several patrons stood, pointing at me in alarm. Dan, the Secret Service agent rushed to me just as I collapsed. The waiter started yelling something. People were shouting until I could no longer make out what they were saying. My vision turned gray and I pointed madly at my throat, when I felt strong arms circling my waist from behind, hauling me into an upright position.

Slash.

He gripped me tight and thrust his clasped fists into my lower diaphragm.

Once.

I tried to cough or breathe, but nothing. It was still stuck.

He adjusted his grip and thrust again. Twice.

Still nothing. After all that work on my "Little Black Cloud" spreadsheet and the long list of things that had happened to me, including kidnapping, plane and car crashes, wild boat rides and being chased by the Chinese, the Russians, Slash's ex-girlfriend and the mob, I would end up dead, felled by a giant raspberry.

Figures.

Slash thrust his fists into my diaphragm a third time and finally the raspberry expelled from my trachea with the force of a speeding bullet. It shot across the room, directly into the plate in front of the guy who sat two tables over. He looked at his plate, then back to us in astonishment.

Slash pulled me into his chest, his hand on the back of my head. His hands were shaking. "*Mio Dio*, are you okay, *cara*? What happened?"

I coughed. "I'm okay… I think. I'm sorry. I snuck a bite of the mousse and choked on a giant raspberry."

He glanced over at the table, the partially eaten mousse and then me. A strange sort of understanding crossed his face and he closed his eyes for a moment.

The waiter rushed us to us, horrified. "Are you okay, ma'am? Should I call an ambulance?"

"No, no." I waved a hand. My throat was sore and the episode had scared me, but I was breathing again and was in no danger of dying. For the moment.

Dan put a hand on my shoulder. "You okay there, ma'am? You gave all of us quite a scare."

"I'm good. Thanks. Sorry to cause a scene."

Everyone in the restaurant was looking at us. Agent Ricollo stood in a protective stance, his arms out, his eyes scanning the restaurant just in case someone else decided to jump up and shove another raspberry down my throat.

You seriously couldn't take me anywhere.

Slash released me and walked over to the guy whose dinner was now ruined. After speaking to the man in a low voice, Slash stuck his hand in the man's food and retrieved the raspberry. I didn't think the guy would have finished his dinner, with or without the raspberry, but it was nice of Slash to remove it for him.

The guy gave Slash his napkin. Slash slid his hand into the cloth and left the table still carrying it. A waiter rushed over to remove the man's plate and speak softly to him.

Slash steered me back to our table, pulled out my chair and had me sit back down. The other patrons began to turn their attention back to their own meals.

I sunk into the chair, grateful to be alive. I took a couple more drinks of water, coughed a few times and leaned back in my chair, rolling my neck. "Wow. Thanks for saving my life, Slash."

"Did I hurt you?"

"What? No. You *saved* me. That was one heck of a raspberry."

Slash sighed and looked remarkably unhappy. "It wasn't a raspberry."

"It wasn't?"

He laid the napkin on the table and opened it up. Nestled on the soft cotton was a ring. The band was polished gold and had two entwining hands that met at a circle of several small diamonds surrounded a gorgeous light blue stone.

I looked at Slash in astonishment. "Whoa. How did *that* get in my mousse?"

"I suspect the chef put it there on my request," he said. "Except it was supposed to be in the champagne, not the mousse, and I should have been at the table to make sure you didn't try to drink it. It was for presentation purposes only. Obviously, this is not going according to plan."

"What plan? Slash, why would you do that?"

He let out a breath. "Because of tradition. That's how Nonno, my grandfather, proposed to Nonna. I wanted to honor her, honor the family tradition of a proposal. Although, I'm totally messing this up. That's what happens to me any time I allow sentiment and emotion to overrule logic. I don't know why anyone thinks it's a good idea to mix food and jewelry." He shook his head in exasperation, as if berating himself.

I barely heard his words. My brain had done a full stop, completely fixating on one word.

"Slash, did you say…proposal? Are you—?"

"Si." He reached over and took my hand. "I talked to your father while you were gone. I asked his permission to request your hand in marriage, although it's just

a formality. I didn't expect to ask you so soon after we moved in, but the truth is, I don't want to wait any longer. I love you, *cara*. My heart knew it the first moment I saw you in your bedroom in that ridiculous T-shirt, challenging me to a hack. My head was more cautious, but it didn't take long. Now, every day that passes is another day I regret I didn't have the courage to speak what is in my heart. I'm asking you to marry me. I want you, our families and friends to know just how serious I am about our future together."

Holy freaking cow.

Slash was proposing? *Now?*

After what might have been several seconds, or perhaps minutes—it was hard to say which because my brain wasn't working properly—Slash finally spoke.

"What are you thinking, *cara*?" His brows were drawn tight, his eyes serious, somber and perhaps a bit concerned. It was almost as if we were discussing the fate of the world, which we'd done before, so I was familiar with that look. But now it was *our* fate, which, in my opinion, made it a million times more important.

I struggled to get my head together. What the heck *was* I thinking? My thoughts were like a computer on overload, whizzing through every circuit in my brain at dizzying speed, lighting up neurons like a Christmas tree. I recalled, with excruciating detail, the moment I'd first met him in my bedroom, when I'd been fast asleep in a ratty old T-shirt. Elvis and Xavier had summoned him to help me, but I hadn't even believed Slash existed. I thought he was nothing more than a myth created by the NSA to discourage hackers. I'd challenged him to a hack, right there on my bed. We sort of became friends after that, as much as that was possible for two loners.

Then one day he showed up at my apartment with a bottle of wine, promising we would open it the day we first made love. More moments flashed through my mind—our first kiss, learning his real name, listening to him play the piano, dancing with him in a dark room, watching him take a bullet to protect me and the people I loved, coding side by side with our wrists and fingers aching, but our eyes mirroring our shared passion for it.

Like minds.

Like hearts.

Finally, my mind screeched to a halt on the image of Slash standing in front of me in the disguise of a middle-aged man. I remembered the moment I looked into his eyes and realized I'd always love him, no matter what age we were.

I managed to form a sentence. "Slash, I'm thinking about us. And, to be honest, I'm also thinking about the spreadsheet."

He looked a bit taken aback. "The spreadsheet?"

I nodded.

He sighed, rubbing the back of his neck. "*Cara*, I know you think things are moving too fast. We've just moved in together and now I'm asking you to take it to the next level—the ultimate level. I'm not pressuring you to decide. That's not what this is about. You can take as much time as you need. But you deserve to know this is what I want for us—where I'm headed. So, if that's *not* what you want, you're going to have to let me know."

Gah! I wasn't expressing myself well. Not that it was a surprise. Conversation was hard for me under normal circumstances, and this conversation was about as far away from normal as we could get. I pressed my fingers against my temple and tried to get my words to match what was in my heart.

Instead, I blurted out, "The ring... Slash, where did you get it? It looks antique."

"Nonna gave it to me when we were in Rome. She didn't say anything, she just gave it to me. Even she knew. This ring has been in our family for four generations. She loves to tell the story of how Nonno proposed to her by presenting her with a ring in her champagne, and how his father had done the same." He looked down at the ring. "No one has ever choked on the ring before."

I sighed. "Leave it to me to be the first."

A slight smile touched his lips as he reached out and touched my hand. "I just didn't want to wait any longer to let you know how I feel. Not one, single day more."

He paused, as if he had more to say, but wasn't sure how to say it. As the silence stretched on, I finally managed to get my head in the right place. This time, I would do it right. I set my hands on the table and leaned forward.

"I'm sorry, Slash. I'm not handling this well. It's just, you took me completely by surprise. I want you to know *why* I'm thinking about the spreadsheet. Even without a full analysis, I know full well the data on my 'Little Black Cloud' spreadsheet indicates that before I had a social life, my existence was safe, conventional and static until I let new people and experiences into my life, including you. There's no question this past year has been extremely hazardous to my health. To say that change has been scary for me would be an understatement. But it's also been incredibly amazing. When I add you to that mix, it's also been magical."

He watched me without saying anything.

I rubbed my throat with my fingertips. "But just because the data proves a little black cloud follows me around, it doesn't mean I should resist change. It means I need to adjust my perspective on how to *manage* that change. All along I've been trying to figure out what's normal, when I've already been living it. You are my normal now. I can't *ever* go back to who I was before I met you. I wouldn't want to."

It was my turn to surprise him. I saw a flash of it in his eyes. I could tell he was trying to figure out where I was going with this.

I took a sip of water and summoned my courage. "So, because of the spreadsheet and the data compiled within, I have an answer to your proposal. The answer is yes, Slash, I'll marry you. Not today, and maybe not next week, but I agree there's no one in the world better suited to me than you. You deserve to know that—and understand that's where *I'm* headed. You're my future, or at least a big part of it. So, there you have it."

He smiled, closed his eyes for a moment, then reached under his shirt and pulled out the gold cross. He gave it a quick kiss before picking up my left hand and sliding the ring onto my finger.

Several people at the tables nearest us started clapping. Dan and Agent Ricollo stood and clapped the hardest. The waiters paused their service, watching us with beaming faces. I hadn't realized we had an audience. Slash apparently hadn't either, but it didn't appear to damper his happiness or mine.

I had no idea how much of our conversation everyone heard, but I squeezed his hand in a show of unity, realizing, with astonishment, it was damp. Slash had been nervous? Had he really thought I might say no? Somehow that made my heart melt just a little bit more.

I leaned across the table and smiled at him. "Can I just say that even though I almost died a few minutes ago, this is officially the best day of my life? As much as I hate the beach, it seems to be the location of the most transformative moments in my life."

Slash chuckled. "Ah, *cara*, I don't know what I've done in my life to deserve you, but I refuse to question it. What do you think of the ring?"

"It's the most beautiful ring I've ever seen. I can't believe I almost swallowed it. What's the blue stone? I've never seen anything like it before."

"It's a blue diamond. It's small because they are exceptionally rare. A rare stone for a rare woman. I can get you a different ring if you prefer."

"I would not prefer. It's perfect. I'm beyond honored, although admittedly worried, you're entrusting me with such a valuable family heirloom, especially given my proclivity to klutziness. As it is, I've eaten it, choked on it and spit it into someone's soup. I haven't even had it for fifteen minutes yet. Are you sure about this?"

"More than anything in my entire life." His mouth curved into a smile. "*Mio Dio*, my heart stopped when I saw you choking. I'm *so* sorry."

"It's okay. Did you really talk to my father?"

"I did. I admit I was more nervous doing that than I was facing a dozen terrorists armed with live grenades and a bomb. He took it better than I expected. After only one hour and twenty-eight minutes of intense grilling about my entire life, most of which was classified, he grudgingly agreed to bestow his blessing as long as you agreed."

"Ouch. I'm certain he appreciated the gesture, though. It was a smart move, Slash, and awfully courageous, if I do say so. My dad can be kind of old-fashioned about these things. My take on it is that if you left the house alive, you should consider it a good omen. How did my mom take it?"

"I'm afraid I tuned out after she started recommending caterers and venues."

"Ugh."

He laughed. "I promise you, *cara*, it was worth every damn minute."

I lifted my champagne glass. "Shall we toast to us, then?"

"We shall." He wrapped his fingers around the stem of the glass and waited for me to continue.

I paused, wanting to say the right thing while preserving this moment in my memory. Slash didn't rush me. He kept his eyes on mine while I studied his strong jaw, intelligent eyes, those elegant hacker hands that could do magic on me, as well as a keyboard. Now, he was going to be my partner in life. It was both a terrifying and thrilling thought.

Never a dull moment.

No. Our life would never be simple or easy because of who we were, but it *would* be worth it. Now, I couldn't imagine it any other way.

I looked down at the bubbling champagne, hoping for inspiration, when the right toast came to me. I smiled at Slash. "I'm not going to make a long toast in honor of our engagement. Since we both like it simple…here goes. I love you, Slash, and I'm excited to spend the rest of my life with you. Let's toast to no looking back and…no regrets."

He smiled and lifted his glass. "No regrets. Ever."

We finished off the champagne with a strange kind of giddy happiness. After I set down my glass, I rested my chin on my fist, the diamond on my hand sparkling in the candlelight. "I do have one more question about the ring, however."

Slash lifted an eyebrow. "Which is?"

"It's not bugged, right?"

THIRTY-EIGHT

AFTER ANOTHER FULL day of questioning by the local authorities and the FBI, Slash and I were permitted to leave the British Virgin Islands. The last twenty-four hours had been the best time in our lives together. We took long walks on the beach, and I didn't even mind the sand in my toes or the Secret Service agents who discreetly trailed us. We made love at sunset and sunrise, streamed several sci-fi movies, and gamed until late into the night. I kept looking at the beautiful ring on my finger and marveling at the direction life was taking me. I rarely wore jewelry other than earrings, so it was an unusual, but not unwelcome, feeling on my hand.

We never did see Basia and Xavier again, although I told Slash I still felt bad for being a third wheel on their honeymoon.

"No worries, *cara*," he said. "I gifted them a week on the Italian Riviera as a wedding present. They can have a second honeymoon whenever they want."

"Wow." I looked at him in surprise. "That kind of makes my toaster oven pale in comparison."

He laughed, twirled a finger around my ponytail. "Have I mentioned today how much I adore you?"

"Maybe once or twice. But don't let me stop you from continuing."

Our ferry ride back to the US Virgin Islands for our

flight home was uneventful. No one even looked my way with Slash and his Secret Service detail in tow.

We were silent in his car on the way home from the airport. When we reached the house, I grabbed the mail while he inserted the alarm code and opened the door. I pulled my suitcase across the threshold and left it at the bottom of the stairs. Slash walked into the kitchen and grabbed a bottle of water from the refrigerator as I tossed the mail on the counter. As I did, something caught my eye. I pulled out a white envelope and studied it.

"Slash."

Something in my tone must have alarmed him, because he paused mid-drink, looking at me with a puzzled expression. "What's wrong?"

I held out the letter to him. He put down the water bottle and took the envelope from me. It was addressed to him, but in his real name—a name known to only his family and a handful of his closest associates, including me. There was no return address. A small corner of the envelope had already been torn open.

"If there were any dangerous substances in there, they would be gone by now," he said quietly.

That was the nature of our lives. Something as simple as a letter could signal a deadly threat to our well-being. The fact that his real name and his current address was on that envelope was more disturbing than I could say. I know he felt the same way.

I nodded as he took a knife from the kitchen drawer and slit open the envelope the rest of the way. Despite his words regarding the danger, he used a pair of tongs to extract the single piece of paper contained within. He smoothed it flat with the tongs. I stood next to him, my head on his shoulder, my hand on his waist. We'd face this together, whatever it was.

Typed in bold letters on the paper were five words: *I know who you are.*

Dread settled in my stomach as I stepped back. "What does it mean?" My voice was shaky.

Slash raised his gaze from the paper to meet my eyes. His expression was grim as he shook his head.

"I don't know, *cara*. But I intend to find out."

* * * * *

ACKNOWLEDGMENT

I AM GREATLY indebted to the wonderful team that comes together to make my books happen, especially my amazing family (Donna, Bill, Brad, Beth, Sandy and Scott), as well as my children, Alexander and Lucas, whose wise, hilarious and observant reflections on life often make their way into one of my books. Thanks also to Victor Sim for suggesting the title. Kudos are due also to my incredibly talented editor, Alissa Davis, who has the keenest eye and always makes my manuscripts better. Thanks also to the Carina Press administrative and marketing team for their amazing support of me and Lexi. Each book really is a team effort!

ABOUT THE AUTHOR

JULIE MOFFETT IS a bestselling author and writes in the genres of mystery, young adult, historical romance and paranormal romance. She has won numerous awards, including the 2014 Mystery & Mayhem Award for Best YA/New Adult Mystery, the prestigious 2014 HOLT Award for Best Novel with Romantic Elements, a HOLT Merit Award for Best Novel by a Virginia Author (twice!), the 2016 Award of Excellence, a PRISM Award for Best Romantic Time-Travel AND Best of the Best Paranormal Books of 2002, and the 2011 EPIC Award for Best Action/Adventure Novel. She has also garnered additional nominations for the 2016 Bookseller's Best Award, Daphne du Maurier Award and the Gayle Wilson Award of Excellence. Her book *A Double-Edged Blade* was an Amazon #1 Bestselling Novel.

Julie is a military brat (Air Force) and has traveled extensively. Her more exciting exploits include attending high school in Okinawa, Japan; backpacking around Europe and Scandinavia for several months; a yearlong college graduate study in Warsaw, Poland; and a wonderful trip to Scotland and Ireland where she fell in love with castles, kilts and brogues.

Julie has a BA in Political Science and Russian Language from Colorado College, an MA in International Affairs from the George Washington University in Washington, DC, and an MEd from Liberty University. She has worked as a proposal writer, journalist, teacher, librarian and researcher. Julie speaks Russian and Polish and has two sons.

Visit Julie's website at www.juliemoffett.com.

Watch the Lexi Carmichael series book trailer at www.YouTube.com/watch?v=memhgojYeXM.

Follow Julie on Social Media:

Facebook: www.Facebook.com/JulieMoffettAuthor

Twitter: www.Twitter.com/JMoffettAuthor

Instagram: www.Instagram.com/julie_moffett

Pinterest: www.Pinterest.com/JMoffettAuthor

Get 4 FREE REWARDS!

We'll send you 2 FREE Books plus 2 FREE Mystery Gifts.

FREE
Value Over
$20

Both the **Romance** and **Suspense** collections feature compelling novels written by many of today's best-selling authors.

YES! Please send me 2 FREE novels from the Essential Romance or Essential Suspense Collection and my 2 FREE gifts (gifts are worth about $10 retail). After receiving them, if I don't wish to receive any more books, I can return the shipping statement marked "cancel." If I don't cancel, I will receive 4 brand-new novels every month and be billed just $6.74 each in the U.S. or $7.24 each in Canada. That's a savings of at least 16% off the cover price. It's quite a bargain! Shipping and handling is just 50¢ per book in the U.S. and 75¢ per book in Canada.* I understand that accepting the 2 free books and gifts places me under no obligation to buy anything. I can always return a shipment and cancel at any time. The free books and gifts are mine to keep no matter what I decide.

Choose one: ☐ **Essential Romance**   ☐ **Essential Suspense**
                 (194/394 MDN GMY7)   (191/391 MDN GMY7)

Name (please print)

Address   Apt. #

City   State/Province   Zip/Postal Code

Mail to the **Reader Service**:
IN U.S.A.: P.O. Box 1341, Buffalo, NY 14240-8531
IN CANADA: P.O. Box 603, Fort Erie, Ontario L2A 5X3

Want to try 2 free books from another series? Call 1-800-873-8635 or visit www.ReaderService.com.

---

*Terms and prices subject to change without notice. Prices do not include sales taxes, which will be charged (if applicable) based on your state or country of residence. Canadian residents will be charged applicable taxes. Offer not valid in Quebec. This offer is limited to one order per household. Books received may not be as shown. Not valid for current subscribers to the Essential Romance or Essential Suspense Collection. All orders subject to approval. Credit or debit balances in a customer's account(s) may be offset by any outstanding balance owed by or to the customer. Please allow 4 to 6 weeks for delivery. Offer available while quantities last.

Your Privacy—The Reader Service is committed to protecting your privacy. Our Privacy Policy is available online at www.ReaderService.com or upon request from the Reader Service. We make a portion of our mailing list available to reputable third parties that offer products we believe may interest you. If you prefer that we not exchange your name with third parties, or if you wish to clarify or modify your communication preferences, please visit us at www.ReaderService.com/consumerschoice or write to us at Reader Service Preference Service, P.O. Box 9062, Buffalo, NY 14240-9062. Include your complete name and address.

STRS19R2